"Don't you believe in curses?" Bridget asked, walking across the foyer beside him.

"I'm not sure how to answer that."

"Why?"

Karl stepped aside at the doorway so she could enter the room, but kept his hand on her back as he walked in behind her. "Because if I say yes, you'll tell me why I shouldn't, and if I say no, you'll tell me why I should."

She held in a giggle, but knew he was right. She liked how they could tease each other, just somewhat, now and again. It was fun. And right now, he needed some fun. Needed to have a light heart to deal with what he had to do. Spinning, she looked up at him. "That's because some curses need to be believed in, and others don't." Leaning closer, she whispered, "The trick is knowing the difference."

He caught her waist with both hands again. "How would I know the difference?"

She gave him a secretive look. "You'd need the luck of the Irish to know that."

"I think I have found that."

Her breath stalled, and so did her heart as he leaned closer until their lips met.

Author Note

News of the sinking of the *Titanic* shocked the world. Early reports claimed there were no survivors, and other reports claimed there were no casualties. It wasn't until the *Carpathia*, the ship that rushed to the site of the sinking and rescued survivors, arrived in New York that the truth was known. A little over 30 percent of the people aboard the state-of-the-art luxury liner survived. They arrived in New York with nothing but the clothes on their backs.

Having always been someone who has wondered *what happened next?* I was excited when given the opportunity to create a story in the aftermath of this historic event.

I hope you enjoy Bridget and Karl's story!

LAURI ROBINSON

A Family for the Titanic Survivor

HARLEQUIN
HISTORICAL

**HARLEQUIN®
HISTORICAL™**

ISBN-13: 978-1-335-50598-9

A Family for the Titanic Survivor

Copyright © 2020 by Lauri Robinson

This edition published by arrangement with Harlequin Books S.A.

For questions and comments about the quality of this book,
please contact us at CustomerService@Harlequin.com.

Harlequin Enterprises ULC
22 Adelaide St. West, 40th Floor
Toronto, Ontario M5H 4E3, Canada
www.Harlequin.com

Printed in U.S.A.

Recycling programs
for this product may
not exist in your area.

A lover of fairy tales and history, **Lauri Robinson** can't imagine a better profession than penning happily-ever-after stories about men and women in days gone past. Her favorite settings include World War II, the Roaring Twenties and the Old West. Lauri and her husband raised three sons in their rural Minnesota home and are now getting their just rewards by spoiling their grandchildren. Visit her at laurirobinson.blogspot.com, Facebook.com/lauri.robinson1 or Twitter.com/laurir.

Books by Lauri Robinson

Harlequin Historical

Diary of a War Bride
A Family for the Titanic Survivor

Sisters of the Roaring Twenties

The Flapper's Fake Fiancé
The Flapper's Baby Scandal
The Flapper's Scandalous Elopement

Brides of the Roaring Twenties

Baby on His Hollywood Doorstep
Stolen Kiss with the Hollywood Starlet

Oak Grove

Mail-Order Brides of Oak Grove
"Surprise Bride for the Cowboy"
Winning the Mail-Order Bride
In the Sheriff's Protection

Visit the Author Profile page
at Harlequin.com for more titles.

To Ashley, who will forever believe there was plenty of room on that door for two.

Chapter One

1912

Bridget McGowen had always known that this day would come, but now that it had arrived, a mixture of emotions as thick as a pot of stew that had simmered too long filled her stomach. America. Da had saved every penny possible for this dream to come true. To send her to America. It was the dream of nearly every Irish family—saving enough money to send a child across the ocean.

Not to become a household servant or laborer, but to rise above, like others had, including Da's cousin Martha.

Martha had become a wealthy woman, a successful woman, all on her own.

A heavy and long sigh slowly seeped out of Bridget.

Today was so bittersweet.

Leaving everything she'd ever known to embark upon a voyage across the sea and arrive in a new country, an entirely new world.

It was exciting—the jubilance of so many people

surrounding her, talking, cheering, giddy about their adventure, made it so. But to her, it was also sorrowful.

Da had died last week.

That pain was still strong, still so consuming it made her eyes sting. If anyone was to notice, they might think it was the mist from the salty sea air. A silly thought, indeed. Everyone was too busy, too excited to board the steamer, to notice she had tears in her eyes, or a broken heart in her chest.

In Da's last breaths, he'd told her to lift a board beneath his bed and take out the metal box hidden there. She had, and she'd cried because she'd known the significance of the money in that box. It was for her trip to America. The pennies, nickels and dimes he'd pinched, saved and hidden away for her to have this opportunity.

I'm here, Da, in Southampton, and will soon set sail for America. I'll make your dream come true.

Da had made her promise that she'd do just this. Travel to America and open a boardinghouse like his cousin Martha had done in Chicago. Martha had returned to Ireland several times dressed in the latest finery and touting to friends and family that the opportunities in America were endless.

Bridget had promised to go, but not until Da no longer needed her.

A nudge in the center of her back urged her forward, shuffling shoulder to shoulder and toe to heel with a crowd the likes of which she'd never seen, up the angled wooden pier that creaked and swayed with the weight it upheld as people made their way aboard the *Titanic*. A ship so massive, so long and wide and tall, Bridget had a hard time believing it could float.

She also had a hard time believing she was boarding it. The greatest luxury liner ever built. The greatest luxury she'd ever known was when there was a slow night at the pub and she'd slip away to enjoy a long soak in a hot tub of water, reading until the water grew cold.

Uncle Matt had claimed the *Titanic* had a bathtub made of pure gold. She'd heard him say that from the kitchen of the pub, where she'd been washing the constant flow of mugs and cups used by the patrons, just as she had for as long as she could remember. Da had always said that Uncle Matt had kissed the Blarney Stone more than once; that's why he could talk at the rate of two men. Normally the constant rattle of Uncle Matt's voice had entered one ear and gone out the other without taking any sort of root in her mind.

That night though, mere days after they'd put Da in the ground, the way Uncle Matt had been boasting made her step away from the wash pan and move closer to the door. She'd heard of the great ship. Of its maiden voyage. Men had been peddling tickets for the ocean liner for months. Just as they had for every ship heading for America. The *Titanic* had been built in Ireland, which gave Uncle Matt more to brag about.

Disbelief had entered her when she'd heard him boast about securing a ticket on the ocean liner.

For himself.

That's when her disbelief had turned into something more. She'd hurried up the stairway in the back room, to the living quarters she and her father had shared above the pub, and into the room that was barely large enough for her bed and chest of drawers. Upon opening the top drawer, digging past her ironed and folded aprons, anger like she'd never known had coiled into a hard knot in her stomach.

It had been taken. The metal box. Her money.

Back downstairs, with the room full of men—family, friends, foes and strangers—she'd demanded her money. The money that Da had saved for her and that had been in her dresser drawer until her uncle, her very own flesh and blood, had stolen it.

It had a been a row, one that had made her squeamish, because of the shame it had brought upon her family, that her very uncle would steal from her, but she'd gotten her money back.

Right there.

Right then.

Uncle Matt claimed he'd only been teasing her, testing her so that she'd put the money in a safer spot, but she knew blarney when she heard it. That night, upon closing and locking the doors of the pub, she'd packed her bag and had left early the next morning. Upon securing a ticket, she'd taken the ferry and train all the way to Southampton, and now would travel upon the *Titanic* across the Atlantic to start a new life. In America. Where she would make all those dreams, all those hopes Da had had for her, come true.

Another nudge urged her forward again, although it was merely half a step up the packed walkway. The entire wharf was crowded, full of women wearing dresses and hats as fancy and frivolous as those seen in pictures, and men who looked just as dapper in their suit coats and shined shoes. There were plenty of people dressed like her, too, wearing what had to be their best clothes, homespun and home sewn serviceable clothing.

While huge nets full of traveling trunks and suitcases were being hoisted high in the air and over the edge of the ship, the people on this pier were like her, carrying various bags and cases that held all the earthly belongings they were taking along for their journey.

The trunks and suitcases in those overhead nets belonged to the people on the piers and stairways above her, boarding the ship in their fancy clothes and hats—first-class passengers.

Their walkway was high overhead. Below that was the second-class pier, and below that was where she stood. On the third-class pier. The separation was designed to keep people in their rightful places. She wasn't bitter or surprised by that; it was the way of the world. There was the upper class and lower class in everything. Cousin Martha had said things were different in America, though. Bridget was a bit concerned about that because different could mean a lot of things. In this instance, she hoped different meant everyone had the same opportunity to achieve their dreams. Humble beginnings were food for the soul, but they shouldn't rule a person's life.

They shouldn't make them want to steal from their family, either. Uncle Matt and Da came from the same place, the same womb, but they sure had been different. Da had been the salt of the earth. Honest, kind, loving. He'd taught her the importance of those things, too.

So, although she had taken her money, that which was rightfully hers, she had also left a note for Uncle Matt, bequeathing him her share of the Green Door, her half of the pub that she'd inherited upon her father's death. And more importantly, she forgave him. Uncle Matt was family.

The faint shrill of a child's scream shattered Bridget's thoughts. There was so much noise she wasn't sure where it had come from. There didn't seem to be a commotion on the pier. Yet, she'd distinctly heard a child scream.

Glancing up, she spied something tumbling through the air. Without concern or thought to the people around her, she leaped onto the piped handrail of the pier and stretched out an arm just in time to grasp ahold of a corner of the fluttering material and draw it close.

A doll. A cherub-faced doll with bright blue eyes and pink cheeks wearing a ruffled, white eyelet dress. Memories filled her as she glanced up, saw the small arm of a little girl extended over a man's shoulder as the man entered the doorway of the ship on the first-class pier. She'd had a similar doll, years ago, that she had loved dearly.

Set upon entering themselves, no one on her pier seemed to have noticed her rescue, or if they had, they weren't concerned, nor did they make room to allow her to step off the rail, to gain a spot back in the boarding line.

A young man finally paused. Thanking him, she stepped off the rail and kept a tight hold on the doll while the ushering aboard continued, along with the inspection of boarding cards and the shouting of stewards for passengers to proceed to the D, E, F or G decks. Once inside, the sound of the crowd, the stewards shouting and the rumbling of the engines echoed between the heavy walls and vibrated in her ears. The process seemed to take hours, and by the time she finally found her berth, Bridget's nerves were frayed.

A crowd at the Green Door had meant two, maybe three dozen people, not thousands, and she'd already been traveling for over a day and a half.

Opening the door, a tiny gasp caught in her throat.

The cabin was small, but certainly accommodating. A set of bunk beds, complete with linens and blankets, were connected to one wall, a sink and mirror on the far wall, and two folding chairs sat along the wall across from the beds. The floor was pink, the walls painted white, and there were small white towels folded so they stood up on top of the holding tank above the sink and below the mirror.

Closing the door, the first thing she did was examine those towels. They were truly the fanciest things she'd ever seen.

When the time came, she would do that with towels at her boardinghouse. Fold them so they stood up, looking pretty while waiting for use.

She set her bag and the doll on the top bunk, leaving the easier-to-access lower bed for whoever her berth mate might be, and removed her wool coat, which had caused her to grow warm during all the hustle and bustle of boarding and finding her cabin. After hanging the coat on a hook, she made sure the small, crocheted purse holding her money was still safely tucked in her skirt pocket, then picked the doll off the bed.

The ocean liner was very large, and once she'd entered the inside of the ship, she'd taken so many turns, walked along so many hallways, that she wasn't sure which way was north, east, south or west, but there was a little girl who was sure to be worried about her doll.

Opening the door, she stepped into the hallway and pulled closed the door she'd been so relieved to find only moments ago. Lines of people filled the corridors at both ends of the hallway. She chose the direction from which she hadn't trekked to arrive at her berth, hoping the steward down there would be a bit more friendly.

The line extended the length of the corridor, and it took a long time before someone allowed her to squeeze in and start shuffling forward. Upon arriving at an intersection of corridors, she waited for her turn to speak to the young steward directing the persons in line as to which way to proceed. Left or right.

"Excuse me," she said, "a child from first class dropped this doll. Would you be able to see it's delivered to her?"

Without looking her way, he said, "No." He glanced at the card the person behind her held over her head. "Left."

She held the frustration that bubbled inside her as she said, "I'm sure the child was upset and—"

"Where's your boarding card?" He glanced at another person's card. "Right."

"In my berth," she answered.

"Then return there until we set sail," he snapped, and went on shouting left and right as people showed him their boarding cards.

Frustration filled his voice and actions. It filled the faces of those around her, as well. There was a set of steps behind the steward, so, with no other option, she turned, excused her way through the line of people proceeding that way, and once across the hall, quickly climbed a different set of stairs.

She requested help from more stewards, with the same luck as the first, and therefore continued working her way through crowds and up stairways. The higher the sets of stairs took her, the more changes she noticed. Painted white walls and doors along the corridors became solid wood doors and the pink flooring became carpet that muffled her footsteps. Higher yet, the walls of the corridors had wooden wainscoting with wall-papered walls above it, and the doors were elegantly carved with gold number plates rather than painted on numbers.

The final set of stairs led her down a hallway that ended in a large foyer, with the grandest staircase she'd ever set eyes on. The double set of steps led to a massive landing of two open corridors and the arched windows filled the ship with sunlight, making everything sparkle and shine.

Awed, she crossed the room to the very center, then turned a complete circle, pausing to watch people stepping in and out of the elevators before completing her turn to face the stairway again. Impressively carved woodwork surrounded an elegant clock at the top of the steps where the corridors met. It was all so gorgeous.

Oh, Da, you wouldn't believe this.

"Excuse me, miss, I believe you must be lost."

She twisted, nodded, then shook her head. "No, no, I'm not lost." At least she hoped she'd find her way back to her berth. "I'm in need of some assistance."

"There are stewards that can help you on your deck," said the man, who was dressed in a black-and-white formal suit.

"No, they couldn't help me," Bridget said, easing the hold on the doll still clutched to her chest. "I believe a child boarding on the first-class walkway dropped this doll. I need to return it to her."

"Very well, I will see to that." He held out his hand.

She was about to hand the doll over but, having encountered so many stewards who weren't concerned about the doll, became suspicious. "How?"

"How?"

"Yes, how will you see the child gets her doll?"

He stiffened, lifted his chin a bit higher. "I will inquire if anyone has reported one missing."

"All right."

He reached for the doll.

She clutched it to her chest again. "I'll wait while you inquire."

The look he cast down his nose was full of disgust. "I will inquire after we set sail. You need to return to your berth."

"Why can't you inquire now?"

"Because not everyone has boarded. Now if you will just—"

"The child has," Bridget interrupted. She normally wouldn't be so rude, but this man wasn't being any more helpful than the others had been. No one seemed to care about anything but setting sail. "A man was carrying her. Wearing a black coat. Her coat was pink."

"Miss, do you have any idea how many—"

"Betsy! Betsy!"

Bridget stepped around the steward. A little girl was rushing down the massive staircase as fast as her little legs would let her, closely followed by a man and woman. Certain this was the doll's owner, Bridget knelt down and held out the doll.

"Betsy! Oh, Betsy!" Long brown hair bounced on her shoulders as the girl jumped off the bottom step and ran forward, arms out.

Bridget's heart swelled as she handed the doll to the girl, who clutched the toy tight to her chest as tiny tears fell from big brown eyes.

"Oh, how are we ever going to thank you?" the woman asked, kneeling down beside the girl.

"How did you find her?" the man asked, kneeling down on the other side of the child.

"I saw her fall," Bridget said. "And caught her."

"I hadn't known she'd fallen—what had made Elsie scream—until we were inside." The man shook his head and then whispered over the child's head. "I was sure she'd fallen in the water."

Bridget shook her head. "She fell right into my arms."

"She did?" the girl asked, still hugging her doll.

"She did," Bridget answered. "And I told her that I'd help her find you."

The steward cleared his throat. "Excuse me, sir."

The man nodded, stood and picked up the little girl. "I'm Benjamin Wingard. This is my wife, Annette, and our daughter, Elsie," he said to Bridget.

"And you've already met Betsy," the wife said. "Elsie's uncle Karl gave Betsy to Elsie for Christmas, and she hasn't let the doll out of her sight since. We are so grateful to you. What is your name?"

Bridget was about to introduce herself, but the steward cleared his throat again.

"We were on our way to the café for a refreshment," Mr. Wingard said. "Please join us."

The steward cleared his throat yet again, louder.

Tall, with brown hair and eyes, like his daughter, Mr. Wingard looked at the steward. "Thank you, your services are no longer needed."

The steward stiffened. "The café is reserved for first-class passengers only, Mr. Wingard."

"This young woman is our guest," Mr. Wingard said.

Bridget shook her head, fully prepared to find her

way back to her cabin now that Elsie had been reunited with Betsy.

"She most certainly is," Mrs. Wingard said, looping an arm through Bridget's. "We promised Elsie cookies and lemonade. Please join us."

Bridget saw the scowl on the steward's face, but she was already being pulled along by Mrs. Wingard.

"What is your name?" the woman asked.

"Bridget McGowen."

"Bridget, what a lovely name, and you are a true angel. There was no consoling Elsie over the loss of Betsy. Benjamin and I tried everything. We were relieved when she finally agreed to a cookie, and then seeing you with Betsy…" She patted the corner of one eye. "I just can't thank you enough."

"I'm glad the two are reunited," Bridget answered, gradually slowing her footsteps as they neared the entrance to the café. "I really should return to my deck."

"Is someone waiting on you?"

"No, I—" She swallowed because it still hurt to say, especially seeing how loving the Wingards were to their daughter. "I'm alone." Alone in the world. That was still hard to admit.

"Then you simply must join us for lemonade, or tea, or whatever you prefer."

Bridget's insides bubbled at the pleading in the other woman's blue eyes beneath her stylish purple hat that was encircled with a wide band of white silk, and matched her purple and white dress. Bridget's dress was blue, a dull blue, and not nearly as stylish. Most certainly not stylish enough for a first-class café. She wasn't stylish enough, either.

Not wanting to disappoint anyone, yet, knowing her place, Bridget whispered, "I'm not allowed in there."

"Nonsense," Mr. Wingard said, walking on the other side of his wife and still carrying Elsie. "You are our guest."

"It will be fine," Annette said. "Benjamin and his brother are bankers. They are the reason this ship was built."

The only banker Bridget had ever known was George O'Reilly, and Da claimed George was so greedy he'd rob a blind man.

Mr. Wingard laughed at his wife's claim. "My brother and I did assist in gaining capital for the White Star Line to build this magnificent ship, but we are not the reason it was built." He winked at his wife. "But I agree with my wife. You must join us for a refreshment."

"Is that why you're on the maiden voyage?" Bridget asked.

Annette's eyes grew sad. "No, it's just a coincidence. We are going home. We've been here for a month. My father was ill and died two weeks ago."

"I'm sorry," Bridget said. "My Da died last week."

"Oh, I'm so sorry." Annette's hold on Bridget's arm tightened. "It's terrible, isn't it? Being an orphan? I know I'm an adult, but that's how I feel with both my mother and father gone now."

Bridget did, too, and couldn't say if it was their common losses, or her part in reuniting Elsie with her doll, but from that moment on, she felt a connection to the Wingards.

The four days that followed were truly wonderful. Benjamin and Annette had several dinners and events they had been invited to attend, and because Elsie's nanny had broken her foot while they'd been in England and had remained behind, Bridget offered to watch Elsie whenever they needed her during the voyage.

Because she was a friend of theirs, Bridget was also able to join the Wingards, seeing sections of the ship that were only for first-class passengers. The restaurants, library, even the swimming pool. Each night, she would share her daily adventures with Catherine, her berth mate, who was also from Ireland and traveling to America with her brother Sean. He was traveling as a steerage passenger, sleeping and eating in a large bunk room for single men.

"I sincerely wish I could convince you to stay in New York," Annette said one night while getting ready to go to an evening party. "Mrs. Conrad is a dear, but she was Benjamin and Karl's nanny, and just doesn't have the energy for a four-year-old. Elsie adores you."

"And I adore her," Bridget replied, placing the final pin in the back of Annette's hair. Elsie was such a little darling, and Annette and Benjamin were two of the kindest, most generous people imaginable. "But I can't stay in New York. I promised my Da I'd go to Chicago, to his cousin Martha's boardinghouse, and eventually start my own boardinghouse."

Annette sighed, but smiled into the mirror. "I understand, and I'm happy for you." She turned around on the stool. "I'm just going to miss you. It's silly, but I feel like you're the sister I never had. An aunt for Elsie."

Bridget was truly touched, because she felt much the same way. "I'm going to miss you, too. We can visit each other, and write."

"We certainly can." Annette stood. "So often we'll

wear out the train tracks between Chicago and New York."

"Yes, we will!" Bridget gave her a tight hug and then stepped back. "You look stunning."

"It's just part of being Benjamin's wife. There is always a function to go to, but it's worth it. He's such a wonderful man. Meeting him was the luckiest day of my life." She pressed a hand to her heart. "He'd traveled to London to meet with my father about investments, and the moment I saw him, I fell in love. We were married a month later. That was five years ago. We haven't been separated a day since then."

Bridget had never heard such a loving story.

"I'm so lucky," Annette said. "Benjamin is so good to me, so good to Elsie."

"She's lucky to have such wonderful parents."

"And to have you. The person who rescued Betsy," Annette said. "She'll never forget you. None of us will."

"Of course not," Bridget said. "Because we'll see each other often. Now, you better go or you'll be late."

"You're right." Annette stood and draped a shawl around her shoulders. "I've already ordered the evening meal to be delivered to the cabin for you and Elsie."

"We'll visit the library after eating and return here to read the books she chooses," Bridget said, walking beside Annette to the door. "She and Betsy will be sound asleep in bed when you return."

"This is so nice of you, to give up your evening for us," Annette said.

"I would simply be sitting in my berth otherwise. I truly don't mind," Bridget replied, opening the door that led into the sitting room of their suite, which also had a second bedroom and a full bath.

Once Benjamin and Annette had hugged and kissed Elsie, they left the suite and Bridget took ahold of Elsie's hand. "What would you like to do, Poppet? Play with Betsy or a game of knucklebones or—"

"Knucklebones!" Elsie exclaimed.

"Then knucklebones it is."

"I'll get it!" Elsie ran to the room she slept in to collect the little bag.

Moments later, they were sitting on the floor, bouncing the rubber ball and picking up the small metal knob-ended jacks before the ball bounced a second time. Elsie's giggles filled the room when the ball would bounce away before either of them could catch it. Bridget was fully enamored by the little girl and loved every moment she spent with her.

After eating the evening meal upon its delivery, they visited the massive first-class library where Elsie, clutching Betsy, snuggled on Bridget's lap in one of the large chairs while she read the child a couple of stories from a children's book.

"Time to go back to your room, Poppet," Bridget said when Elsie started yawning. "We'll read some more there," she added when Elsie frowned.

"Yippie!" Elsie said, getting a second wind.

Her second wind didn't last long after Bridget had helped her into her nightgown and lay down on the bed beside her to read another story. When Elsie was sound asleep, Bridget eased off the bed, kissed Elsie's forehead and then sneaked out of the room. In the sitting room, she nestled into a corner on the sofa to read a book she'd chosen for herself. The story was good, but she found herself wondering about the Wingards. Wondering if all the people in America were as nice as them, including Benjamin's brother, whom they spoke of so fondly. Karl Wingard. He was older than Benjamin. Twenty-eight, and unmarried. He sounded nice, and he had bought Betsy for Elsie. Annette said they all lived in the Wingard family home, because it was so large, and because they didn't want Karl to live alone.

She couldn't help but wonder about that. About him.

When her eyes snapped open, Bridget questioned what had awakened her, then was appalled that she'd dared to fall asleep! The room was silent. Annette and Benjamin had not yet returned. She rose to check on Elsie, but felt oddly off-balance, as if the ship itself was somehow faulty.

Attributing it to falling asleep, she checked on Elsie, who was still fast asleep. Feeling something was out of place, or simply awkward, Bridget returned to the sitting room.

Everything felt oddly still.

Or had she grown so used to the movement of the ship, she simply no longer noticed it?

Bridget was about to sit back down on the sofa when the cabin door opened.

"Good evening, ma'am," the steward said, walking directly to a closet. "The captain has ordered all passengers put on their life belts." He pulled a white life belt off the closet shelf and held it out to her. "And proceed to the sundeck."

Her heart stalled. "Life belts? Why?"

He dropped the belt over her head. "Just a precaution, ma'am. How many people are in the cabin?" He talked fast, yet calmly, and with quick steps, crossed the room and opened the door to Annette's bedroom.

"Two," Bridget answered, fastening the life belt as

she hurried into Elsie's room. "Mr. and Mrs. Wingard are at a private party in the—"

"Get the child," he said, standing at Elsie's door. "And come along. Hurry."

"What's happening?"

"Just a precaution, ma'am." He handed her another life belt. "Put this on the child. Get your coats. Hurry."

Scared and flustered, she grabbed Elsie's coat from the small closet. "Why do we need to hurry if it's just a precaution?"

"Captain's orders. Please hurry. I have other passengers to alert," he said.

"Can you please find Mr. and Mrs. Benjamin Wingard, let them know?"

"Yes, now hurry to the sundeck."

"Thank…" Her words trailed off because he was already gone, leaving the bedroom door and the door to the corridor open.

The noise that filtered in, of other passengers scurrying along the corridor, sent her heart racing. Not wanting to scare Elsie, she gently awakened her. "Sit up, Poppet. I need to put your coat on."

"I'm not cold, Bridget," Elsie said, with one eye open. "I'm in bed."

"I know you are darling, but we need to go up on the deck, and it will be chilly up there," she said while putting on Elsie's coat and buttoning it. "I need you to put on this life belt, too."

The white cork-filled vests were cumbersome, but with Elsie in her arms, Bridget picked up the doll. "Here, you hold on to Betsy." Then, concerned because Elsie didn't have on any socks or shoes, Bridget pulled a blanket off the bed and quickly tucked it around the child.

She left the cabin and followed other vest-wearing passengers up to the sundeck, all the while assuring Elsie that everything was fine.

"It's just a drill," a woman wearing a fur coat said. "They canceled the life boat drill this morning."

"Why are they doing it at this hour?" another woman asked. "It's ludicrous."

Others agreed and discontent grew as they were ushered along the deck toward the lifeboats. Uniformed men were racing back and forth, shouting for people to hurry to the lifeboats. Passengers returned with shouts that they were not getting in a boat. That there was no reason to if it was just a precaution.

Bridget bustled alongside the protesters, her arms trembling at the difficulty of holding Elsie with both of them wearing the bulky life vests, and shivering as the cold air penetrated her thin dress. Every time she stopped, or saw a seaman, she asked them to find Annette and Benjamin.

"Women and children first!" shipmates were yelling. "Women and children first!"

One of the ship's men grasped her shoulders from behind, shoved her toward a lifeboat. "Here! Woman and child! Here!" He pushed harder to get her through the group. "Step aside! Step aside!"

Elsie was slipping from her hold due to the jostling. Bridget hoisted her higher, fumbling to hold on to the blanket in the process. "Please," she said to the shipmate over her shoulder. "The child's parents are at a party. With the captain. Captain Smith. You must let them know where we are. Mr. and Mrs. Benjamin Wingard. Annette and Benjamin Wingard!"

"Sure, sure," he said. "Get in the boat."

Still trying to get a solid grip on Elsie, Bridget shook her head. "Her parents—"

The man grabbed her, lifted her, along with Elsie in her arms, over the edge of the boat and dropped them inside.

She landed on the wooden seat so hard it made her backside sting, but her concern was Elsie. "Are you all right, Poppet?" she asked, twisting Elsie about on her lap so her leg wasn't squished between her and the woman beside them. "Where's Betsy?"

Elsie lifted the doll so her head popped up over the blanket.

"Good." Bridget kissed the top of Elsie's head and tucked the blanket snugly around her little feet and legs. "It's going to be fine. We are just going to sit here for a little bit, then we'll get you back in bed."

Chapter Two

One by one, raindrops slowly inched their way down the window, leaving long narrow streaks, but Karl Wingard didn't see them. Not the drops. Not the streaks. He didn't see anything. On purpose. He was forcing his mind to go blank, to not see what was before him or what his mind was conjuring up.

He turned from the window, adjusted his focus and settled his gaze on the man standing on the other side of the desk. "I want to know the very moment you know more. The very moment."

"Of course, Karl." Daniel Brock nodded. "I have reporters collecting every ship to shore message. As I said, knowing Benjamin and his family were on the maiden voyage, I wanted you to hear what I'd heard so far. Novice operators are filling the airways, causing a lot of interference, and there hasn't been a solid confirmation yet of what happened, other than she sank."

Karl's throat muscles tightened as he tried to swallow. The *Titanic* couldn't have sunk. Couldn't have. The White Star Line… He huffed out a breath as other consequences rushed across his mind. Investors. He'd invested funds in the line, and had brought along many others while building capital for the White Star Line. So had Benjamin. It had been a solid investment. Comfort. Luxury. Speed. That's what the world wanted. The White Star Line had promised all of that, along with safety. The *Titanic* had watertight compartments. She couldn't have sunk. Couldn't have.

"Hellish news to receive on a Monday morning," Daniel said.

Karl nodded, still not believing what he'd heard. It was impossible. "Telephone me as soon as you hear more."

Daniel planted his tweed hat on his head, still wet from when he'd run through the rain to knock on the door. "I will." Nodding, he glanced at the floor and shook his head. "It's days like this when I don't like owning a newspaper."

"Thank you again for coming over," Karl said while crossing the room and opening the door.

Willard was right outside it, waiting to escort Daniel to the front door, just as he'd escorted him inside a short time ago. To the dining room, where Karl had been eating breakfast and thinking about Benjamin. That's what had awoken him this morning, thoughts of Benjamin.

His brother had been in Europe for over a month, along with Annette and Elsie. Annette's father had been ill, and had died while they'd been in London. Benjamin's last letter had said they'd be returning home on the *Titanic*, and that his firsthand account of traveling on the luxury liner was sure to impress clients who had invested in the line.

Karl grinned recalling Benjamin's letter as he walked across the room and sat down behind his desk. His little brother always found a way to make everything sound like he was working, doing his share. From the time he'd been little, following in Karl's every step, Benjamin had always wanted to do his share. Karl had caught on to that way back then, but had never let Benjamin know.

Benjamin was his little brother. Taking care of him had been his job for as long as he could remember. Father had been busy building the investment banking company that had made a fortune—and continued to—and their mother, well, she'd given birth to both him and Benjamin. That's the most credit he'd give her.

"Master Karl?"

He let out a breath and lifted his head, looked at the doorway of his office, the room he'd brought Daniel to when the newspaper owner had said he needed to speak with him. He'd never in a million years have expected Daniel to deliver the news that he had. Swallowing, Karl answered, "Yes, Willard?"

"Is it true?" Willard asked, his normally stiff shoulders sagging. "The ship Master Benjamin, Mistress Annette, Miss Elsie and Mrs. Conrad were traveling on board sank?"

"That is the report as of right now," Karl answered, his throat burning. Willard used to carry Benjamin, and him, on those square shoulders when they were little. Without Mrs. Conrad knowing, of course. "After midnight last night. Mr. Brock doesn't know more than that. He will keep us informed. Telephone as soon as he knows more."

Willard's shoulders drooped even more. "Oh, dear Lord." Then as if remembering his role, he straightened. "We will hope for the best."

"Yes, we will," Karl replied. "The ship was equipped

with lifeboats. I'm certain Benjamin and his family boarded one before——" He couldn't say more because he refused to believe it was possible. There were numerous ocean liners crossing the Atlantic from England to the United States. It could have been another ship and the reports were merely saying it was the *Titanic* because her maiden voyage was so popularized.

"Yes, sir, they most definitely would have." Willard put his hands behind his back and assumed his butler stance. "Will you be returning to the dining room to complete your breakfast?"

"No."

"Very well, sir." With a bow, Willard backed out of the room and shut the door.

Karl stared at the door for a moment, thinking about all the roles Willard had played in his life over the years. Playmate. Disciplinarian. Confidant. Far more than simply a butler. He and his wife, Mary, were far more than employees.

Just like Benjamin had been far more than simply a younger brother. With their father working and their mother gone, they'd only had each other.

Karl closed his eyes and fought against the odd feeling inside him, as if something was missing.

He'd felt that before, when his father had died just over a year ago. Heart attack. Just like that. His heart had been beating one minute and not the next.

That's how it was with death—here one minute, gone the next—but Father's had been so unexpected. No illness. No nothing. He'd been on the sidewalk, walking to his office at the bank building downtown.

That was Karl's office now. He'd taken over the chairmanship role. Just like this was his desk now, here at home. A lot had changed this last year, even the company name. It was now Wingard Brothers instead of Wingard and Sons. The name couldn't change again. Benjamin had to be fine. Had to be. Along with Annette and Elsie and Mrs. Conrad.

Karl pushed away from the desk and, needing a way to release the tension inside him, to stop the wild roaming of his mind, he left the office, making his way through the house and out to the woodshed behind the carriage house.

That had been his job as a child, chopping wood to keep the fireplaces in the big house glowing with warmth during the long winters. He still maintained that job. The wood he purchased could be delivered spilt, but he requested logs.

Ignoring the rain dripping off his hair, he stepped beneath the outstretched roof of the woodshed, tugged the ax out of the chopping block and grabbed a log.

Swinging the ax made him focus. Not think, just focus on the logs, on splitting them in twos, then fours and tossing them into a pile.

He continued, even as his biceps began to burn, his back began to sting, his legs, and knees throbbed. He kept swinging the ax, splitting the logs, tossing aside the wood and repeating the actions, all the while refusing to think of anything else.

Anything else.

When his entire body ached and the physical pain consumed his thoughts, he planted the ax blade deep in the cutting block and stepped out from beneath the roof, letting the cold April rain wash over him. Wash away the sweat pouring down his forehead, his back, his arms.

There, standing in the cold wet rain, he wanted to, but couldn't deny that deep inside, past his aching and burning muscles, he felt something else.

An emptiness.

Like a part of him was gone.

That feeling hung with him throughout a day that became a living nightmare.

The telephone rang practically nonstop. Other newspaper owners called, besides Daniel. Some reported that there had been no casualties, that everyone aboard the *Titanic* had been rescued; others reported that there were no survivors, and others had numbers that went from one survivor to two thousand.

He placed calls, too, to the White Star Line offices and other investors, not caring about the financial aspects—he needed real numbers, real names. Benjamin hadn't been the only millionaire on the *Titanic*. Moguls, tycoons and entrepreneurs from around the world had booked passage on the ship's maiden voyage. Someone had to know something.

Their answers were as obscure and different as the newspapers. Special editions of newspapers up and down the coastline were being printed and distributed with headlines about the ship, all wanting to be the first to break the news to the world.

Karl's nerves became frayed, his gut churned harder and his anger built throughout the day.

It was after midnight and he was still sitting at his desk when the phone rang again. The only solid, continuous report he'd heard all day was that an ocean liner bound for the Mediterranean, the *Carpathia*, had responded to the distress calls of the *Titanic* and was returning to New York with survivors on board.

Karl grabbed the earpiece of the candlestick telephone with one hand and the speaker with the other. "Hello."

"Karl, it's Daniel. The captain of the *Carpathia* has refused all contact from the press, but has transmitted a list of first- and second-class survivors to the White Star office. It's being sent to me on another line as we speak. My secretary is writing them down."

Karl squeezed onto both pieces of the telephone harder. "How many?"

"Over six hundred," Daniel said.

Hope rose inside him, but he held his silence, assuming the list would be alphabetical and it may take time to get to the *W*'s.

"I've decided that we won't publish the list until the *Carpathia* arrives in port," Daniel said. "But I will contact any relatives in the interim."

"It's appreciated, Daniel," Karl said. Of all the phone calls he'd made and taken today, Daniel had been the one most dedicated to only providing verified information. "Very appreciated."

"Wingard! It says Wingard, Karl!" Daniel's shout echoed in the earpiece. "Right here! Elsie Wingard! Plus one!"

Karl's heart soared at hearing his niece's name, even as he asked, "Plus one? Who is the one?"

"It says, 'nanny.'"

"Mrs. Conrad," Karl said, still hopeful. "Elsie's nanny, she'd traveled with them to England." He held his breath for a moment. "Any other names?"

Daniel's silence said more than words ever could.

Karl's throat grew thick, burned, and he clenched his teeth in response to the burning in his nose behind his eyes.

"They are on second class now," Daniel said humbly. "They could have the…"

Karl lowered the earpiece and speaker as he drew in a long breath of air and held it against the pain encompassing his chest.

After a moment, knowing there was no use listening, waiting, he put the earpiece back to his ear, and the speaker to his mouth, "Thanks, Daniel."

"I'll call once the list is complete, if I have more news," Daniel said somberly.

"Thanks." Karl hung the earpiece on the candlestick holder and set it on the desk, then he bowed his head, pressed a hand to his forehead and no longer tried to stop the pain. The loss.

Over the next few days, Karl had moments of hope that Benjamin and Annette had survived, but those moments were completely shattered when he received a telephone call from the White Star Line office. Benjamin and Annette's bodies had been recovered and would be brought back to New York.

Elsie then became the sole subject of his thoughts. He was the only family she had left, and he couldn't help but believe she would also have perished if not for Mrs. Conrad.

The *Carpathia* was due to arrive in New York by nine o'clock that night, and at seven that evening, he instructed Willard to drive to the docks. Karl assumed others would be there for the ship's arrival and wanted

Willard to be there in plenty of time to see Elsie and Mrs. Conrad as soon as they stepped off the ramp.

By ten-thirty, Karl was pacing the floor, and by eleven, he climbed in his automobile to go see what was taking so long.

A mass of traffic and people appeared well before he reached the docks, filling the streets and sidewalks. He turned around, searched for other ways to get to the dock, but couldn't get any closer for the crowds of people. "You there!" Karl shouted out his window at a constable. "What is the meaning of this?"

"The *Carpathia* has arrived!" the man shouted in return.

"Hours ago!"

The constable walked closer. "No, sir. She went to Pier Fifty-Nine first, to drop off the lifeboats and employees of the White Star Line. She arrived at Pier Fifty-Four about an hour ago. Her passengers disembarked first, then the survivors."

"Good Lord," Karl muttered, glancing at his watch. It was after midnight now! He waved an arm at the sea of people as far as he could see. "Why are all these people here?"

"To meet the survivors! By the thousands!"

Karl shook his head, stunned by the crowd and also flustered. He shut the automobile off, left it in the middle of the street and proceeded on foot, searching for Willard, Elsie and Mrs. Conrad.

At first, he excused himself while shouldering around people through the massive crowd, but soon that was getting him nowhere and he resorted to pushing his way forward, block after block toward the docks.

He could smell the seawater—see the flags atop the masts of the ship—when someone grabbed his shoulder.

"Karl?"

Pivoting on one heel, he was relieved to see a familiar face. A friend he'd known since school. "Reggie! Have you seen Willard?" He had to shout over the noise of the crowd.

"Yes! Some time ago! He was in your Studebaker, taking Elsie home!" Reggie then clamped his shoulder harder. "He told me about Benjamin and Annette. I'm so sorry."

Karl's heart lurched, and he held his breath to hold in the pain. He'd have to get used to the loss, just as he'd gotten used to his father's death. "We all are," he replied, putting his thoughts toward his niece. "Did you see Elsie? Was she all right?"

"She was in the back seat, wrapped in a blanket," Reggie said. "I walked ahead of him, clearing the street so he could head home."

"Thank you!" Karl said, desperately hoping she wasn't ill. Desperately hoping.

He squeezed and pushed his way back through the crowd to his automobile, climbed in and laid on the horn, warning people to step out of the way as he maneuvered along the street and around the block until he was headed away from the docks. When the street before him was finally clear, he pressed his foot harder on the gas pedal, anxious to get home.

The carriage house doors were open, the Studebaker parked inside. Karl pulled his Packard next to the Studebaker and climbed out.

"I'm sorry it took so long that you felt the need to go look for us," Willard said, appearing at the carriage house door. "It was so crowded. I've never seen so many people."

"I saw that," Karl replied, and quickly swung the left door closed as Willard did the right one. "I'm glad you found them."

"I wouldn't have if Miss McGowen hadn't been shouting your name," Willard said.

"Elsie?" Karl asked, his focus still on his niece. "Is she ill? Why was she wrapped in a blanket? I saw Reggie Peters."

"No, she's not ill," Willard replied, as they hurried to the house. "Miss McGowen kept her wrapped in a blanket to protect her from the rain."

Rain. It was misting. Karl hadn't taken that into consideration. It had been cold and raining all day. All week. Inside him as well as on the outside. "Where is she? In her bed?"

"I knew you'd want to see her," Willard said, holding open the house door. "She and Miss McGowen are in the front room, near the fireplace. They were both chilled to the bone. Miss McGowen—"

"Who?" Karl asked as the name Willard had used several times struck his hearing. He froze then. "Where's Mrs. Conrad?"

"She's still in England. She'd broken her foot and stayed behind," Willard said. "Miss McGowen took care of Elsie on the ship."

"Oh." He removed his coat and handed it to Willard. Karl hurried down the hallway to the front room, his footsteps faltering as he spied the woman sitting on the sofa, cradling Elsie in her lap.

Her head was down, one cheek resting on Elsie's head, eyes closed. Dark, nearly blue-black hair was tied back, or had been. The wind and rain had released several long strands from the restraint, leaving it to fall in thin clumps from her temple.

As if she heard his footsteps, or the creak of the old floors beneath the carpet, she slowly lifted her head, opened her eyes.

His steps nearly faltered again as thickly lashed, dark blue eyes settled on him and a soft smile formed on her lips. She looked tired and worn out, but could still very well be the most beautiful woman he'd ever seen.

It took effort to pull his eyes away and get his thoughts in order. He'd expected someone like Mrs. Conrad, not a young... He cleared his throat as he quietly crossed the room. "Miss McGowen, I assume."

She nodded, her smile making her high cheekbones more prominent. "And you are Uncle Karl. You and your brother favored each other."

The pain inside him sharpened. "We did."

After folding back the blanket covering Elsie, Miss McGowen used one knuckle to softly rub Elsie's cheek. "Poppet, wake up. Wake up. There's someone here to see you."

Karl's heart tumbled as Elsie lifted sleepy lids and smiled. He stepped closer to the sofa, knelt down.

"Look, Poppet," Miss McGowen whispered softly, pointing her finger at him. "Look who is here."

Karl would never have considered himself a sentimental man, but the way his niece softly cried out his name and flung her arms around his neck, brought more than a sting to his eyes. Picking Elsie off the woman's lap, he held her tight, stood and turned around as moisture formed in his eyes. The pain inside him was greater than ever because she'd lost so much, endured so much. There was also thankfulness inside him, because she had survived.

Her hold around his neck tightened. "I dropped Betsy off the boat," she whimpered.

"That's all right, darling. We will get you a new doll," he whispered, kissing the top of her head.

"Bridget saved her."

He grinned. "That's good." Although he had no idea who Bridget was, he asked, "So you don't need a new dolly?"

She shook her head and then leaned back, looked at him.

Her rosy face was so precious, so cute. He kissed her forehead. "I'm happy you're home."

"Mommy and Daddy weren't on the new boat." Her tiny lips quivered.

His heart constricted. "I know, sweetie."

A tiny frown formed as she looked at him seriously. "It was dark. And cold. And there was no bed."

The stinging in his eyes intensified. "You are home now." If there was a way he could erase her memory of the past few days, he would. "Where it is warm and you have your very own bed."

She nodded, yawned and laid her head on his shoulder. "And Bridget and Betsy."

"And Bridget and Betsy," he said in agreement, assuming Bridget must be another doll. Elsie adored the one he'd given her for Christmas. As soon as she'd opened it, she'd named the doll Betsy and never went anywhere without her. "I'll carry you up there now and tuck you in."

She nodded and let out a long sigh.

The poor little thing had to be exhausted. It was after

one in the morning, as the chiming mantel clock had just alerted. He turned toward the sofa. Nodded. "Miss McGowen, would you bring her dolls, please?"

Nodding, she collected the Betsy doll off the sofa and gathered the blanket in her other hand as she stood.

Assuming the Bridget doll was inside the blanket, he nodded toward the doorway. She began walking, and her slow, almost unstable footsteps showed how exhausted she had to be, too.

"You can use Mrs. Conrad's room for the time being," he said.

"Thank you," she said quietly. "I appreciate a place to sleep tonight."

Elsie's hold had relaxed and her even breathing said she'd already fallen back to sleep. He nodded at Willard, who stood in the doorway and told the nanny, "Follow Willard. I'll be right behind you."

Willard led the way up the steps, and as Karl followed, he figured the young Irish girl must have been the only nanny Benjamin and Annette could find on short notice. That would be the only reason to hire someone so young. Over the years, Mary Andrews, Willard's wife and cook, who also oversaw the household staff, had hired young maids. It had never worked out. The experience they'd had with some that young had been that they'd been looking to become more than a maid.

Thank goodness Mary had found Mildred Dahl. An older woman who came in, cleaned and left. He'd only seen her a couple of times in the past three years, ever since she'd been hired. The young maid before her, he'd found in his bed, waiting for him one night.

Women would do anything to get what they wanted.

His mother had. For the right price, she'd sold him and Benjamin to their father. More than once. She was the reason he'd sworn off women years ago. For himself. Marriage was the last thing he'd ever need, ever want.

Willard led them directly to Elsie's room, and Karl laid her down on the bed where the covers had already been turned down. He held out his hand toward Miss McGowen.

She handed him Betsy.

He tucked the doll next to Elsie and held out his hand again.

"This is a blanket off the *Titanic*," she said. "And needs to be laundered."

"Where's her other doll? The one she called Bridget?"

"I'm Bridget," she said.

His spine shivered slightly as he folded the covers up over Elsie and the doll, kissed Elsie's head. Without glancing at the new nanny, he told Willard, "Show her to Mrs. Conrad's room for now."

"Yes, sir."

Karl left the room, wondering what his brother had been thinking by hiring someone so young, so beautiful.

Chapter Three

So tired she could barely stand, Bridget locked her knees to keep herself upright as she waited for Karl Wingard to leave the room. His looks had surprised her. She'd known he was Benjamin's brother, but hadn't expected them to look so similar in some ways. The dark eyes and hair mainly. Karl's eyes were just like Elsie's. As dark as fresh brewed coffee. But he also looked different than his brother. More handsome. Older, perhaps, and most certainly more aloof.

As soon as he left the room, she leaned closer to Willard, whose very soul must be at the right hand of God, because he'd been as kind as they come from the moment he'd approached her at the dock. "If you don't mind, I'd prefer to sleep here, with Elsie. The poor little poppet hasn't slept well, and I don't want her to be alone if she awakes in the middle of the night." The first couple of nights, Elsie had missed her parents so much she'd whimpered for them in her sleep. It was beyond heart-wrenching.

Willard's kind blue eyes softened as he nodded. "That will be perfectly fine, miss, perfectly fine."

"Thank you."

He winked one eye. "I will just go get the items my Mary has put in the room for you."

"I'm right here," his wife said, walking in the door with an armload of clothes.

Mrs. Andrews, Mary, had been as kind as her husband, serving hot tea as soon as they'd arrived at the house, and another cup as she'd waited for Karl to return home, in the front room, where she'd fought to stay awake. She'd promised Elsie that she wouldn't let her go until she put her in her uncle Karl's arms. And she hadn't. Since that terrible, terrible night when the lifeboat they'd been put in had been lowered into the water, she hadn't let go of Elsie for a moment. Not a single moment.

"Here, now," Mary said. "I have a nightgown for you, and some underthings as well as a dress for in the morning. They are mine, so they might be a bit big, but they will do until we can get you something else to wear. I know you're tired, but I will sit with the little miss while you use the water closet across the hall. You go take yourself a hot bath. You'll sleep better afterward."

Bridget sighed—a bath sounded so wonderful—yet she glanced at the bed. "Elsie needs a bath, too."

"She'll get one in the morning," Mary said. "Now, scoot. I know you'll feel better afterward, and I'll be right here if she wakes."

The workers and passengers on the *Carpathia* had been very kind, but the ship had already been at capacity. Adding another seven hundred people had meant there was no opportunity for bathing, or beds for that matter. She'd slept sitting against the wall in one of the corridors with Elsie on her lap the past three nights.

The idea of scrubbing clean was enough to bring tears to her eyes. She just wished she could scrub clean the nightmarish memories as easily.

"Thank you," she said, taking the items from Mary. "I won't be long."

The couple looked as tired as she felt. They were older, older than Da even, and had openly wept while hugging after she'd carried Elsie inside the solid, huge home of brick and thick lumber.

Karl Wingard had wept, too. He'd turned away, so she wouldn't notice. She had, but would never say a word because men were that way. They'd rather drown their sorrows in a pint than let a tear fall.

Her heart had gone out to him, though, at how he'd held his niece so tenderly, as he'd silently wept.

She entered the water closet, a room as elegant as the ones on the *Titanic*. Her eyes slammed shut, closing out the memory. *Help me forget, dear, sweet Lord, just help me forget some things. They don't do anyone any good.*

She gave herself a moment for the prayer to be sent and received, and then quickly undressed and climbed in the tub while the water was still running. After a thorough scrubbing, including soaping her hair twice, she rinsed, stepped out and toweled dry. Touched that Mary had even remembered to loan her a brush and comb, she removed the snarls from her hair, which took longer than she'd wished because she was worried about Elsie. Once her hair hung smoothly down her back, she dressed in the soft cotton nightgown and then left the room.

"I'll take your dirty things," Mary said. "Have them washed tomorrow."

Bridget would like to never see that dull blue dress

again, but knew that wasn't possible. She had to be even more practical than ever. All of her belongings, including her crocheted pouch of money, were now on the bottom of the Atlantic, with so, so many other items worth far more.

"Thank you," she said, once again wishing she could block her memories. Block her mind from the sights and sounds of that night. Of watching the lights on the massive ship disappear, row by row by row. Of seeing the ship break apart, then completely vanish. The shouts, the screams, had been horrific, so had the complete silence that had then followed.

"You crawl into bed, now," Mary said. "Everything is going to be fine. Just fine."

Bridget nodded, her throat was swelling too fast to speak. For the first time since that night, she didn't feel helpless. Hopeless.

She'd survived, but more importantly, Elsie had survived. There was guilt inside for surviving when so many hadn't, but only for herself, not for Elsie. She was extremely grateful for Elsie's survival. She was also very grateful that Karl had sent Willard to the docks to collect them. Stepping off the *Carpathia* had been overwhelming. All she could think of was to shout his name, and was so thankful Willard had heard her.

Mary waved a hand at the bed, and knowing the older woman wouldn't leave until she was tucked in, Bridget climbed in beside Elsie and snuggled her close.

The room went dark and the door closed with a soft click. Bridget held her breath for a moment, then, unable to hold them back, let the tears flow.

It was such a relief to be here, on solid ground, off the ocean. Yet, much like boarding the huge ocean liner had been, it was bittersweet. She'd delivered Elsie home, and tomorrow would need to leave. Figure out how to get to Chicago.

She would miss the little poppet as much as she'd ever missed anyone in her life. More, perhaps. It was comforting to know Elsie had so many people who loved her, especially her uncle Karl. Bridget hadn't known what to expect, but upon seeing the tall, broad-shouldered man kneel down and then embrace the child so lovingly, a great comfort had overcome her. She had forgiven her uncle Matt, and during the past few days she'd grown thankful that it had been her on the *Titanic* and not her uncle. He wouldn't have survived. So few men had, only a very small portion of those from third class and steerage. The sinking of the *Titanic* had created lifeboats full of widows. So many widows.

When her eyes popped open, it took her senses a moment to catch up, figure out where she was before Bridget could let out a sigh of relief. Sunlight was streaming in through the windows, and it was a welcome sight. A truly welcome sight.

Carefully, to not wake Elsie, Bridget scooted off the bed and quietly put on the dress Mary had loaned her. The dress was big in the shoulders, breast and waist, and so short her shins were exposed, but it was clean and a lovely shade of orange, almost a peach color, with a lace collar.

The clean stockings felt as near to heaven as anything she could imagine. It was strange how little things, things that were so common, so taken for granted, could become such major issues. Water had splashed into the boat when it had been lowered, and her feet had become soaked through that night, so cold they still ached.

She pushed the thought aside, put on her shoes and brushed her hair while walking around the lovely room that held everything a little girl could want. There was a small painted white desk, a pink cradle for Betsy, a tiny wooden table with two spindle-backed chairs and set with a blue and white child's tea service, shelves of books and other toys, and a closet full of colorful clothes. The walls were covered in wallpaper of tiny pink roses, and sheer pink curtains hung over two large windows.

"Bridget, we're home."

She turned and smiled at the little girl rubbing her eyes. "Yes, Poppet, we are." Holding out her hand, she continued, "Come, pick out a dress to wear so we can pop you in the bathtub before breakfast." That had become her routine the past few days, quickly finding things to keep Elsie's little mind from focusing on her mommy and daddy and the perilous situations they'd encountered.

A short time later, with Elsie sparkling clean, wearing socks and shoes for the first time in days, and carrying Betsy, who also was wearing a clean dress, they ventured downstairs.

The big house had plastered and painted walls, dark polished woodwork, thick, colorfully patterned carpets and enough rooms that a person could get as lost as she had her first day on the *Titanic*, while looking for Betsy's owner.

She pushed out a sigh, truly wishing she could forget, but knew that would take time. Some things, she doubted she'd ever forget, so learning to live with them was what she would have to do.

"Uncle Karl!"

Bridget released Elsie's hand and watched as the girl ran across the dining room, into the arms of the man kneeling down to catch her. It warmed her heart to know that last night hadn't been a onetime occurrence, when he'd knelt down and embraced Elsie. The poor little poppet would need him more than ever now.

"What are you doing up so early?" he asked, hoisting Elsie up off the floor.

"I had a bath," she said. "Bridget put a bow in my hair and in Betsy's hair."

"I see that," he said. "A pretty pink bow for both of you."

"It matches our dresses."

"Yes, they do." He set her on a chair. "You and Betsy can join me for breakfast."

"And Bridget," Elsie said.

"Yes, and Bridget, too." He grasped the back of the chair next to Elsie's and then nodded her way. "Miss McGowen."

The dining room, with its massive table, high-backed wooden chairs, long drawered credenza along the back wall and low-hanging light fixture with several small electric lights flicking softly was like the rest of the house. *Elegant* was the word that came to mind. There was a soft carpet beneath her feet as she walked to the table, and her heart thudded oddly as their gazes locked briefly before she sat in the chair he held for her.

"Thank you," she heard herself say in a voice that didn't sound like her own. She'd lived in a pub that was full of men on a daily basis her entire life, but something about Karl made her nervous. He had last night, too, but she'd been too exhausted to give it much thought.

Or perhaps it was the surroundings. Much like when she'd ventured into areas only for the first-class passengers on the *Titanic*, Bridget knew when she was out of her station in life. Whether things were different in America or not, she was still the same, and some things were simply foreign to her, in ways that had nothing to do with the country or continent.

"I hope you slept well," he said, taking a seat at the head of the table, on the other side of Elsie.

"We did," Bridget answered, smiling down at a nodding Elsie, holding Betsy on her lap. Delight filled her at seeing the little girl clean and smiling, but as she looked up and met Karl's intense gaze, her delight wavered. A man like him was as foreign to her as the surroundings.

"Will you be having company for breakfast this morning, Master Karl?" Willard asked, smiling brightly as he entered the room carrying a platter.

"Yes, Willard," Karl answered. "Miss Elsie, Betsy and Miss McGowen will be joining me. You can hold my meal and serve us all at the same time, and perhaps you can find a box for Miss Elsie to sit upon."

"Right away." Willard carried the platter back through the door.

"Does Elsie normally not join you for breakfast?" Bridget asked, confused.

He looked at her with a small frown tugging his dark brows downward for several moments before stating, "Children normally take their meals in the kitchen, or their rooms."

Bridget found what he said and the way he said it

somewhat terse—unusual—but refrained from questioning why.

He picked up his blue and white china cup and took a sip before asking, "I'm assuming you were hired in England, employed as a replacement for the trip home, while Mrs. Conrad recuperated?"

It was clear that he chose his words carefully as to not remind Elsie of the tragedy. Bridget appreciated that, his thoughtfulness. She too had talked around the bush while on the *Carpathia* and looking for Benjamin and Annette, not wanting to upset Elsie. Therefore, she simply replied, "No."

He lifted a dark brow. "Oh? When then?"

"Never."

His frown was back, darker, as he glanced from her to Elsie and back again. "How is that so?"

"I was never hired or employed." She smiled down at Elsie.

The door opened and Willard entered the room again, this time carrying a wooden box. His smile was still as bright. There was something about him that reminded her of Da. His short stature, ring of curly gray hair below his balding center, or the twinkle in his eyes. Maybe all of it.

"I believe this will work for our little miss," he said.

Bridget lifted Elsie and held her as Willard positioned the box on the chair.

Settling Elsie on the box, she whispered, "Look at that, Poppet, now you're as tall as me."

Elsie giggled and set Betsy on the box beside her. "There's room for Betsy, too."

"There most certainly is." Willard patted Elsie's head.

"What do you say?" Bridget whispered to Elsie.

"Thank you, Willard, and Betsy says thank you, too."

"You are both very welcome." He winked one eye. "Your breakfast will be served directly."

"Thank you," Bridget answered.

Willard went to the credenza and promptly set napkins, silverware, cups and glasses before her and Elsie. Having waited on others her entire life, Bridget felt uncomfortable having him wait on her. While on the ship, she'd eaten at a restaurant, but that had been different— she'd paid for the service there.

"Would you prefer coffee or tea, Miss McGowen?" he asked while setting down a blue and white china cup and saucer.

"Coffee is fine," she said, knowing that the urn on the table contained coffee.

While filling her cup, he asked, "Cream or sugar, miss?"

"No, thank you."

He left the room, and she kept her eyes averted, feeling Karl watching her.

Willard returned a moment later, with a larger tray that held three plates and a pitcher of milk for Elsie. After serving them, he asked if there would be anything else.

"Yes," Karl said. "Once we've eaten, perhaps Elsie could join Mrs. Andrews in the kitchen while Miss McGowen and I speak privately."

"Of course, sir," Willard said.

The eggs and pancakes were delicious, as was the coffee, and Bridget was hungry, yet the food sat heavy in her stomach at the idea of speaking privately with

Karl. It was understandable he wanted to know all that had happened; she just wasn't ready to relive it. Her entire life seemed to be a series of reliving things. There had always been issues at the pub, where she'd had to explain what had happened and when. Brawls, broken tables and bottles. Da's illness and death.

This was different, though. There was something about him that kept making her heart thud oddly.

The meal proceeded with an unnatural slowness, and when it was over, Bridget, as she had most of her life, squared her shoulders to face what she had to face. Coming to America had been her father's dream; having a life where she wasn't confronted with one disaster after the other was what she dreamed of.

She'd have that someday. In Chicago, while running her own boardinghouse. She'd be in control then.

After Elsie had been delivered to the kitchen, Bridget left the dining room with Karl. Seated in a room hosting a large wooden desk, a set of wood chairs, a large, brown leather davenport and heavy brocade drapes hanging beside the tall windows, she kept her chin up, waiting for Karl to speak.

He'd been silent since they'd entered the room. She wondered if he wanted her to talk first, but she had no idea where to start.

"Am I to understand that you were not hired to be Elsie's nanny?" he finally said.

"Yes, I was never hired or employed by—to be her nanny." She had been asked, several times, but refused because that wasn't what Da had wanted for her.

"Then where is her nanny?" he asked, standing near the window, across the large room from where she sat on the davenport. "The list of survivors that I received from the *Carpathia*, specifically stated Elsie Wingard and her nanny."

"I did say that I was her nanny to the people on the *Carpathia* because people kept assuming I was her mother." Her heart ached as she continued, "I spent the entire first day, from the moment we were on board the ship until night fell, searching for her parents." The hope of finding Benjamin had vanished almost immediately. The lifeboats had been full of widows, sobbing and crying for their husbands. She had held out hope for Annette and continued to search the survivors every day. In the small ship's hospital, she had found her berth mate, Catherine, and Catherine's brother Sean, but other than that, the ship had been full of strangers.

He walked to the desk and leaned his arms on the back of the chair. "How did Elsie come to be in your care?"

"While boarding the ship in Southampton, I saw a doll falling from the first-class pier and caught it before it fell in the water. After boarding, I found Elsie and gave her the doll." She took a breath, and told herself to relate the story as simply as possible. "When Annette explained that Mrs. Conrad had broken her foot, I offered to watch Elsie during some of the events that Benjamin and Annette were committed to attending. One of those events was the night of the accident. Elsie and I were put in a lifeboat, together."

"You never saw Benjamin and Annette that night?"

She bit her lips together for a moment while shaking her head. "Not after they left the cabin at seven."

"Where are you from?"

"A small village north of Dublin."

"Am I correct in assuming you were emigrating to America?"

"Yes. To Chicago. I have distant family there."

"Are they expecting you?" He scratched the side of his face, near his temple, as if thinking. "Did they know you were aboard the *Titanic*?"

Her skin shivered slightly at his question. "No. Why?"

He walked around the chair and leaned a hip against the side of the desk. "As you can see, Miss McGowen, without Mrs. Conrad, my home is not sufficiently staffed to take care of Elsie properly. Each of the household employees have specific duties to see to that keep them busy. Since you have already formed a relationship with Elsie, I shall employee you to be her nanny until the return of Mrs. Conrad."

She had started shaking her head as soon as she'd understood what he'd been about to suggest. "I can't."

"Why not?"

"Because I have things to do." So many things. "I need to continue on to Chicago."

"How? Do you have the means?"

Her skin shivered. She didn't have the means to do anything, but she had the will. "I will find the means. It's what I have to do."

"If your family isn't waiting on you, a month or so won't matter," he said sternly. "Furthermore, as I've said, you've already formed a relationship with Elsie. She likes you."

"I like her, but I cannot—"

"Yes, you can." He walked back around the corner of the desk and sat in the chair. "I'll pay you the same salary as Mrs. Conard." With somewhat of a nod toward the door, he said, "Thank you, Miss McGowen."

Thank you? Did he think this was the end of the conversation? She took a moment, half wondering if she'd said something for him to assume that, but knew she hadn't. "No, you won't, Mr. Wingard, because I can't stay." She had thought he was like Annette and Benjamin, but he was far more like most of the other men she'd met over the years. A horse's arse for assuming she'd do exactly what they asked, when they asked it. She wasn't anyone's servant, and never would be.

"What do you suggest I do, Miss McGowen?"

Stop calling her Miss McGowen in that tone for one. It was stiffening her spine. "Hire a nanny."

"I don't have time. There's an inquiry starting today concerning the sinking of the *Titanic*, at the Waldorf Astoria Hotel, and I will be in attendance." His tone grew colder, firmer, as he spoke. "I will be in attendance every day until I find out exactly how and why my brother and his wife died. That commitment will not permit me the time to put the proper attention toward advertising, interviewing and hiring a nanny. If you believe the wage I'm offering is below you, you are mistaken."

"Below me?" Anger drove her to her feet. This was the very thing she had not wanted to encounter in America. "I do not believe anything is above or below anyone. God created all races, all nations, from one blood, for his purposes! It is men, bigoted men, who, like you, believe they are above others!"

"It is the way of the world, Miss McGowen."

There it was again, that tone. The way he said her

name. As if he had to spit it out. "That does not make it right, *Mr. Wingard*." She spit his name out in return.

"Neither is my niece going without a nanny because of your stubbornness."

"My stubbornness?" Thoroughly irritated, she muttered a curse on him. *"Ualach sé chapall de chré na h-úire ort."*

He stared at her for a long moment and then laughed.

She glared at him, not finding humor in any of this.

"Do you believe you are the first Irish person to set foot in America?" he asked. "To toss out a curse like you are holier than thou?"

She lifted her chin. No, she did not believe that, but he deserved to be cursed for filling her with guilt. Elsie did need a nanny; it just couldn't be her.

"Six horse loads of graveyard clay upon you," he said. "That is what you just cursed me with, is it not?"

She stared at him without blinking, flustered he'd understood her completely. There was also a sting of guilt inside her that she'd have said that particular curse. He'd just lost his brother and sister-in-law, so she shouldn't have said graveyard clay. He'd just irritated her to her wit's end.

He licked his lips and glanced away, which she was thankful for so she could close her eyes for a moment in order to collect her decorum. Da always said she riled too easily. That she needed to learn to control her temper and hold her tongue. It had caused more than one patron to stomp out of the pub, threatening to never return. Da had said it wasn't proper for her to curse others, either.

"What I meant," he said, "and what you mistook, was that Mrs. Conrad has been with my family for many,

many years, and her salary, the same which I am willing to pay you, is far higher than you will find elsewhere."

She had not thought that was what he meant. Not at all.

"I was also being truthful when I said that I will be very busy the next few weeks. I will be. I have no idea how long the inquiry will continue, but I will be there. Every day."

That, too, irritated her. Elsie was alive, Annette and Benjamin weren't. He should be focused on his niece, on what she needed, not on his brother and sister-in-law. No matter what he did, he couldn't bring them back. If he didn't realize that, she felt inclined to point it out. "Elsie needs attention right now. She has been through so much. She needs to know she's not alone."

"I understand that," he said, "which is why I'm asking you to provide her the utmost attention, right now, when she needs it. I can't be two places at once."

He was still thinking about himself. That shouldn't surprise her. *Men.* She had certainly had her fill of them during her twenty-two years of life. No matter where they lived, men seemed to be the same.

"I need to leave in half an hour, Miss McGowen," he said. "Can I trust you will remain here, with Elsie, during my absence?"

Was he insinuating she'd leave Elsie alone? She hadn't done that for days, and wouldn't now! "I will be here," she said, anger still running through her blood, especially at the way he said her name. "Not because you hired me, because you didn't. I will be here because Elsie needs love and affection right now. Something you not only don't have time for, you appear incapable of even understanding what that is!" Needing to prove that, she added, "Children shouldn't eat in the kitchen. They should eat with their family!"

Karl pinched his lips together, watching as she marched toward the door. He hadn't felt like smiling in days, but she was so full of spit and fire, it was hard not to. That had surprised him. She'd appeared timid last night and during breakfast.

"And," she said, spinning to look at him while opening the door, "my name is Bridget, not *Miss McGowen*."

"Very well, Bridget," he said. His smile broke loose as her long black hair flipped and flopped as she spun again and marched out of his office, shutting the door firmly in her wake. In that moment, he found great appreciation for Bridget McGowen, for he doubted anyone would have protected his niece with more passion the past several days than her.

He hadn't meant to insult her, and had been surprised that she'd refused his offer. She was right in the fact that he didn't have time right now, and that he didn't know what children needed. He was an uncle. Not a father. Benjamin and Annette had set the schedule of Elsie eating in the kitchen. Or maybe Mrs. Conrad had. He truly had no idea. He and Benjamin had eaten with their father for as long as he could remember. They may have eaten in the kitchen when very small, before their mother left, but… Ah, hell, it didn't matter. He needed to leave. A special subcommittee of the Senate had organized hearings to begin this morning and he wasn't going to miss a minute of testimony. Someone was responsible for his brother's death. For leaving his niece an orphan. For leaving him in a situation he was ill prepared to undertake. Including hiring a nanny!

He grabbed his jacket and headed for the door. Nannies should be old and crotchety, not young, pretty and stubborn.

Chapter Four

The expansive ballroom had been arranged in a court-like setting, with a panel of senators seated at the front of the room, chairs for interviewees positioned before them and row upon row of heavy upholstered chairs for spectators.

There were plenty of those, spectators, from all over, and a literal plethora of reporters. Karl took a seat next to several other major investors of the White Star Line. Frustration coiled in his stomach knowing many of them were there because of money, not the lives that had been lost.

He had to wonder if he'd be here, like them, with the same interests they had, if not for Benjamin and Annette. That left him unsettled. He'd been born into wealth and had worked on building that wealth his entire life, but at this moment, he would give it all up to have Benjamin and Annette alive. Here with their daughter. Able to watch her grow. Guide her through life.

They weren't. This inquiry wouldn't change that, but if there was something that could be done to prevent another disaster like this, he had to be a part of it. For them. So that their lives hadn't been taken in vain.

He had to do that for Elsie.

The inquiry didn't get underway until after ten that morning. Karl listened to the opening remarks and took notes on all the subjects that would be discussed over the next few days. Following that was a long report about the White Star Line, including those who had invested in capital for the *Titanic* and her sister ships. That list included his name, and Benjamin's, which caused people to glance his way and murmur.

As a report on the building of the *Titanic* and the testing of her waterproof compartments began, Karl's mind drifted. He'd read a similar report months ago, and as he glanced around the room, at survivors who'd been asked to testify, his thoughts drifted to Miss McGowen.

Bridget.

He withheld the smile that tried to form as he thought of her informing him that was her name while stomping out of his office this morning, the hem of her skirt swishing around her shins. His thoughts paused on that. Shins, not ankles. He hadn't realized at the time, but her dress had been too large in places, while also being too short. It must have been borrowed. Mary must have loaned it to her. Of course, she had, because Bridget had lost everything except for the clothes on her back during the sinking.

Why hadn't he realized that? Elsie had returned home to a closet full of clothes, but Bridget hadn't. He settled a thoughtful gaze on some of the survivors in the room. Although they too had lost everything, they had the means to obtain new clothes.

The first witness called to testify was the managing

director of the White Star Line, followed by the captain of the *Carpathia*. The captain's report of the field of icebergs he'd encountered, and how the passengers of the *Carpathia* shared whatever they could with the survivors—from blankets to extra clothing and shoes—had Karl's throat going dry at the terrifying ordeal Elsie and Bridget had lived through.

The committee adjourned for a lunch break after the captain's account, and the first thing Karl did was find a telephone.

Julia Robertson, an integral part of why the Wingard Brothers office continued to operate to the highest level whether he was in the office or not, answered his call. After a short discussion about the inquiry and the amount of a donation she should send to the Red Cross on behalf of the company, he said, "I would like you to complete a personal errand for me."

"Of course, sir," Julia replied. "What do you need?"

"My niece's nanny remained in England, and the woman who took care of Elsie during the voyage will remain with Elsie until Mrs. Conrad returns home. She lost everything during the voyage. I'd like you to go shopping for her and have the items delivered to the house."

"Certainly. What does she need?"

"All the necessities," he said, not knowing exactly what that all entailed. If today was an indication of anything, it suggested the hearing would take far more than a week. "Everything she might need on a daily basis. Clothes, shoes, hats, coats. I don't have a list, but anything, everything you can think of that a woman needs for at least a month."

"Do you know her size?" Julia asked. "Never mind,

I know you're busy. I'll call your home. Speak to Mrs. Andrews."

"Yes, do that, and have the items delivered as soon as possible."

"Of course. Is there anything else?"

He searched his mind, but still wasn't sure of what was truly needed. "Just make sure there is plenty of everything and make sure they are nice." Something else Bridget had said registered, and he added, "And see if you can find a stool so Elsie can comfortably sit at the dining room table."

"I'll have everything delivered today, sir."

He hung up, ate and made his way back into the inquiry room. The afternoon witnesses included the Second Officer of the *Titanic*. As had happened that morning, when the managing director of the White Star Line had been sworn in, rumbles spread through the crowd, questioning how these men had survived when so many other prominent men and women hadn't. Karl couldn't deny those thoughts entered his mind, but were overshadowed by other thoughts, mainly of Elsie and Bridget.

They had to have been so terrified, so cold, so uncertain. He wanted to leave, to go home and confirm that they were safe. Alive.

He grinned to himself. She'd probably curse him again.

Karl remained at the inquiry, taking notes because he was not sure he would remember all that was being said. The final person to testify for the day was a bedroom steward, whose account of truly horrifying incidents had Karl's full attention. Adjournment was called at ten-thirty that night. Prior to leaving, Karl found the young steward and shook his hand.

"You played a major role in saving the life of my niece, and I just wanted to thank you," Karl said.

"You're welcome, sir," the man said, his eyes filling with moisture. "May I ask your niece's name?"

"Elsie Wingard."

The man nodded as a reverent smile appeared on his face. "Your niece's rescue can be more attributed to her nanny than to me, sir. Even while rowing, Miss McGowen never let go of Elsie. She kept her on her lap. Others offered to hold the child, but she refused." He bowed his head slightly while adding, "Will you please offer her my condolences? She'd asked me to find Elsie's parents, tell them they'd been put in a life boat, but there wasn't time. I didn't have the heart to tell her, not even while on the *Carpathia*."

Karl maintained his composure as he nodded. "I will. Thank you, again."

He left the hotel and drove home with a heavy heart and mind. Bridget's heart and mind must be even heavier. She'd lived through it. He'd only heard other people's accounts of what had happened. Bits and pieces of what she'd encountered.

An enormous, almost overwhelming debt of gratitude, but also respect for Bridget, filled him. That was uncannily rare for him. His mother had instilled an indifference toward women. She'd done that by the way she'd sold—there was no other word for it—him and Benjamin to their father for a large sum of money, and then, when that was gone, she'd returned, demanding more. Every year. On their birthdays. The irony of that never failed to goad him. He remembered one such incident clearly, and had come to hate birthdays after that year.

His mother had once said that his father had invested in her just like he had other ventures, and that she'd supplied what he'd wanted—children—and that she should be paid yearly for that. Dividends on what she'd produced.

Lights shone in the house windows as he pulled into the drive, and Willard was waiting to close the carriage house doors when he turned off his Packard.

"Bri—Miss McGowen is waiting for you in the main living room," Willard said as they walked to the house.

Karl's heartbeat quickened. "Why?"

"She said she needed to speak with you before going to bed," Willard replied.

Karl buried the flash of anger that raised inside him, certain Bridget was going to say she was leaving. Just like his mother had left when he'd been Elsie's age and Benjamin an infant.

Bridget was once again seated on the burgundy sofa near the fireplace and offered a tentative smile as he entered the room. His heart thudded oddly at the sight of her. No woman did that to him, and he wasn't impressed that she did.

"Hello," she said.

"Is everything all right?" he asked, forcing his feet to walk across the room. She was still wearing the borrowed dress from this morning, and he clenched his teeth. Was that meant to be a sign she was leaving?

She shook her head, then nodded. "Elsie is fine. She had a wonderful day and is sleeping." Folding her hands on her lap, she continued, "I owe you an apology and couldn't go to bed without offering it. My Da always said to never let the sun go down on your anger."

An apology. He didn't know how to respond to that, and sat down in the chair adjacent to the sofa to consider it. "You're not still angry at me?"

She looked down and then up at him, with sincerity filling those blue eyes. "No, and I shouldn't have been angry with you this morning. I apologize for that and hope you can forgive me. I just—"

"I accept." He didn't like apologies and chose to get this over with as quickly as possible. "I apologize, as well. I hadn't meant to upset you."

Her face softened and he was once again struck by how lovely she was, even in a borrowed dress. Oddly, her sincerity had evoked his own. That was a rarity, but the truth. He hadn't meant to upset her. "I was being selfish this morning. I was thinking of the only thing I can do for Elsie, and how I couldn't do that without her being properly looked after."

Her dark brows tugged together above the bridge of her nose. "Do for Elsie?"

"Yes, this inquiry." Recalling all he'd heard today, he leaned forward, laid a hand atop of hers. The touch made his hand tingle, but he kept it there. "I can't change what happened. I can't bring her parents back. I can never give her the life she would have had with them." He clamped his back teeth together as the pain of his brother's death struck again. "What I can do is find out what happened and hopefully work on a way to prevent it from ever happening again. Hopefully, someday, that will ease her pain, to know her parents hadn't died in vain."

Bridget let what he'd said filter through her mind for a moment, much like she had her own anger this morning. Throughout the day, she'd realized just how quick she'd been to jump to conclusions. He was concerned about his niece. The stool he'd had delivered to the house was only a small piece of evidence of that. The way he'd gone to the docks looking for them last night was another one. Annette and Benjamin had spoken highly of him, so had Willard and Mary throughout the day, and she herself had to face her own hour of truth. How she'd been more to blame than him this morning.

She glanced at his hand. The warmth of his palm was radiating up her arm, straight to her heart. He'd not only accepted her apology, but offered his own. Which truly wasn't necessary, nor was there anything he could do about Benjamin's and Annette's deaths.

Yet, he thought there was, because of his own pain. She could see it on his face and felt bad for him. So bad. "The *Titanic* hit an iceberg," she said quietly. "It was an accident."

The pressure of his hand increased. "True, but the ship had been warned that there were icebergs in the area and to take caution."

"It had been?"

"Yes." He shifted in his chair, leaned closer. "There might be something that can be done to prevent that in the future, or some of the other issues that occurred. I need to be at this inquiry, to learn all I can, and in order to do so, I need your help. Need you to be here with Elsie. I don't want her to have more changes. More loss. Not right now."

"I don't want her to, either," Bridget admitted. That's

what nearly tore her heart in two. Elsie did need her, but she had to fulfill the promises she made to Da. "It's just that I made promises, too."

"To whom?"

"My Da. He'd pinched pennies for years so that I could come to America."

"I understand, and if you will stay here with Elsie until Mrs. Conrad returns, I will personally see that you get to Chicago. To your family there. It shouldn't be more than four or six weeks."

She closed her eyes, trying to tell herself she could do that, but at the same time, she knew herself. The longer she stayed, the harder it would be to leave. There was more to it, too. "I want to stay, I want to help you and her, but my Da made me promise that when I finally got here, I wouldn't become a servant. That happened to others that we knew, and for many of them, their lives here were no better than back home." Da had also said she didn't have the temperament to be a servant.

He nodded. "So that's why I can't hire you."

"Yes. That's why I wouldn't let Annette hire me, either." She drew in a deep breath, glad she'd finally voiced her true concerns, even though it didn't bring a conclusion to anything. Da had worked so hard for her to get here, she had to keep her promise. "Da believed, and I believe, a person should work hard for their money, but they shouldn't be indentured."

"Indentured servitude is illegal in America," he said. "Has been for years."

She shook her head. "But it's still happening. There are road agents selling contracts every day in Ireland."

He sat back in his chair. "I never thought of that, Bridget, but I believe you. There are some things, no matter how many laws are passed, that we just can't seem to escape, aren't there?"

"Yes." She let out a long sigh, having no idea what to do. "Da said that when you commit your life to someone else, you lose your own."

"Does your father know you survived the accident?"

For the first time since his death, she was glad he wasn't here, that he wasn't in Ireland wondering if she'd lived or died. "No. He died the week before I left."

"I'm sorry."

She nodded in acknowledgment, and then said, "I'm sorry for your loss. Losing people we love is very hard."

He looked away and cleared his throat before asking, "What sort of work did your father do?"

Understanding that everyone dealt with death differently, she answered, "He owned a pub. The Green Door. It's a small pub, a stop for travelers between Dublin and Drogheda, and a place where fishermen would gather to share their tales."

"Did you work there? At the pub?"

"Yes, my entire life."

A soft smile curved the corners of his lips upward. "How old are you?"

"Twenty-two." She pushed out a sigh, partially because his smile made him look friendly, handsome and like someone she didn't want to disappoint. Perhaps talking about her father would help him understand that talking about his brother might help him. "Da wanted me to leave, come to America years ago, but I refused. He needed me. Then he grew ill. Grew slower, tired. He had the cancer poison. There was nothing we could do about it. He needed me to stay, to be with him, help him, and I promised I would leave, when the time came."

"That had to have been difficult."

She nodded. "It was some days, seeing him so sickly, knowing he wanted a different life for me than working in a pub."

"He let you work in a pub, but didn't want you to be a servant?"

He made it sound like they were nearly the same thing. They weren't even close. "Yes. He owned the pub. It's what provided the means for me to leave. I needed to work there, help him, so he could save the money for me to leave."

Nodding, he said, "I see what you're saying, and I hope you understand what I'm saying. I need your help, so does Elsie." He rubbed his chin. "And, as I see it, you need a place to stay until the White Star Line compensates you for your losses, so you can continue on to Chicago. I should think we could come up with something that works for both of us."

What he said was true, but as she nodded, her thoughts stalled. "What do you mean compensates my losses?"

"The shipping line had insurance, a policy in place to cover losses, to the line and the passengers."

She hadn't known anything about an insurance policy. If she could get her money back, she could go to Chicago as soon as possible. Today, while lamenting over her anger this morning, she'd realized why she'd gotten so angry, so quickly. She was afraid. Afraid of staying with Elsie any longer than necessary. She already cared about Elsie so dearly that leaving her was going to be difficult. But she had to. The night of the accident, she remembered taking her money pouch out of her pocket and setting it on the table next to the sofa before she'd fallen asleep. "How long will that take?"

"I'm not sure, but it shouldn't take long. As soon as I know, I will let you know." He cocked his head sideways, looking at her. "I feel the need to point out that the people who work for me have never been indentured servants. Willard, Mrs. Andrews and Mrs. Dahl are employees. Paid a fair wage for their time, their work, just like the employees of my company. It's no different than working somewhere else."

Bridget nodded as she considered that. Da hadn't wanted her to become a servant, but she did wonder if he'd think taking care of Elsie would be all right. He'd surely have realized that it was only because she did need a place to stay and a way to earn money until being compensated for her losses.

Karl stood up and held out a hand. "It's late. The hearings won't resume until ten-thirty tomorrow morning. We can discuss this again before I leave."

She laid her hand in his, accepting his assistance to rise off the sofa.

He released her hand and gently cupped her elbow to escort her out of the room. It reminded her of how his brother had done that with Annette. It was something she'd never experienced.

"Your brother spoke highly of you," she said. "So did Annette."

He gave a slight nod. "The items I had delivered to the house today, for you, are gifts. Tokens of appreciation. I truly believe that if not for you, I would not have my niece right now. Her life means more to me than anything else on this earth. By accepting, using the gifts, it will prove that you feel that way, too."

She held in her sigh, recognizing he wasn't ready to talk about his brother. The items he'd sent to the house for her were something they'd need to discuss. More dresses, underclothes, coats, hats, shoes and socks than she'd owned her entire life, along with other things—a hairbrush, mirror, comb, even face powders and creams. She'd only had three dresses with her on the ship, not a dozen.

Because she did need something to wear, she would accept a couple of the dresses, but saying that accepting them would prove how much Elsie meant to her, made him sound like he'd kissed the Blarney Stone. That made her smile rather than irritated her. He wasn't the type of man who would kiss a stone. He was too stiff, too proper for that.

She caught him glancing down at her, or maybe it was the other way around. Pinching her lips together to hide the smile, she shook her head.

"I do believe I was right about one thing this morning," he said.

"Oh?"

He nodded and winked. "That you are stubborn."

Her smile broke loose. "Now, that is the kettle calling the pot black if I ever heard one."

"Perhaps, but we are both looking out for Elsie. That we can agree on."

That *was* something she could agree on.

They continued walking side by side to the staircase that ran along the wall of the wide hallway that went from the front door all the way to the back door. The kitchen and dining rooms were near the back while the front living room and his office were near the front. Another hallway past his office led to two small sitting rooms and a water closet and what Willard referred to as his and Mary's "living quarters." The upstairs had six very large bedrooms and two water closets. The home was enchanting, as was the backyard that Elsie had played in during the warmth of the day. It had a black iron fence that separated the yard from the houses on either side and a large porch where a high-back swing, large enough for two people, hung on heavy ropes.

"You have a lovely home," she said as they climbed the steps. Even more lovely than Annette had made it sound.

"Thank you, but I don't deserve any credit. It was built long before I was born," he answered. "My ancestors came to America before the Revolutionary War. They fought in it, and the Civil War. My grandfather bought this house, raised his family here. He owned a merchant shipping company and divided it four ways, to my father and each of his brothers. They all four sold their ships. My father stayed here, became a banker and my uncles all went west. Montana, Colorado, and California. Cattle, gold and textiles. That's what they invested in and have done very well. They and their families traveled here last year, when my father died."

Annette had told her about that, how Elsie didn't have any grandparents. "I'm sorry that you recently lost your father, too."

"It's been over a year now," he replied as they arrived at the top of the stairs. With a nod, he said, "Sleep well, and we'll talk after breakfast."

"Good night." She went right down the hall while he went left, and she forced herself not to look over her shoulder when she arrived at Elsie's bedroom. There was something about him that warmed her insides in a peculiar and unfamiliar way. She had to be cautious of that because she was known to care too much about others. That's what Da said.

She slept in the room adjacent to Elsie's that night, in Mrs. Conrad's bed, knowing she had to allow the child to become accustomed to sleeping alone again, to know she was home and safe.

Bridget felt safe, too, and wondered if Da, if he knew all the details, would have said she could work for Karl, be Elsie's nanny for a few weeks. Da was a reasonable man, and she herself had already admitted that she needed to be practical. It wasn't as if she was totally breaking her promise. She would still go to Chicago as soon as possible. Until she had the means, working for Karl wouldn't be so different than working for Da had been. Da had been so against her becoming a household worker because he'd said it would be like a trap, that once a person started, they never got out.

She'd just have to make sure that didn't happen to her.

Karl wasn't at the breakfast table the following morning. Willard explained he was in his office, taking telephone calls. Bridget sensed something was wrong, but didn't ask questions, not in front of Elsie. Before breakfast was done, she heard a door slam.

Then another.

Later, as she sent Elsie into the downstairs water closet to wash after eating, she asked Willard where Karl had gone, knowing the second door had been the front door of the house.

"He received terrible news this morning, Bridget. Just terrible," he replied, his entire face showing his misery. "They were to return Benjamin's and Annette's remains here, to be buried, but Karl just got word that they will be buried in Nova Scotia."

There were times when he spoke like a servant and others when he dropped the miss, mistress and master titles and sounded like a family member. Laying a comforting hand on his arm, she asked, "Why?"

He shook his head, blinked at the wetness in his eyes. "Because they were too far gone, the bodies…" He shook his head again, unable to say more.

Her heart ached for him, for Karl and Elsie. She wrapped her arms around him. "I'm so sorry, Willard."

"Karl insisted he will have them brought home. That the little miss needs a place to go, to…"

"I understand," she said, hugging him tighter. "There has just been so much tragedy with all of this. So much tragedy."

"For you, too." He released her and patted her upper arms. "You must have known others on the ship."

Whether she knew others or not didn't make the loss of so many less sorrowful, yet she nodded. "I did. Not many other than my berth mate and her brother. They both survived, but were very ill on the *Carpathia*. I do hope, do pray, that they are receiving care now."

Willard squared his shoulders. "What are their names? I shall find out for you. The paper listed the hospitals where people were taken. I will call them."

Her heart skipped a beat. She had wondered about Catherine and Sean since saying goodbye to them before the *Carpathia* had docked.

"Please, let me find them for you," Willard said earnestly. "I've felt as if my hands have been tied, not able to help with anything."

She smiled at him and his sincerity. "Catherine and Sean O'Malley. It would be good to know where they are."

Within the hour, he entered the sitting room where she and Elsie were sitting on the floor drawing pictures.

"My Mary will keep an eye on the little miss while I take you to see your friends," Willard said.

Bridget pressed a hand to her chest at the thumping of her heart. "You found them? Are they all right?"

He was beaming with pride. "Yes, I did, and I will drive you there to see them."

She would love to see Catherine, but shook her head as she glanced at Elsie.

"My Mary has watched Miss Elsie many times for Mrs. Conrad." He took her hand. "There is nothing to worry about. Now, go put on one of those nice hats that arrived yesterday for you."

She wasn't sure if it was for herself, or him, but her decision was made. "I need to go with Willard for a while," she told Elsie.

"All right." Elsie nodded to her drawing. "I will finish your picture for you."

Willard gave her a smile.

She grinned in return. "I'll be right back," she told him, and then hurried upstairs to put on a hat and a thin coat over her dress. It was one of the new ones. A yellow and white striped one, with a lacy collar and cuffs. She had on new shoes, too, and for the first day since the accident, her feet didn't hurt.

If only she had a few more hairpins, so she could pin up her hair rather than just pin back the sides, but the wind on the *Carpathia* had caused her to lose all but three. After making sure the three pins were secure, she brushed the ends of her hair and then picked out a hat and coat from several in the closet in the bedroom across the hall from Elsie's. There were also purses, but she didn't have anything to put in one. Still, she took one, a white one, and a pair of white gloves, which she put in the purse as she hurried back downstairs. She'd never owned such stylish clothes and felt a bit vain at how much she admired herself in the mirror. A hat had only been something she'd dreamed of owning, and she couldn't stop from glancing at her reflection in the windows as she walked to the sitting room.

"You look pretty, Bridget," Elsie said, still on the floor drawing pictures.

"Very pretty," Mary said from where she sat on the floral sofa. "Willard is pulling the automobile out of the carriage house. You take your time. Enjoy visiting with your friends. We will be just fine."

"Thank you, very much." Bridget leaned down and kissed the top of Elsie's head. "You be a good girl."

"I will," Elsie agreed.

Bridget told herself she should be glad that Elsie was so comfortable with her leaving. That was how it should be. It was her that had the problem with it. Not just in leaving Elsie, but in leaving the house. It was frightening. The last time she'd left home it had been to board the *Titanic*.

This wasn't her home, so the comparison was silly.

She drew in a deep breath, called herself a ninny and left the room.

Willard met her in the hallway and explained that both Catherine and Sean were at a hospital only a couple of miles away and that the report he was given said that they there were both making very good progress.

The only other time she'd ridden in an automobile was the night Willard had picked her up at the docks. She sat in the back seat again, because that was the door he'd opened for her. As they backed away from the house, she thought how different it looked in the light of day. The red bricks, white framed windows, front pillars and black shutters all shimmered in the sunlight, making it look welcoming. It was a welcoming home, and she needed to be thankful for that. Without Karl Wingard's generosity, she had no idea where she'd be right now.

Willard pointed out homes of friends and neighbors as he drove along the street, and other things that she listened to, but didn't really hear because she was thinking about Karl. Not only how he'd offered her a place to stay, but a job that she needed for the time being. A way for her to stay with Elsie.

"I hope you don't get in trouble for taking me today," she said.

"Trouble? By whom?"

"Ka—Mr. Wingard."

He laughed. "Master Karl won't mind in the least. Mary and I often go places during the day, and evenings. Last month we were gone for over two weeks. We drove up the coast and stayed in a cottage the family owns. With the rest of the Wingard family gone, there wasn't much we needed to see to."

"What about Karl? Who cooked for him?"

"Mrs. Dahl made sure there were meals, but she also went out, visited friends."

She had never been away from the pub for more than a day until leaving. "How long have you worked for him?"

"Longer than he's been alive." Willard laughed again. "I worked for his father, so did Mary. We raised our two children in the house. Our Marie is now a school-teacher, and our son, James, works for Karl's bank. We have six grandchildren between the two of them. They are getting older now, too. Growing up. Moving on."

"Did you ever work anywhere else?"

"Oh, yes. Several jobs. I met Karl's father when I was delivering milk. His father was still alive then. He asked if I wanted a job. I told him that I had a wife and two children. He said bring them with you. I did and have never regretted it. I've enjoyed my years with the Wingards very much. It's been a fine job. The finest."

Bridget wondered what Da would think of Willard and how he felt about working for Karl until the auto-mobile stopped and Willard opened her door to lead her inside a very large building. The largest she'd ever been in. She'd never seen so many sick people, either.

Chapter Five

Because it was Saturday, the inquiry recessed in the early afternoon, which suited Karl just fine. Besides hearing the same questions over and over, and often the same answers, his anger at the White Star Line had grown to mammoth proportions. He'd visited the offices this morning, demanded to have Benjamin's and Annette's remains returned home. It was like the day he'd heard of the sinking. Each person he'd spoken too had told him something different. Yes, that could happen. No, that was impossible.

It was infuriating.

He no longer believed anything anyone said.

Leaving there, he'd gone to the inquiry only to hear a senator confront the press about printing half-truths. How could they not? That's the information they'd been given. Everything seemed to be a half-truth, from everyone.

Everyone.

Upon arriving home, he threw several sheets of paper on his desk. The list of casualties, directly from the White Star Line's office.

The name Bridget McGowen was on that list.

This at least was something he could confront.

He was still standing at his desk, staring at the papers a moment later when a knock sounded on the door. "Come in."

The door opened slowly and his breath caught as Bridget stepped into the room. She wore a yellow and white dress that fit her to perfection, from the collar of lace around her slender neck, to the hem that stopped just above the heeled low-sided shoes covering her feet. His eyes followed the line of white buttons that went from her waist up to her face, framed by her long, wavy black hair. A slight frown tugged the corners of her dark eyebrows down slightly above her blue eyes.

"Willard said you wanted to speak to me," she said.

He swallowed, nodded and looked away for a moment. The fact she was wearing a new dress should please him—it's why he'd purchased them. He was simply so angry right now, at the world, that nothing pleased him.

Most certainly not a liar, no matter how lovely she may be. His mother always looked pretty, and she was the world's greatest liar.

"Yes," he said. "Please close the door."

She twisted, closed the door, then turned, started to walk toward him.

Her frown grew as her gaze met his again. She stopped, midstep, staring harder.

It was as if the room went still as they stood there, face-to-face. His lungs grew hard and he pushed out the air. He sucked in another breath. Why had he thought she'd be any different? Hell, he'd entrusted Elsie's care to her.

Folly on him for believing a woman, any woman, could be truthful.

"What is it? What did you want to see me about?"

Her voice was soft, lyrical with her accent, and that made his neck muscles tighten. "I have a question to ask you, and mind you, I've been lied to all day and will not tolerate another one." It wasn't as if he was giving her a second chance, it was merely a warning.

"All right."

She still hadn't moved, stood halfway across the room from him. It wasn't possible for her to see the print on the paper, but still, he lifted a sheet off his desk. "What is your name?"

Her head moved, just slightly, back and forth, as if shaking her head at the question before she said, "Bridget Louise McGowen." Still frowning, she added, "My father's name was Patrick and my mother's name was Annie. She died when I was eight."

He didn't need to know that. Didn't want to know that. He'd wanted the truth. Holding up the paper, he explained, "This is a list of casualties from the *Titanic*. Verified by the White Star Line's list of boarding passes from Southampton."

Still frowning, she gave a slight nod.

"Would you care to explain why Bridget McGowen is on this list? Before you do, let me remind you that I'd already said I wouldn't tolerate another lie."

If he'd expected outrage, a show of the feisty anger he'd seen before, he'd have been disappointed. Instead, the color drained from her face as she stepped forward.

"Where?" she asked softly, walking to the desk.

His lungs stalled again, making the air he breathed in and out, hurt. He jerked his head sideways, unlocking their gazes, and held up the paper. "Right there. Bridget McGowen."

She took the paper.

He took a step back, but it was too late, the quick whiff of a scent as soft, as lovely as her, was already locked in his mind.

"That's a bit unnerving," she said. "Seeing yourself listed as deceased."

The paper in her hand fluttered slightly, because her hand was shaking. He took the paper. It was either that or take her hand and he couldn't do that. She was trying to fool him. Make him care. He'd never do that again. Care about a woman. His mother had taught him that lesson too well. Taught him that the one who cares the least has the most power. He'd never forget that.

She pressed two trembling fingers to her temple. "Oh, dear, my uncle Matt. Friends from the pub, they are all going to think I died. Why didn't I think of that? Mrs. Flannagan. I promised I'd write when I arrived." Her fingers went to her lips. "She's going to be so… Oh, dear, and she will tell the entire village. Everyone will believe I'm dead."

Her voice was barely a whisper, and the gaze she lifted, cast toward him, was as if she was in a haze. Of pain.

He stiffened, planted his feet firmer against the floor, committed to not falling for her act.

Shaking her head, she continued, "I never went to the third-class line. I was so concerned for Elsie, wanting to make sure she was on the list of survivors. If Annette or Benjamin had somehow survived, I wanted them to get word that she was alive."

"What line?"

"On the *Carpathia*, when they separated us to collect our names. I never went to the third-class line. I went to the first-class line because I knew that is where Elsie's name would be listed. I told them my name, but when they asked if I was her mother, I said no, her nanny." She laid her hands on the desktop, as if needing help to stand. "Every time I went back, to check to see if they had new names, it was to the first-class line, knowing that's where Annette would have gone. I never thought..." Looking at him, she said, "I need to get word home. Let them know I'm not dead."

She wobbled, and the moment he thought she might collapse onto the floor, something inside him snapped. Not anger. Compassion. A compassion he'd never experienced. He stepped forward, took ahold of her arm to steady her.

"They have to be so worried," she whispered.

"We'll get a message to them," he said. "They may not have seen this list yet."

She nodded and then shook her head. "Yes, they would have. Mrs. Flanagan lives next door to the pub. She sorts the town's mail, postings, newspapers—she was so much help when Da died. I promised her I'd write."

"You can still do that. A letter wouldn't have arrived there yet."

"But the news has." She pressed a hand against her mouth as a tiny sob escaped.

His heart constricted, knowing what she'd been through on the ship, and now he'd caused her more grief. He grasped her other arm, twisted her and pulled her against his chest. "It's not your fault. Mistaken reports are everywhere," he said, wrapping his arms around her. "Your friends, your uncle, will be glad to hear the truth, that you are alive, fine and well."

The side of her face was pressed to his chest, her arms around his waist holding on as she continued to tremble. He didn't want to care about her, to care about anyone because it led to pain. His mother, his father, his brother. So much pain, at this moment, he didn't want her to feel that pain, either, and held her tighter.

"I never thought," she whispered. "I just kept thinking about Elsie."

Her trim, firm curves were melded against his, creating a warmth, a comfort he'd never known, and an awareness. A heated, significant awareness.

"I feel so thoughtless for letting this happen," she whispered.

"It's going to be fine." He bit his lips together to stop from brushing his lips to the top of her head, but it didn't help. The desire to comfort her was stronger than all else and he gently kissed the top of her hair.

Her arms slipped from around his waist and she slowly took a step back. Color had returned to her face. Her cheeks were tinged pink.

Blood was flowing through his body faster than normal, too. He shouldn't have done that. Held her or kissed her hair.

"Thank you for telling me about this," she said, chin up but wobbling slightly.

She was thanking him for thinking the worst of her. He'd been so angry, so sure she'd lied to him. Now the only anger he felt was at himself. Actually, it was more disgust than anger. He let his hands slide off her shoulders, drop to his sides, and for a man who'd been yelling at people nearly all day, he was suddenly tongue-tied.

"I'm sorry for being so foolish," she said. "For causing such confusion."

"I'm sorry, too." It was the least he could say.

"You don't have anything to be sorry about." She huffed out a breath and took several steps away. "You must think I'm a—"

"I'm the fool," he said. That was the truth. "For—" He stopped and shook his head.

"For what?"

It wasn't flattering, but it was him. That much he had to admit. "I thought you were trying to trick me."

"Trick you? How? Why?"

"I don't know, Bridget, and that's the truth." He walked around his desk, putting a solid barrier between them because having his arms around her felt too right. Too good. "I've been lied to all day, and seeing your name on that list." He shrugged. "I—"

"You thought I'd lied to you, too." Her frown overtook her entire face. "That I wasn't really Bridget Mc-Gowen."

He nodded. Shame was not something he'd known before, and he wondered why she brought that out in him. Why she seemed to bring other things out in him, too. Things that he wasn't accustomed to.

She crossed the room, slowly, gracefully and sat down on the davenport near the fireplace. Back straight, chin up, she asked, "Who has been lying to you all day?"

He shook his head. "Who hasn't?" Knowing that wasn't an answer, he continued, "The White Star Line, witnesses at the inquiry, their stories don't match. The senators, blaming the newspapers for printing incomplete news, when they are the ones censoring what can and can't be printed."

"What are the witnesses saying?" she asked. "What doesn't match?"

Everything, yet he didn't want to tell her that. He didn't want to tell her any of it. Didn't want her to have to relive it. He walked to the fireplace, set a foot on the hearth and a hand on the mantel. "It doesn't matter."

"I was there. I can tell you what I know. If it will help."

"No, that's not necessary."

"I believe it is." A gentle smile formed. "I have a favor to ask of you, but first, I'd like to discuss what upset you so much today." Compassion filled her eyes as she added, "Willard told me about Annette and Benjamin being buried in Nova Scotia."

It wasn't something he wanted to discuss. "There's no need to ask a favor, I'll contact the White Star Line and have your name taken off that list."

She grimaced slightly. "Thank you. I'll write letters this evening to mail home."

"I'll post them for you."

She nodded and nibbled on her bottom lip before asking, "Did they find Annette and Benjamin?"

The weight on his shoulders grew heavy. "Honestly, I don't know. I've been told they have, and I've been told they haven't." There was still a portion of anger inside him, but a larger portion of frustration. It was like there was nothing he could do. He'd loved his brother. He missed him. He'd always taken care of Benjamin. At a time when he should have been being a kid, he'd been more focused on Benjamin. With their father at work, and their mother gone, he was the only person Benjamin could count on, and had to be now, too.

"There were so many," she said quietly. "So, so many. The water was white with life vests. At first, I thought they were icebergs, because that's what we'd been encountering while rowing toward the other ship, but it wasn't icebergs. It was life vests. Unmoving. Just bobbing in the waves."

His skin shivered at her description.

She closed her eyes.

Empathy filled him and he crossed the room, sat down beside her on the davenport. "Don't, Bridget." He shouldn't, but put an arm around her. "Don't think about it."

"I can't stop thinking about it." She lifted her head, looked at him with sorrowful eyes. "I've tried, but can't. It would be nothing shy of a miracle for Annette and Benjamin to be found. There were so, so many. But if it helps, Annette was wearing a green dress, with gold stitching. It was velvet. Benjamin had on a suit, black, with a white shirt, gold vest and green tie."

He wished he hadn't subjected her to these memories. "Thank you," he said, not knowing what else to say while trying to come up with a way out of this mess that he'd created with his anger.

"They both looked so fetching that evening," she said. "Annette was excited to attend the party. They were having the evening meal with the captain, a party to celebrate how well the voyage was going. Benjamin asked me if I'd watch Elsie so Annette could attend with him. I had watched Elsie a few other times, but mainly in the afternoons, to put her down for her naps so Annette and Benjamin could accept other invitations. There were a lot of people they knew on the ship."

"I'm sure there were, but—"

"I'm sorry," she said, laying a hand on his thigh. "I don't mean to upset you. It just feels good to talk about it, not keep it locked inside." Shaking her head, she added, "I tried so hard to not say anything in front of Elsie."

His heart softened, even as the touch of her hand made his leg burn. "If it helps, you can tell me anything, but I don't mean to upset you."

She shook her head. "It feels as if the memories want out."

He could understand that, and with his arm still around her shoulder, sat back against the davenport, pulling her back, as well. "Then let it out."

She leaned her head back, on his arm, and closed her eyes. He tried not to think about how exquisite her skin was—flawless except for a faint, thin scar high on the side of her cheek—or how pleasant she smelled, like springtime when the flowers in the park were blooming.

"I'd fallen asleep on the sofa," she said, opening her eyes and staring up at the ceiling.

There was moisture on her lashes. Tears. Unable to look away, he asked. "Where?"

The memories were flowing, stronger than ever, yet Bridget felt oddly quiet inside. There was no stirring of nausea, no overwhelming fear. Karl's arm around her shoulders, his nearness, was so comforting, like it had been earlier, when she'd learned about her name on the list of the deceased. And like last night, when he'd laid his hand atop of hers.

"In the sitting room of Annette and Benjamin's cabin," she said. "Elsie was in bed, had been asleep for hours. It was after midnight. I don't know what woke me, but I remember something felt odd when I stood up. Still and quiet. I thought maybe I'd just gotten used to the constant movement. After checking on Elsie I went back to the sitting room and that's when a steward entered the cabin. I don't remember if he knocked. He grabbed a life vest out of the closet and dropped it over my head, told me to get Elsie, put a life vest on her and go to the sundeck."

A pang of guilt struck and she pressed a hand to her stomach. "I should have put on her socks and shoes, too, not just her coat, but people were rushing down the corridor. I just grabbed a blanket off the bed, wrapped it around her legs and left the cabin. The steward had said it was just a precaution. That's what others were saying, too. That it was because the lifeboat drill had been canceled that morning. People were upset that they were doing it then, in the middle of the night."

"That's what they said was happening?" he asked, frowning.

"I don't know who said it for sure. I was more worried about Annette and Benjamin knowing where Elsie was, and kept asking for them to be found, asking anyone who had on a uniform. But the seamen were busy, shouting for women and children. One shoved us forward, then picked me up, with Elsie in my arms, and put us in a boat. Someone told two stewards to get in with us and then they lowered the boat into the water. It wasn't full, but they still lowered it. The stewards didn't even know how to put the oars in the oarlocks. One of them was the same one who'd told us to leave our cabin. I showed him how to put the oar in the lock and then showed him how to row."

A gentle smile formed on Karl's face as he said, "I met him."

"You did? Where?"

"At the inquiry."

She nodded and admitted what she'd realized that night. "He didn't want me to recognize him, not in the lifeboat or on the *Carpathia*. I think because he'd never found Annette and Benjamin. It wasn't his fault. There hadn't been time. It wasn't his fault that he didn't know how to row, either. He was a cabin steward, not a seaman."

Karl's smile remained as he nodded. "That was exactly why he didn't want you to recognize him. He asked me to give you his condolences."

That was not something she'd expected to hear and had to blink slightly at the moisture that created in her eyes. "He did all he could. Rowed until he was nearly exhausted, but the ship we were rowing toward kept getting farther away instead of closer."

A frown formed as he looked at her for a silent moment. "What ship? The *Carpathia*?"

"No, this was long before the *Carpathia* arrived. It was when they lowered us into the water. The ship was off in the distance. We could see the lights, but it was sailing away from us. I guess it never saw the flares the *Titanic* kept sending up. We finally gave up, and not knowing what else to do, we just drifted." She closed her eyes briefly at the memories coming forth, including those of being so cold. So tired from rowing. "I kept trying not to look, but it was hard not to. The rows of lights on the lower decks, they just kept disappearing into the water, sinking row by row. I kept the blanket over Elsie, even her head. The sounds carried on the water, through the night air. The flares. The screams. Splashes. Creaks and bangs and booms."

The memories would have overwhelmed her, if she hadn't been sitting here, on the davenport next to him. Safe.

She huffed out the air in her lungs as an image formed that she'd never forget. "Then, it was as if the ship broke in half, because part of it stood straight up in the water and then it all disappeared. Completely sank. We started rowing that direction, to all the people in the water. We had room for more in our boat. But as we approached another lifeboat, a seaman told us we couldn't get any closer. Some of the people in that boat transferred into ours, and the seaman rowed the emptier boat toward the people, pulled them out of the water. It wasn't long, though, before the screams stopped and everything went completely silent. Even the crying from those in the lifeboats seemed to stop."

Her throat thickened and a shiver rippled her spine at that memory.

His arm around her tightened and he tugged her closer. She eased her head onto his shoulder, let it rest there as those memories slowly faded. Letting those memories out was like a weight had been lifted off her chest.

She lifted her head, sat straight in order to finish. "We were adrift. Maybe it was the pull from the *Titanic* sinking, but we ended up closer again, to where the water was full of bodies. Other lifeboats. Debris, all kinds of things. Someone, I don't know who, said we had to start rowing again, that a rescue boat was on its way, so we did. We rowed and rowed and rowed. It was almost daylight when the *Carpathia* arrived."

Holding in the urge to lean against him again, she glanced his way, attempted to smile.

He held her gaze while asking, "What?"

His eyes were so kind. He was so caring. "It seems silly, but that was the scariest part."

"What was?"

"Climbing aboard the *Carpathia*. We had to climb a rope ladder, the adults. The children were lifted up in mailbags. I was so afraid when I put Elsie in that bag. I don't remember climbing up the ladder. I just knew I had to be at the top, to be there when they lifted her out of that bag."

"And you were, weren't you?"

His smile warmed her heart, made her smile. "Yes, I was."

He gave her shoulder a squeeze. "Once again, thank you. If not for you, I wouldn't have my niece."

She nodded, but had to be honest. "I wish your brother and his wife were here, instead of me."

Gently, he grasped the side of her face, forced her to look at him. "Don't wish that. Don't ever wish that."

Deep inside, in crevices she didn't know existed, she felt his words, and it produced an odd longing. A private, personal one that she'd never experienced. She had to look away because a part of that longing including kissing him.

A short time ago, when he'd hugged her over by his desk, for a moment, she'd thought he'd kissed the top of her head, but then had realized she must have imagined it. He was being kind. So kind, and she shouldn't have such silly thoughts.

Chapter Six

Karl pulled his eyes, and his hands, off Bridget and stood, drawing in a deep breath. Not from what she'd told him, but because of how she made him feel. He didn't need any more issues. Especially where a young immigrant was involved. Her retelling of that night made him care, and he couldn't have that. "I will contact the White Star Line. Someone should still be in the office. I'll have them remove your name from that list."

She nodded without looking up at him.

He hadn't ever wanted to kiss someone, to hold them close, like he did right now. So he crossed the room to his desk and pulled the phone close. The less he cared, the better. He'd learned that when he'd attempted to make his mother stay once, on his birthday. His father had been mad. Spanked him. Told him to never do that again. His mother hadn't cared. Therefore, from that moment on, he told himself that he didn't care either, until it had become true. The only person he had cared about then was Benjamin.

"Before you call them, may I ask a favor?"

Releasing the phone, he turned, nodded. "Yes."

Her breasts rose and fell as she drew in a breath.

He looked away, questioning all over again why everything about her affected him so strongly. So deeply.

"I went to the hospital today, to see my berth mate and her brother, Catherine and Sean O'Malley, and they told me that a representative from the White Star Line was in to see them. With papers to sign."

His attention sparked. "What sort of papers?"

"I'm not sure." She shook her head. "They weren't sure either, but Willard was with me and said they shouldn't sign anything, and that I needed to talk to you." She rose from the davenport and walked closer. "Could you find out what sort of papers they are? Catherine said that signing the papers was worth twenty-five dollars."

The anger he'd held earlier was still inside him. It had simply been buried while sitting next to her, talking with her. Now, it rose back up with a vengeance. "What hospital?"

"Um, the—"

"Never mind." Finally, there was something he could do. Leaving the desk, he grasped her hand and headed for the door.

"Where are we going?" she asked.

"To the hospital. To see your friends."

"I can't. Elsie is napping and—"

"Willard and Mary are here—she'll be fine." Pulling open the office door, he shouted, "Willard!"

The man appeared in the hallway instantly. "Yes?"

"What hospital are her friends at?" Recognizing the name Willard provided, Karl then said. "We'll be back in a few hours."

"I'll get Miss Bridget's hat and coat and then go pull your Packard out," Willard said.

"I'll go pull the automobile out." Karl then nodded at Bridget. "Get your coat and hat."

A fraction of frustration entered him as he made his way out to the carriage house. He wanted action now, and women took forever to get ready to go anywhere.

He needed to eat those words a moment later, while opening the driver's door, and saw Bridget standing near the edge of the driveway, waiting.

"I didn't mean you needed to go see them," she said as he walked around the automobile to open her door.

"I know. But I want to talk with them, find out exactly what was said to them." He opened the door, waited until she was seated, then closed the door and walked around to the driver's side.

"Tell me about them," he said once in the driver's seat and backing out of the driveway. "Why are they in the hospital?"

"Because they were in the water so long," she answered, glancing around the automobile, the front seat and the back.

"Is something wrong?" he asked.

Shaking her head, she answered, "This isn't the same one that I rode in with Willard."

"This one is mine, the other one is Willard's."

"He has his own automobile?"

"Well, technically it belongs to me, but it's Willard's to use as he wishes." Changing back to the subject at hand, he asked, "Why had they been in the water so long?"

"The lifeboats were all gone by the time they got to the sundeck. Those on lower decks hadn't been told to board the lifeboats as quickly as those in first class. Both Catherine and Sean had life vests and jumped in the water while the ship was sinking. They held on to debris, a table if I recall correctly, and were eventually picked up by one of the lifeboats. While on the *Carpathia* they became very ill and were taken to the hospital upon docking. They are both feeling better. I was grateful to learn that today."

"I'm sure you were," he answered, knowing her well enough to know that was true. "Did you know them before boarding the ship?"

"No. My ticket was for a double berth, and Catherine happened to be my berth mate. Her brother Sean was in steerage." She was quiet for a moment before saying, "Catherine's ticket was like mine, third-class."

He didn't like the way she sounded. After turning the corner, he glanced her way. "There is nothing wrong with that. Third class."

She nodded. "I know. It's just that if Elsie hadn't dropped her doll, and if I hadn't caught it, I—" She shook her head. "I just have to wonder why things happened the way they did."

"I don't know." He reached over and gave the hands folded in her lap a quick squeeze. It was as if once he'd touched her, now he couldn't stop. "But I'm glad she did drop Betsy and that you are the one who caught her." At that moment, when she glanced his way, he knew he'd never spoken truer words in his life.

He returned his hand to the steering wheel and focused on the road while his mind focused on things it shouldn't. Like how adorable she looked in her white hat. She was a very pretty woman. Very pretty. He'd realized that the first night he'd seen her, sitting on the sofa and holding Elsie. Even worn out, her hair wind-blown and her cheeks chafed, she'd been so lovely it had startled him. Had made his footsteps falter.

She'd been so quiet and shy, still was, but he had to bite back a smile every time he thought about how quick to anger she'd been when he'd tried hiring her. She hadn't been afraid of showing it, either.

"What is it you are going to do in Chicago?" he asked.

"Open my own boardinghouse," she said instantly, and with pride that lifted her chin.

"A boardinghouse?"

Her profile showed how her lips twitched, fighting back a smile. "Yes. Da's cousin Martha did that and became a very accomplished woman. She'd traveled back to Ireland several times, telling everyone stories about America. How one can achieve anything they want to here. Da said that's what I was going to do. Become a very accomplished woman."

He nodded while contemplating how her father didn't want her to become a servant, yet had let her work in his pub. How he wanted her to have her own board-inghouse, which, in a major city like Chicago, or any-where for that fact, could be dangerous for a woman on her own.

"A boardinghouse will take hard work," he said.

"I'm not afraid of hard work."

There was a definite hint of testiness in her tone. "I didn't say you were," he replied, not bothering to hide his smile. Still, the idea of a boardinghouse disturbed him slightly. "What about strangers? Will having so many live in the same home frighten you?"

"No. They won't be strangers for long. Just like you weren't a stranger for long."

She was right about that, and he doubted there was much she was afraid of. Other than putting Elsie in that mailbag. That had shown on her face when she'd told him about that. "How were you treated on the *Carpathia*?"

"Very well. The crew and passengers were very kind and helpful. A dear older man gave me a pair of socks for Elsie. There were no children on the *Carpathia*, other than those rescued. The socks were much too large for her, but I found a way to tie them on so they wouldn't slip off. The cabins were all full, but many of the passengers invited others to sleep inside them, wherever there was space."

"Were you and Elsie invited to sleep inside one?"

She turned, looked out her side of the automobile. She may have nodded, but may not have. He couldn't tell. "Were you?" he asked.

"Yes, but I declined."

"Why?"

She turned from the window and glanced at him with apprehension in her eyes, yet pursed lips, as if irritated. "Because of who provided the invitation."

He was instantly irritated for her. "Why? Who was it?"

"I don't know her name. She was an elderly passenger, with a maid. A young girl whom she didn't treat very well."

That didn't surprise him. The *Carpathia* was designed to haul immigrants and cargo to America, and over the years, to maximize on profitability, they'd began to carry American vacationers to the Mediterranean. Tickets were relatively inexpensive and catered to older, frugal clients.

"Is that why you said no?"

"No." She huffed out a breath. "She'd heard me asking about Annette and Benjamin and told me to bring Elsie to her cabin. I'd said no, because lifeboats were still being unloaded. Still being spotted. She'd found me again later, toward evening, and told me that I needed to give Elsie to her. That her parents weren't on the ship. Elsie was missing her mommy and daddy greatly by then, and that woman wouldn't stop talking about how they'd…they'd perished. Elsie was crying and I was so mad that I walked away from her, but she found me again later."

Her breasts were rising and falling with every hard breath she heaved in and out, displaying her annoyance. He'd seen it before from her.

"And?" he asked.

"And she had a steward with her, from the *Carpathia*, and said that I needed to give her Elsie."

His anger was easily aroused, and became so again. "Why?"

"She said she knew Elsie's grandmother and that she'd take care of *the child* until her grandmother could be contacted." Bridget folded her arms across her chest. "I knew Elsie didn't have any grandparents. That she only had you. Annette had told me that her mother died when she was very young and about her father and your father dying, and that she'd never met your mother."

His gut churned as his anger hit a boiling point. He'd already thought about his mother and how, as soon as she got word of Benjamin, she'd show up. He hadn't seen her in over a year. Since his father's will had been read. She hadn't been at the funeral, but had been there for the reading of the will and to receive her payment. He'd told her to be satisfied with what she'd received because now that his father was dead, she wouldn't be getting any more.

"The steward asked who I was, how I knew Elsie," Bridget was saying. "I told him that I was her nanny. A crowd had gathered and the steward that you met, the one who told us to leave the cabin, who rowed the boat, arrived and said that I was Elsie's nanny, that he'd seen me with Elsie on the *Titanic*."

His back teeth were clamped so hard they stung. "What happened then?"

"The woman said she was going to speak to the captain because I was trying to steal Elsie." With a sheepish expression, she bowed her head. "I avoided her from then on, and when the captain questioned me, I told him I was her nanny and that the only person I'd deliver her to was you. I'd promised Elsie that already, but now that I think about it, it does explain why my name was on the deceased list. I never told him my name. I just said I was her nanny."

"I'm very glad you did exactly that," he said, whilst knowing full well he had to warn her about an occurrence that could happen at any time. Any moment. It was also the last thing he needed right now. His mother would know that, and that was exactly why she'd show up now.

He waited until they arrived at the hospital and turned off the Packard. "I need to tell you something."

"What?"

He held in the heavy sigh pressing at his lungs. Making every breath burn as if his lungs were on fire. That's what even a thought of his mother did to him. "Elsie does have a grandmother. My mother. Harriette Apperson."

Her eyes grew wide and her chin dropped. "I—I didn't know. Annette said—"

"That she never met her," he interrupted. "That is correct. Benjamin made sure that didn't happen. Our mother left when we were young. Benjamin was an infant. She remarried, but returned every year while we were growing up. To see our father."

"Why?"

There was no reason to hide the sordid details. "For money."

Frowning, she asked, "What about you? And Benjamin? Didn't she want to see her children?"

"She pretended to. She made those visits on our birthdays." His anger kept growing. "But we weren't children to her. We were products. Something she expected to be paid for. And I will not allow her to have anything to do with Elsie." Fury was now living inside him. "That much I can do for my brother."

Bridget watched him climb out of the automobile and walk around to her door. She'd heard of bringing out the beast in someone, but she'd never seen loathing like she had on Karl's face. It made her tremble. Inside and out.

He opened her door, took her hand and helped her out of the automobile. After closing the door, he took her elbow, but didn't take a step. Instead, he stood still before her.

"I'm sorry. I didn't mean to take my wrath out on you," he said.

His hold on her arm was light. His words sincere. Her

trembles eased. "You didn't take it out on me," she said softly, honestly. "But it certainly came out."

He laughed, and she could practically see the tension leave his face. "You certainly aren't afraid of calling a pot black, are you?"

She shrugged, then shook her head. "I've seen a lot of black pots."

He nodded. "Working in the pub?"

"Yes." She was thinking of him, not the men from the pub when she answered, "Men are interesting creatures."

"So are women."

"I suspect so," she agreed.

He took a step sideways. "Let's go see your friends now."

Although he was no longer blocking her way, she didn't move. "Will your mother want to see Elsie?"

Looking at her, he lifted a brow. "I suspect so."

Any woman who thought of her children as products, something to be paid for, didn't deserve to have children, or grandchildren. If this woman did return, did want to see Elsie, someone needed to be there. To protect Elsie. Lifting her chin, Bridget made a solid decision. "I will work for you. If you still want to hire me to be Elsie's nanny."

He laughed. A real, happy-sounding laugh. "I do. You're hired."

Bridget made another decision while walking into the hospital. Karl wasn't like other men she'd known, and for that alone, she liked him. If Da was alive, he'd completely agree with her decisions. She would still go to Chicago, still open a boardinghouse. It would just take a bit longer.

* * *

They met with Catherine first, and Bridget was happy to note that there was more color in Catherine's face. With her curly red hair and freckles, she was pale to begin with, but aboard the *Carpathia* she and Sean had been a ghostly blue-gray. Sean had fair skin with red hair, like his sister, and, also like Catherine, looked better.

Brother and sister shared the same story with Karl as they had her. That a man stating he was representing the White Star Line had visited them, asking them to sign papers. He wouldn't leave the papers behind, but had visited with all of the patients in the hospital who had been on the *Titanic*. Sean went into more details, explaining how the man had said the papers were from the insurance company, that the twenty-five dollars they would receive was reimbursement for their tickets. He went on to explain that between the two of them, their tickets had cost more than that. His had been twenty dollars and Catherine's had been forty.

Bridget confirmed her ticket had been forty, as well.

By the end of the visit, Karl had not only said they shouldn't sign anything, he assured Catherine and Sean that they were both entitled to more than twenty-five dollars and that he would help them. Bridget didn't remember a time she had been so proud to be at someone's side.

"Thank you so very much," she said as they were leaving the hospital, after he'd spoken to several hospital workers about not allowing any patients to sign papers presented by representatives of the White Star Line.

Holding the door for her to exit, he said, "Thank you for bringing this to my attention."

Another wave of pride, or affection for him, filled her. "You like helping others, don't you?"

"I've never really done it before."

"Yes, you have. You're a banker. You help people all the time." Annette had told her that, along with other things about him and his brother.

"I do offer solid investments for clients, so I guess I do," he said. "I never thought of it that way before."

This time, when she looked up at him, she allowed herself to think about how very handsome he was. She'd realized that before, with his dark eyes and hair, his straight nose and somewhat pointed chin, but hadn't let herself dwell on it because it shouldn't matter. He was Elsie's uncle. That was how she'd told herself to think about him, but right now, she was thinking about him as her friend. A very nice man. A very handsome and nice man whom she was proud to know.

A sense of quiet, of peace, filled her. It may have been because she shared so much about the sinking with him, or simply because of him. How he was helping Catherine and Sean, and her.

That evening, after putting Elsie to bed, Bridget wrote several letters home, apologizing for her name mistakenly being on the list of deceased. She explained that she was in New York, but would be traveling to Chicago as soon as possible and would write again when she arrived there. She then penned a letter to cousin Martha, explaining the same thing.

As she sealed the envelopes, she found herself reflecting on the fact that a mere week ago, right now—Saturday night—the *Titanic* was still afloat, steaming toward America. It seemed like a lifetime ago. As if too many things had happened for it only to have been seven days.

She sighed, leaned back in the chair that matched the writing desk in the bedroom. This wasn't Mrs. Conrad's room. Hers was next to Elsie's. This one was across and down the hall a short distance from Elsie's room. Large, with pale green and white striped wallpaper that shimmered like silk in the overhead light and plush dark green carpet that was as soft to walk on as the thick grass on the hills behind the pub back home.

The bed, big enough for two—if not more—and covered with a flowered quilt, was the softest she'd ever slept on, and the number of pillows was close to outrageous. Four large and two small. There was also a dressing table with a mirror and stool, a wardrobe, bookcase and the writing desk. The curtains over the two large windows were sheer white, with heavy green drapes to pull across and block out any drafts, and there were two lovely paintings of roses and tulips hanging on the walls.

Each room in the house was fully furnished and stylishly decorated, just waiting for occupants to settle in. She would make sure that was how her boardinghouse was. Stylish. Welcoming.

Karl had said a boardinghouse would take hard work. She wasn't afraid of that. Everything worth doing took effort. However, she did wonder about living with strangers. They wouldn't be strangers for long, just as she'd said, but how would she know if she wanted them in her boardinghouse?

She'd told Karl that he hadn't been a stranger for long, but that was different. Annette and Benjamin had spoken highly of him, and Elsie had been anxious to get home to him.

Then again, she hadn't known Catherine before becoming berth mates, and they'd gotten along very well upon meeting.

She shook her head and picked up the envelopes. All this pondering was unneeded. As soon as she had the means and the way, and Mrs. Conrad had returned, she'd go to Chicago and open her boardinghouse. Truly begin her new life in America, just as Da had wanted.

Pushing away from the desk, she stood and determined she would miss Karl. With a shake of her head, she corrected that she would miss Elsie. She sighed. And Karl. She would miss him, and she did like him. Not just because he was helping her, but because he was likable. Just like Willard and Mary. She would miss them, too.

However, just like she and Annette had talked about, she could travel back to see them. The trip would be much shorter than Martha's trips all the way back to Ireland to see family. Karl and Elsie weren't family, but they had become dear to Bridget. They had become a part of her life that she'd never forget.

Chapter Seven

Karl released a yawn as he pulled into Roy Whitney's drive. He'd had a very restless night. His mind hadn't wanted to stop. Benjamin, Annette, Elsie, his mother, the inquiry, the hospital full of patients, all had vied for his attention as he'd lain in his bed, staring at the soft shadows the moon had cast upon his ceiling. But front and center, taking up the most time and space, had been Bridget.

Her blue eyes, dark hair, the tiny scar on her cheek. Never had a woman taken over his mind like she had. He should be glad that she'd agreed to allow him to hire her as Elsie's nanny. She'd proven her abilities during the tragedy, but he'd also seen other skills, mainly how deeply she cared. That worried him. She'd gotten under his skin in an unexplainable way.

He'd care about Elsie, but no one else. It had to stay that way.

While lying there last night, thinking about her, he'd found himself comparing her to women other than his mother. That was a first. It had made him recall how shocked he'd been when Benjamin had returned home from his first trip to England with Annette in tow. They'd already been married. Benjamin hadn't written, hadn't warned him, because he'd wanted to tell him in person. Assure him that Annette was nothing like their mother.

His brother had been right. Annette had been loving, kind, generous, and a wonderful mother to Elsie. Right from the start.

Karl pushed out a sigh.

But even if she hadn't been, he wouldn't have said anything to Benjamin, because his brother didn't remember the day their father had spanked him for not wanting their mother to leave. Karl had made sure Benjamin never knew about it, either, and he had also made sure that their mother never got her claws into Benjamin. He'd been so young when she'd left that he'd never had any memories of her. Karl had, but in one day, he'd wiped any positive ones away for good.

Movement, a door opening, jarred his attention and he killed the engine of his automobile and opened his door.

"Good day, Mr. Wingard," the butler greeted. "Mr. Whitney is waiting for you in his library. I'll show you the way."

"Thank you," Karl replied, walking around the Packard to follow the man into the old brownstone home in New York's Cobble Hill neighborhood. Whitney was the chairman of the marine company that ultimately owned the White Star Line.

"Aw, Karl," Whitney said as the butler opened the door to his library. "Come in, come in. I'm glad you telephoned."

"Hello, Roy," Karl greeted, walking into the room

lined with bookshelves from floor to ceiling. A thin swirl of smoke twirled in the light shining through the one window. "Thank you for agreeing to see me today."

"I can't say it came as a surprise." Whitney, a man of considerable age, one life had been good to, waved the pipe in his hand toward a chair next to the one he sat down in. "Weinstein from the White Star Line offices called me yesterday, said you'd been at the office."

Karl sat. "I had been."

"Tragic. That's what this has been. Tragic. I'm sorry for your loss." Roy took a draw off his pipe. "I only met your brother once, but he appeared to be a fine young man."

"He was," Karl agreed, controlling his emotions. Why couldn't he do that when it came to Bridget? Control his insides, his heart, his mind.

"His wife was with him, I understand," Roy said. "As well as his daughter and her nanny. The two of them survived, am I correct?"

"Yes, you are. Elsie and her nanny are both fine. No injuries."

"There is that, then, isn't there?" Roy's thick, white brows rose.

Karl leaned back and crossed a foot over his knee. "Yes, there is."

Roy knocked the ash out of his pipe into an ashtray and set the pipe on the table between them. "Several ships have been deployed to recover bodies, and instructions have been given to search for specific remains. Your brother and his wife are on that list. The ships have morticians aboard, with supplies and ice for the bodies so they can be delivered to families rather than being buried at sea or in Nova Scotia. If you brother and his wife are found, you have my promise they will be returned to New York."

Karl nodded as his thoughts went to Bridget, to what would have happened to her body had she not survived. "How are they identifying people?"

"They have been provided pictures, descriptions."

"For first-class passengers," Karl said. "What about second- and third-class? Steerage?"

Whitney shook his head. "There are too many."

An ugly knot rolled in his stomach as he recalled how upset Bridget had been about her family learning her name was on the list of casualties. "They have families. Homes."

"There is only so much anyone can do," Roy said, "I'm sure you understand that, Karl."

"I do." He kept his temper in check. "The White Star Line issued a statement that all bodies are being treated equally. That the more prominent citizens are not being separated or being given any special considerations."

Roy folded his arms. "Of course they did. They had to. The accident itself caused an uproar. The line can't have the general public getting out of hand."

"They're lying," Karl said. "Not only in statements to the press, but in the senate inquiry. I've been there. The White Star's chairman and others from the company stated that there were no bodies in the water when the *Carpathia* arrived at the scene, but I've heard differently. At the inquiry, and personally. That isn't going to bode well for them. To be caught in lies."

"Perhaps it's the others who are lying, wanting it to sound worse than it was," Roy said stoically.

Karl clenched his back teeth. He'd been born into a society that looked from the top down, and this was the first time he'd looked at things differently. He wasn't even exactly sure why. It hadn't started out that way, but he couldn't help but think about Bridget and what would have happened to her if she hadn't been watching Elsie that night. "It was a catastrophe of major proportions."

"Yes, but there could have been no survivors."

That was true, and that was his fear. That Bridget would have perished. She hadn't, and she'd saved Elsie. For that he was grateful. "It's my understanding that representatives from the White Star Line are contacting survivors, asking them to sign off from any liability for twenty-five dollars."

Roy nodded. "Which is more money than many of those people would have had in their pockets when they arrived in New York had the ship not sunk."

"So it is just a specific class they are targeting," Karl said.

"Have you been contacted?" Roy asked.

"No."

Leaning forward, Roy frowned. "You seem to be overly concerned about those beneath you, Karl. That's not like you. I understand you've lost your brother and his wife, and assumed that was the issue concerning you."

"I am concerned about them," Karl replied. "About Elsie's parents having a final resting place that she can visit when she's older. However, I wouldn't consider my concern about others on the ship as too much. I would hope the White Star Line would be concerned about all passengers, not just a select group."

"The *Titanic* was also hauling cargo, and the ship itself was a total loss," Roy said. "Other than thirteen lifeboats and a few hundred life vests, there's nothing

"I know, but a house this size, there is always something that needs to be dusted or washed."

"That is why we have a maid."

"I know that, too." She picked a feather duster off his desk and walked toward the fireplace. "Mrs. Dahl does a fine job, but she has a lot to do, so I thought I'd take care of some of it."

"Then we'll have her come in more than two days a week," he said, watching her swipe the duster over the top of the mantel. "There wasn't that much to do with just me living here this past month."

"She can't," Bridget said, now dusting the bricks around the hearth opening. "She's helping her daughter, who just had a baby."

"Then we'll hire another maid."

She moved to dust the credenza behind the davenport. "There's no need. I can help while I'm here, and then Mrs. Dahl will resume her normal schedule." Walking around the davenport, she nodded. "I'm done in here now. I was hoping to finish before you arrived. Sorry."

He grasped her arm as she started toward the door. "...ve you been cleaning every day?"

...r cheeks grew pink. "Only while Elsie's napping."

...ced at the doorway. "I better go check on her."

...tened his hold on her arm and forced himself

...at how cute she looked trying to escape.

...ve you been doing around here? Besides

...breath. "Just some cooking and dish

...elps with that. Everyone should

...w things and wash dishes. She

---

left of a seven-million-dollar investment. An investment you supported. The financial loss of that ship includes you. Do you think the line should go completely bankrupt over this?"

"Every investment I make is a risk. I weigh them and take the risk. At times it works, at times it doesn't," Karl said. "I and my clients understand that. With that said, in a situation like this, everyone should be compensated for their loss, equally. There are widows with children who no longer have a husband and father to provide for them."

Roy shrugged. "Like you, and me, they took a risk. It didn't pay off."

Karl hadn't expected such utter disdain, and wondered if he should have. Men like Whitney hadn't made their money by being compassionate. Karl also wondered what type of man that made him. What type of man he'd always been, and if he continued to want to be that man.

"I've heard the Red Cross has raised a significant amount of money for the survivors," Roy said. "They'll help them."

Karl knew that. His company had made a donation to the Red Cross and this morning at church, with Elsie sitting between him and Bridget, he'd put extra in the collection plate for all the church was doing to help the survivors. He nodded and stood. "Thank you for the visit, Roy. It's been enlightening."

"Karl, you're young, passionate—those are good qualities. Just don't let them get away from you. What your father built, what you've continued to build, takes a man who can see beyond today. Like you said, there is risk in everything. We aren't always going to like every outcome. That's why we look at tomorrow, next year, five years from now."

Karl nodded, understanding the philosophy of Roy's words. In fact, what Roy had said sounded a lot like what his father would likely have said. He held out his hand, shook Roy's. "Thank you again for seeing me."

He left, and though he'd received answers, nothing was settled inside him. It felt as if he was on some sort of bridge, stuck in the middle, and didn't know which way to go because both ends were collapsing.

During the drive home, he spied a man and woman walking along the sidewalk with a young girl before them, holding the leash of a little gray dog.

The weight inside him increased. That could have been Elsie with Benjamin and Annette, but it wasn't. She no longer had her parents. She had no one but him.

And Bridget, for now. She would leave as soon as Mrs. Conrad returned. She'd made that completely clear yesterday when they'd arrived home from the hospital, when they'd discussed her salary and duties.

A boardinghouse. That idea still didn't sit well with him. Her, inviting a plethora of strangers, most likely single men, into a house to live with her. Yet, she was determined to do it, and he doubted anything would stop her. He had to admit he liked that about her. It's what had saved both her and Elsie. He was sure of that.

Before he arrived home, he saw another family walking in the spring sunshine, with another dog. This one was black-and-white. Small, with lots of hair, and on a leash held by a little boy. There was an older boy, walking closer to the parents, and the mother was carrying a cluster of yellow flowers.

He'd never wanted a family, and over the past few years had grown grateful that Benjamin had married as it had taken a lot of pressure off him.

Pressure that had now returned.

Tenfold.

Elsie was his now, and he had to do the best for her. Just as he'd always done for Benjamin.

Upon arriving at the house, he went straight to his office and stood in the open doorway, staring at the sight before him for several moments. Bridget was standing on a chair, practically hidden between the heavy drapes covering the window behind his desk.

"What are you doing?" he finally asked.

The curtains fluttered at her startled jolt, and he shot forward, afraid she was about to fall.

She didn't fall and was smiling down at him when he arrived at the chair.

"Hello," she said. "I didn't hear you come in."

He grasped the back of the chair. The
ing still had his heart poundin~

"Washing wind~

drapes apar
couldn't tell
light, so I clos
"It was a strea

He took he
"Washing wind

She brushed a
back of one hand.
and figured I migl

He released her
his own hand tingle

He was certain that Elsie would enjoy doing any-thing with Bridget. He did. Church this morning, eve-ning meals, even going to the hospital yesterday. She had a way of saying things, of doing things that made him want to smile. Including right now.

"I need to go check on her," she said.

Releasing her arm, he nodded. As she was walking out of the office, he thought of the families he'd seen earlier. "Bridget."

She stopped, turned around.

"Would you and Elsie care to take a walk later?" Feeling odd, he quickly explained, "It's very nice out." What was he thinking? He never went for afternoon walks, yet, it appeared that many families did, so he probably should get used to it.

"We would like that very much," she said. "I'd al-ready promised her that we'd go outside, play in the backyard this afternoon."

A sense of enjoyment that he hadn't felt in a long time filled him. "Good. Thank you."

She nodded and left the room, and with his mind still on those families he'd seen on his drive home, he walked to his desk and picked up the telephone.

Bridget pretended as if her insides weren't fluttering like a bird caught in a cage as she walked up the stair-case. If she could have jumped out the window when he'd arrived in the room, she would have. Mary and Willard had insisted she didn't need to clean or help in the kitchen, but as she'd told them, it was the least she could do for her keep. Besides, she'd never been one to sit around. There had always been something that needed to be done at the pub. The few chores she'd done while being here was nothing compared to all she'd done back home. It wouldn't compare with what she'd be doing once she opened her boardinghouse, either.

Her house wouldn't be this big, but there would be more people. Plenty of people.

It wasn't helping. She was trying to think of anything other than Karl asking if she and Elsie would like to go for a walk. She was excited about that. Elsie needed to be with family, and that was Karl. Only Karl.

A nanny didn't count as family. She'd been thinking about that today, her first day of actually being Elsie's nanny.

She'd also been thinking about Karl's mother. Not about her as much as him, and how angry he'd become when talking about her, thinking about her. The more she'd thought about it, the sadder she'd become, for him. Family shouldn't hate each other, and she feared he hated his mother.

"Bridget! I'm awake!"

A smile filled her face as she pushed the door to Elsie's room the all the way open. "I see that, Poppet." She walked over and picked Elsie off the bed. "And guess what? Your uncle Karl wants you to take a walk with him."

Elsie wrapped her arms around her neck. "Yippie!"

She put Elsie down. "Help me make your bed and then we'll get you ready."

Elsie grabbed the corner of the blanket to pull it over the sheets. "You, too!"

"Me, too." Bridget helped her make the bed and then took her across the hall to wash her face, brush her hair and tie it back with a blue bow that matched her frilly dress. All the while, she wondered if she should let just

Elsie and Karl go on the walk. By the time they were done, she'd convinced herself she would go this time, but not the next.

Karl was waiting in the doorway of his office, and Bridget let go of Elsie's hand so she could run to him and jump into his arms. Which is exactly what happened. Elsie had her arms locked around his neck when Bridget arrived at the door.

He always looked so handsome. He'd removed his suit jacket, and the dark brown color of his vest over his white shirt was the same shade as his hair and eyes, which were twinkling with a secretive gleam.

"Someone is very excited about taking a walk with you," Bridget said, trying to hide how fast her heart was beating.

"I've changed that a small amount," he said. "We are going to take a drive instead." He tickled Elsie's side. "There's something I want this little girl to see."

Giggling, Elsie asked, "What?"

"It's a surprise." He put Elsie down. "Ready?"

Bridget nodded while Elsie shouted, "Yes!"

Elsie sat on the front seat between them, as she had that morning when they'd driven to church, and chatted. It wasn't until they were several blocks away from home that Bridget realized Betsy had been left upstairs, on the bed. She hoped Elsie wouldn't realize, or if she did, wouldn't be overly upset. As a nanny, she should have remembered the doll. She hadn't because her thoughts had been on Karl. That needed to stop. It was hard, though, because there was so much about him that she wanted to know.

He eventually pulled up next to a lovely painted white home with a wide front porch. "We're here."

Bridget had no idea what he wanted to show Elsie, and gave him a curious look as he opened the door for her. He grinned and shrugged, that secretive gleam still in his eyes.

As soon as he'd helped her out, she released his hand and moved aside so he could lift Elsie out of the vehicle.

"Hello!" a blond-haired man greeted as he walked down the steps of the big house.

He looked somewhat familiar to Bridget, and she wasn't sure why.

"Hello, Reggie," Karl said. "Thank you for inviting us over. This is Bridget McGowen, and this—" he jiggled Elsie on his hip to make her giggle "—is Elsie."

"I'm glad you could drive over," Reggie said, walking closer.

"This is Reggie Peters," Karl told her. "An old and dear friend of mine."

"Miss McGowen," Reggie said with a nod as he stopped before them.

She then knew why he looked familiar. "You were at the dock, the night we arrived. Made people move so Willard could drive through the crowd."

"That was me," he said.

"Thank you for that," she said.

"You're very welcome." He then smiled brightly at Elsie. "I have two little girls who are very excited to meet you. Leslie is four and Becky is six. They are in the backyard."

Bridget's heart nearly doubled in size as she looked up at Karl. Playmates for Elsie was even more special than a walk. He winked at her as he took her elbow and, still carrying Elsie, followed Reggie toward the house.

"My wife, Alice, is in the backyard, too," Reggie said. "With refreshments so we can visit while the girls play."

Unable to keep her thoughts to herself, Bridget said to Karl, "This was so thoughtful of you."

"I'm glad you approve," he replied.

She shook her head at him, because the glint in his eyes held a teasing flare.

Reggie led them through a quaint home with shining wood floors, colorful braided rugs and cream-colored wallpaper, out onto a back porch that had a small metal table with chairs and a porch swing.

"Hello, I'm Alice," a tall, thin woman with curly blond hair said as they walked onto the porch.

Reggie made the introductions, and again when two little girls, both with long blond hair ran onto the porch followed by four floppy-eared, copper-colored dogs. Three puppies and one older dog.

Bridget laughed as Elsie wiggled for Karl to let her down. This was truly a delightful surprise, and within minutes, Elsie was running through the green grass in the backyard with Leslie, Becky and all four dogs.

"She is having the time of her life," Bridget said as Karl held a chair for her to be seated.

"So are the girls, and Trixie and her pups." Alice smiled at her husband. "Reggie built them the playhouse last fall, and they were excited to show it to a friend."

Bridget had noticed the little pink and blue gingerbread house in the backyard right away. All three girls were now running in and out of it with the puppies while the mother dog lay down near a tree that hadn't yet completely leafed out. "It's adorable. So are your girls and puppies."

"Luckily, they are all potty-trained," Alice said, laughing.

"The girls and the puppies," Reggie added, laughing, as well.

The conversation flowed from there as the four of them drank coffee and watched the girls play for an extended length of time. Bridget couldn't seem to stop staring at Karl. He looked relaxed, at ease, and was smiling. Remembering good times as he talked about Benjamin, shared stories about when they were young, in school with Reggie and Alice. That warmed her heart as much as the day did, how he'd brought Elsie over here to play with other children.

"Bridget!" Elsie exclaimed, running up the short set of steps, followed closely by a little puppy with a cute little white spot in the center of its forehead. "Come see the house! You, too, Uncle Karl!"

Karl stood and excused them as he pulled out her chair for her.

Walking across the grass, holding one of Elsie's hands while Karl held the other, Bridget realized that she'd never allowed herself to think about something like this. A family, children, a life like Reggie and Alice had. Her focus had been on owning a boardinghouse for as long as she could remember.

The playhouse was adorable. So was the way Elsie showed them the child's table and chair set inside, as well as a rug on the floor, curtains on the windows and hand-drawn pictures hanging on the walls.

Bridget's heart tumbled again at how Karl knelt down, listening to Elsie talk about the playhouse.

When the puppy ran out of the house, Elsie took chase and Karl stood up, laughing.

"You've made one little girl very happy today," Bridget said.

He nodded, and time seemed to stand still for a moment as he looked at her. Bridget could feel a pull inside, toward him. It was unique and made her heart race. Her eyes went to his lips, and she bit hers together as they tingled, as if they wanted to touch his.

"Yes," he said, looking away. "She's very happy."

Bridget took a step back and drew in a deep breath to get her thoughts in order. "You and Benjamin certainly had some fun times together."

He took ahold of her elbow and they started walking toward the house again. "Yes, we did. It's been good to remember them."

Her legs were slightly wobbly and her heart was still racing. "And now you're making good memories with Elsie. She's very lucky to have you."

He nodded. "She's very lucky to have you. We both are."

Chapter Eight

Bridget's heart did an odd flip-flop. Not so much at his statement, but at how he was looking at her. His look was so intent, so focused on her, that her blood warmed. He smiled. She smiled in return, but had no idea how to calm the blood rushing through her veins faster than it should.

"What did you think of the playhouse?" Reggie asked from the porch.

"I didn't know you were a builder," Karl said in jest.

"I'm not," Reggie answered. "I'm a pharmacist, but my father helped me."

By the time they arrived on the porch, Bridget was sure she had her insides under control, but knew the moment she sat down that she didn't, because Karl kept his hand on the back of her chair. The problem was she liked it. She liked having him close. Liked breathing in the scent of his aftershave. Liked him in a way that kept getting deeper and deeper inside her and wondered what all that meant.

The girls joined them a short time later for cookies and lemonade, and shortly thereafter, Karl suggested it was time to leave. Bridget's heart saddened at the disappointment on Elsie's face as she looked at the puppy sleeping on her lap, the one with the white spot that had barely left her side since they'd arrived.

Bridget prepared to stand, to walk over and ease the separation between Elsie and the puppy, but Karl laid a hand on her arm.

"Would you mind if the puppy came home with us?" he asked quietly, leaning even closer.

Her insides nearly melted. "It's not my place to mind," she answered just as quietly.

"Yes, it is," he said, "because I'm certain its care would fall to you. If you don't want that, I'll understand."

She had the greatest urge to kiss his cheek, and withholding it was tremendously difficult. Resting a hand atop his, the one still on her arm, she whispered, "I'd enjoy the duty as much as Elsie would enjoy the puppy."

His gaze was locked on hers and remained there as he whispered, "Thank you."

She closed her eyes briefly as the idea of kissing him grew even stronger. He truly was a very caring man. A very wonderful man. Right now, she knew for sure that Da would approve of her working for him. It was herself now that questioned if that had been a good idea. She had an odd feeling that she could come to care for Karl more than she should.

He gently squeezed her arm. "Shall we go tell her?"

Putting thoughts of Elsie first, she nodded. "Yes."

Within a short time, they were all four in the front seat of Karl's automobile, with Elsie holding the sleeping puppy on her lap sitting between them. The discussion, as he drove, was about the puppy's name. Elsie was trying out several, but having a hard time deciding.

"Four," she said.

"Four?" Karl asked.

"Yes," Elsie said. "Because I'm four."

Swallowing a giggle, Bridget shrugged at the amusing glance Karl gave her over Elsie's head.

"That's true," Karl answered. "You could name him four. But what will happen when you turn five? Will you change his name?"

Elsie frowned, as if contemplating that.

"What about Spot?" Karl offered. "Because of that white spot on his head."

"Or White," Elsie said, excitedly.

Karl chuckled. "Or White," he said glancing over Elsie's head again.

Bridget had to giggle at that, and at his expression. She gave the puppy's soft fur a long pet. "The rest of his hair is copper colored. What about Copper for a name?"

"Copper! I like Copper, Bridget!" Elsie said.

"So do I," Karl said, nodding.

She tapped Elsie's nose. "I like it, too, but you don't have to decide today. You can think about it for a while."

Elsie nodded and gave the puppy a hug. He woke up long enough to lick her chin and yawn, before snuggling his little head back in her lap.

After a quiet moment, Elsie asked, "Uncle Karl, will Mommy and Daddy ever come home?"

Bridget's heart went from being full and joyous to nearly breaking in two. For both Elsie and Karl. He'd gone stiff and stared out of the windshield.

Wrapping an arm around Elsie, Bridget tugged her close and kissed the top of her head. "Remember what

I told you, Poppet," she said softly. "When you want to see your mommy and daddy, you just close your eyes and think about them. Think hard, until you can see them in your mind."

"I do that, Bridget," Elsie said. "And can see them, but I want them to see Copper."

Bridget kissed the top of Elsie's head again and patted the puppy. "Oh, darling, they do see him. They are watching over you all the time."

"Just like your mommy and daddy?" Elsie asked.

"Yes, just like mine." Glancing up at Karl, seeing he was still staring out the windshield, Bridget added, "And just like your uncle Karl's daddy. Your grandpa. They are all up there watching over us."

"That feels good," Elsie said. "Doesn't it, Uncle Karl?"

He reached over and patted Elsie's head. "Yes, it does feel good." He then glanced over Elsie's head and smiled.

Bridget smiled in return and then stroked the puppy again, trying to stop her heart from racing all over again. "So, Copper is his name?"

"Yes," Elsie said. "Copper is his name, and I love him."

Karl stood on the back porch of his house watching Elsie and Copper run across the backyard. Bridget had suggested bringing the puppy out here before taking it inside, so he could smell the ground and know where to do his business. He wouldn't have thought of that, yet that had been the first thing the puppy had done. His business.

She was wise, in so many ways. Wiser than him.

He laid a hand on the small of her back, looked into her deep blue eyes when she glanced up at him. "Thank you for how you handled that earlier, her question about her parents."

Her face softened as she shrugged. "She's been asking those question since that night. I couldn't lie to her. Couldn't give her hope when there isn't any."

He touched the side of her face with one knuckle. "You gave her a way to cope, and that's more important." Having her around was different from all he'd known, a good different. She'd brought out a side of him he'd never known. He'd thought not caring was the only way to cope, but she cared, and had somehow transferred that to him, because he certainly was starting to care. His hand on her waist slipped around her back, keeping their bodies close. Inches apart. "Thank you for that."

Her lashes fluttered as she whispered, "You're welcome."

She sounded breathless, and that increased the desire to kiss her. Made it so strong, so consuming, he tried to look away, to break the spell, but he couldn't. Those thickly lashed blue eyes were so mesmerizing. Her skin so flawless, her lips so enticing. He trailed his knuckle down her cheek, to her chin and lifted her face as he leaned down, brushing his lips over hers.

The simple touch, the feel of her breath on his lips, ignited a stronger desire, a powerful one. He pressed his lips to hers again, more firmly, fully feeling the warmth and softness of her lips. Her response, the way she returned the pressure, made him want to completely explore her lips, claim them, but something—common sense, perhaps—told him to stop. Despite protests from other parts of him, he pulled back, lifted his head.

She wobbled slightly, and he pulled her closer to steady her. Both of her hands landed on his chest and her lips curled up in a soft smile.

It was so endearing, his heart kicked up another notch. He should release her, but couldn't. Not just yet. "I sincerely appreciate you being here."

She nodded and then gave his chest a tiny pat before she looked away, toward the yard.

For whatever reason, a great sense of happiness filled him. He gently pinched her chin. "Have I rendered you speechless?"

She shot him a sideways look and giggled softly, "No."

He dropped both of his hands and took a step away so they both could turn and watch Elsie and Copper. "I think I have," he said teasingly.

"Gobshite!" she said under her breath.

He laughed harder.

She shook her head.

The enjoyment inside him grew. He probably should be questioning his intelligence about kissing her, but not right now. If he started thinking about the how and why, he might do it all over again.

A moment later, the back door opened behind them. "The little miss sure looks happy," Willard said.

"Yes, she does," Karl answered.

"Because she is," Bridget said. "That little puppy is going to make everything that happened so much easier for her."

"How do you know that?" Karl asked, sensing something deeper in her words.

Turning, to look at him, she said, "Because my Da brought me home a puppy after my mum died."

There was a wistfulness in her eyes, and he wondered if it was from their kiss or from the memory of the puppy her father had bought her. A part of him hoped it was their kiss, but the practical part of him said he'd better hope not, because his life didn't need any more complications. He couldn't care about someone that much and certainly didn't need them caring about him.

When a person cares, they lose. He didn't want to lose again, and he didn't want her to, either.

"Excuse me," Willard said, stepping around them. "I'm going to introduce myself to the little pup. We've needed a dog around here for a long time."

"What was your dog's name?" Karl asked.

"Shadow," she said. "Da named him that because he was always in my shadow."

"Ours was Baxter," Karl said. "Our father gave him to us for Christmas one year. A big black Labrador." He nodded toward the porch swing as memories flowed. "We could put a piece of food on his nose, and he'd flick his nose to throw the food up in the air and catch it in his mouth. Benjamin taught him to do that."

"That sounds like quite a trick," she said as they walked to the swing.

"It was, and he'd chase the ball for hours on end." He waited until she sat on the swing seat and then sat down beside her.

"Did Benjamin teach him that, too? How to fetch?" she asked.

Watching Elsie and Willard petting the puppy, he nodded. "Yes, he did."

She laid a hand on his arm, his bare arm, where he could feel the heat of her palm radiating into him.

"Because you taught him," she said softly. "You taught him how to teach Baxter to fetch and how to catch food he tossed in the air with his nose."

He drew in a breath, yet knowing his secret was safe with her, he turned, looked at her. "Yes."

Her smile was knowing, and sweet. Like her lips had been.

He'd already told her more than he'd shared with anyone, yet found he had the need to say more. "Benjamin needed more than I did. He needed reassurance, encouragement. Our father was a good man, but he worked every day. Even Sundays. Mrs. Conrad, Willard and Mary raised us, but that wasn't enough for Benjamin."

"He needed love, and that's what you gave him," she said quietly. "Because of you, he grew into a loving husband and father. I saw that. How much he loved Annette and Elsie. You need to be proud of that, Karl. It's hard to lose people we love, very hard. We miss them so much and wish things could be different, even while knowing they can't be. The best thing we can do for them, and ourselves, is to be honored to have known them. Be proud of who they'd been." She rubbed his arm. "We do that by talking about them. Remembering them."

She was right, as usual. He'd barely spoken about Benjamin to anyone, except today, when she'd encouraged him to after learning that Reggie and Alice had gone to school with him and Benjamin. It had felt good to remember some fun times, and though only time would heal the pain inside him, it wasn't as strong as it had been. Even his anger had eased. That, too, was because of her. She was remarkable in so many ways. "Tell me about your father."

Her eyes fluttered shut for a moment as a smile formed on her lips. "He was about Willard's size, a mite shorter maybe, with the same ring of gray hair around his otherwise bald head. And his eyes, they were deep blue, and they twinkled."

"Like yours," he said.

"No, he always said I had my mother's eyes."

He leaned closer. "Then hers twinkled, too, because yours are right now." They were, and he liked that. "Tell me more."

"He could tell a joke, a story, like no other. The entire pub would go quiet when he started one of his tales because everyone knew it would be a good one and wanted to hear it." She giggled slightly. "It wouldn't be one he'd told before. He never told the same story twice. People would ask him to, and he'd say that was yesterday's news." She sighed. "He didn't believe in yesterdays, only tomorrows. He said that to me, more than once. Said it to others, too, those who had too many pints and he'd had to send home. They'd come in to apologize the next day, and he'd say there was no need for that, it was a new day."

"Because he never let the sun go down on his anger," he said, repeating the words she'd said to him the other night.

She nodded. "He was kind, good to everyone he knew and to anyone who knew him. If there was someone who needed something, he'd go out of his way to find a way to help them." Leaning back, she looked up at the sky. "I'd never seen him angry. I'd seen him stern, cross, but never really angry. He'd told me that

I needed to learn to control my temper, that I riled too easy and that the only person it was hurting was me."

Karl leaned back, too, looked up at the same sky. He'd been angry his entire life. Thanks to his mother. "Have you learned to control it?" he asked.

She laughed. "No. I'm still hoping that will happen someday."

He laughed, too. "You're cute when you're mad."

She laughed harder. "You haven't seen me mad."

The door opened and Mary stepped outside. "So that's why no one has come inside. I told Willard to let you know the meal would be ready to serve twenty minutes ago."

Karl liked times like this, when both Willard and Mary were family, not servants. "We all got a little distracted," he said.

"I can see why. I'll have to add bones to the shopping list." She smiled at him as she walked to the edge of the porch. "You are a very special uncle right now."

"I agree." Bridget patted his arm one last time before she stood. "Elsie, bring Copper inside. It's time to eat."

He stood, touched her arm. "Just for clarification, do dogs eat in the dining room or the kitchen?"

The look she shot him was so saucy he was still smiling hours later, while lying in bed, once again with her on his mind. The day had been an extraordinary one. Elsie adored the puppy and he hoped it would help her over the next few months, and the years following. Lord knows she would need it. The loss of a parent, whether through death or abandonment, affected a child forever.

That's part of what had made the day extraordinary. The things he knew and how they'd affected him over the years. Bridget, in her unknowing way, had made him think about his anger and several other things. After dinner, while Elsie played with her puppy in the living room, and he and Bridget sat nearby watching, she, unbeknownst to him as to exactly how, coaxed more memories out of him about Benjamin. Fun memories that had made him laugh and want to remember more. He had, and that had made him grow thoughtful as they'd retired for the evening.

It was a bit unnerving, the way she made him feel.

He shouldn't have kissed her today. That was a given, and he wouldn't do it again. It had made him want more. More of something he could never have. Benjamin's death changed a lot of things in his life. The business. The family. He was now solely responsible for Elsie's future and everything he did would affect that. She was the next generation of Wingard Brothers Investment Banking. His father had often told him that, how he'd been the next generation of the company. That had been why his father worked so much, and paid his mother to stay away. He hadn't had time for a woman, any woman. Hadn't wanted the interference.

Karl had known that for years and had followed in his father's footsteps. He'd been able to because Benjamin had married Annette, and Elsie had been born. That had secured the next generation. All he had to do was cultivate it, like his father had done for him.

It would be years before Elsie was ready for grooming, but she would become the first woman at the helm of the company, and it was his job to make sure she was fully prepared for that.

Therefore, Bridget was a distraction he didn't need. Even now.

Ultimately, that meant he needed to continue to

provide attention to the inquiry, to having her and her friends compensated for their losses so she could travel on to Chicago, to her family there.

A boardinghouse still didn't please him, neither did her leaving, which was exactly why he had to distance himself from her, focus on getting things settled and get life back to the way it needed to be.

Bridget could not fall asleep. She had gotten used to the comfort of the big bed, the softness of the pillows and the warmth of the thick quilt. None of that had a thing to do with why she couldn't sleep.

It was Karl.

Down the hall.

Probably sound asleep.

She huffed out a breath. He had rendered her speechless on the back porch today. He'd kissed her! That's also why she couldn't sleep. Every time she closed her eyes, she felt his lips on hers all over again.

Many men had kissed her before. Quick pecks on the cheek or her forehead, much like she kissed Elsie all the time. She'd also kissed people. Boys. A couple of them who had asked her father if they could come over, take her on a picnic or a walk. Those kisses had been experiments. To see if they made her heart jump rope inside her chest.

That had been what Da had said would happen when she met the right man. That her heart would jump so hard and fast it would be like it was jumping rope inside her chest. That had never happened, and she'd started to believe Da had been fooling her. Teasing her. Lying to her.

She couldn't believe that he'd ever out-and-out lied

to her—that wasn't Da's way. But he did tease. Up until today, that's what she'd figured the whole jumping rope heart tale had been. A teasing tale so she wouldn't let any man steal her heart.

Today, when Karl had kissed her, she'd discovered exactly what Da had described. It had shocked her, stunned her, and she'd been set upon testing to see if it was really happening, when Karl had ended the kiss.

That's when she'd known it had been real. Her heart had been skipping rope so hard and fast that her knees had gone weak and she'd had to grab ahold of Karl to continue standing. That truly had rendered her speechless.

She had been so thankful that Willard had arrived outside when he had and that she'd been able to distract herself by talking about Copper and her Da as she and Karl had sat on the swing. She had continued to force herself to focus on conversations thereafter, throughout the evening meal and while sitting in the front room, but she'd felt Karl the entire time.

Even now, lying here, she could feel a connection to him. She didn't want to believe it. Couldn't believe it.

"Mercy me," she muttered.

Karl had made her feel things since she'd met him, and today, watching him with Elsie had intensified all of those peculiar sensations.

That's what it had to be. She was so grateful for the way he'd taken Elsie over to Reggie and Alice's, to play with friends, all so she'd see Copper and fall in love with the puppy. Elsie had needed that so she wouldn't have time to dwell on what had happened.

That was exactly what she needed to do, too. Become

so occupied that she wouldn't have time to dwell on Karl, and the way his kiss had made her heart skip rope.

Maybe it truly hadn't.

Maybe she'd just been expecting it to.

Well, that was silly. Why would she expect it to?

Shaking her head, she squeezed her eyes shut and told herself to think about the bed, how comfortable it was, and how she'd have beds like this in her boardinghouse.

When she opened her eyes, early morning sunlight shone in through the window. Karl was still on her mind as she got dressed, but now she also had a full list of reasons why she couldn't fall in love with him. There was just so much she had to do before any man could make her heart jump rope.

After getting Elsie up and dressed for the day, she hurried downstairs with the little girl to let Copper outside before joining Karl in the dining room for breakfast.

Bridget was relieved that upon seeing him her heart did make a small leap, but it certainly didn't jump enough to skip rope. While eating breakfast, she decided that she would just keep as much distance between the two of them as possible. If this week was like last week, he would be at the inquiry until late in the evening, so keeping her distance should be simple enough.

Once breakfast had been consumed, Karl gave Elsie a hug that included a tummy tickle. With Elsie still giggling, he set her down on the floor. "I will see you both tonight," he said.

"Tell your uncle Karl to have a good day, Poppet," Bridget instructed.

"Have a good day," Elsie said.

"You, too." He patted Elsie's head. "And you."

Bridget's heart did another little skip at the way he was looking at her. "And you," she repeated.

It wasn't until he was completely out of the room that she let the air out of her lungs. Guilt struck her then, at how she was thankful he was leaving. Avoiding him, when she wanted him and Elsie to spend time together, would be difficult. Even if it was just evenings.

That same guilt struck harder a short time later, when she and Elsie, wearing their coats, arrived at the front door for Willard to drive them to the store.

"I see you are both ready," he said. "I'm going out to pull the car out of the carriage house right now." He held up a suitcase. "We'll need to make a stop along the way. I have to drop Karl's suitcase off at the train station."

"Why?" Bridget asked.

"He called and said the inquiry is being moved to Washington, D.C.," Willard answered.

"He's going there?" Her heart pounded now, as that guilt increased. All her thoughts about distance didn't mean she wanted him to leave town.

"Yes. Only for a few days," Willard said. "I'll go pull the car out now."

The wave of remorse that washed over her was great, for more than one reason, but she shoved her personal ones aside. She understood that Karl was set on finding out all he could about the accident. He felt it was necessary, but she just couldn't help but worry about him hearing the sordid details of that night. All her thinking last night while trying to fall asleep had led her to question why she was so drawn to him. She'd thought it was his love toward Elsie. She admired that, but that wouldn't give her this deep need to help him. That came from the pain she saw in his eyes. A pain that she felt went deeper than his brother's death.

She and Elsie sat in the back seat as Willard drove to the train station. They got out of the car and joined him in walking to the depot building. It was much, much larger than any train station she'd ever seen. Even the one in Southampton. This depot building was massive, and there were far too many trains to count.

Her hand held tight onto Elsie's as they walked along the side of the building. Little signs hung from poles, with the names of towns. She quickly deduced that's how the people knew which train to board.

Willard led them to the one that said Washington, D.C., and she couldn't help but notice the one marked Chicago as they walked past it. A train she would soon take.

"I see Uncle Karl!"

Bridget saw him, too. His smile made her heart thud, but a sadness filled her at the notion of him leaving. She had a deep sense that what he was looking for, he wouldn't find in Washington, D.C.

"I didn't expect a farewell party," Karl said, taking the suitcase from Willard and setting it on the ground.

"We are going to the store!" Elsie exclaimed. "For a collar and leash for Copper."

"He certainly needs them," Karl said, picking Elsie up.

"Then Bridget and I can take him for walks!"

"Yes, you can." He kissed her cheek and set her back down. "I shouldn't be gone long."

"Why are they moving the inquiry?" Bridget asked, mainly because he was looking at her.

"To make it easier for the senators to be in attendance," he replied. "I suspect it will also limit others from being able to attend."

"Must you attend?" she asked.

He nodded.

Not sure what else to say, she nodded. "Be well."

He reached out and took her hand, gave it a squeeze. "You, too." Then he picked up his suitcase, spoke to Willard about the hotel where he'd be staying and walked onto the waiting train.

The sadness inside her grew heavier as she watched him disappear. Bridget determined that despite the fears she'd had about him making her heart skip rope, about what that might ultimately mean to her, she had to see this through. Karl and Elsie needed her.

There was a full train of people traveling because of the inquiry, but Karl found a seat where he could see Bridget, Elsie and Willard as the train pulled away from the station. The idea of not going to Washington crossed his mind, but he had to go. Not only for his brother and for Elsie, but for himself. Staying away from Bridget was his plan. One he had to stick to. That kiss yesterday was still alive inside him, making him want more. He couldn't do that. Couldn't want more. Couldn't care more. That went against all he knew. All he was.

What he could do was help her get to Chicago.

Upon arriving in Washington, he secured a room at a hotel, then went to the senate office building, and while walking along the hallway, a young man hurried past him.

"Excuse me, Senator," the young man said to a man

walking in front of Karl. "I would like to renew my application to be heard as a representative of a large number of third-class passengers—"

"We have a representative of the third-class on our witness list. That is more than enough," the senator replied.

"Your witness list contains several first-class passengers, but only one third-class passenger," the first man said.

"Of course it does," the other man said sharply. "It's inconceivable there is anything that third-class passengers experienced that didn't affect first-, or even second-class passengers. This inquiry won't become a circus show. Now, excuse me." The senator sped up and then disappeared through a door marked private.

With a knot of growing anger tightening in his stomach, Karl stopped next to the young lawyer. "You're representing a group of third-class passengers?"

The man nodded. "Yes, sir." Then, as if checking his manners, or memory, he said, "I offer you my condolences on the loss of your family in this catastrophe."

Karl gave a nod in acknowledgment, then because he did not recognize the other man, shook his head slowly, "I'm sorry, Mr.?"

"Braddock. Charles Braddock of McCoy and Associates."

"Nice to meet you, Charles." The name of the law firm was very familiar to Karl. He knew William McCoy and the firm well. "I'm interested in adding a name to your client list."

Charles frowned. "I'm representing third-class passengers, Mr. Wingard."

"I understand that." Why hadn't he thought of that?

A class action suit had the potential to carry weight, get Bridget compensated quicker, and others. "It's actually three clients I'd like to add."

By Thursday, Karl had had enough. He'd been in Washington for four days, and the longer he'd been there, the less he'd liked it. The inquiry had a preset determination for its outcome. The interviews he'd sat through made that obvious. The White Star Line would not be deemed responsible for anything.

"They've been trying to cover this up since the moment they hit that iceberg," Charles said with disgust. "They won't accept responsibility for anything."

Karl nodded, glancing out the train window as they rolled along the tracks back to New York. The complete disregard of the full impact to all classes affected by the sinking of the *Titanic* was eating him from the inside out.

He knew why.

Bridget.

He hated the idea that no one cared what she'd been through, or what others had been through.

He also knew he'd missed her the past four days. More than he'd missed someone in a very long time. More than he *should* miss someone.

She was not of his class. He'd never considered the unwritten privileges that came with his station, nor had he realized how he'd taken them for granted, assumed he deserved them while somehow believing others didn't.

That was wrong. He would never have come to that realization if not for her.

"I will call you tomorrow," he told Charles as the

train rolled into New York. "Set up a time for you to meet with Bridget and her friends."

"Are they still in the hospital?" Charles asked.

"I'm not sure. I'll know more once I arrive home."

His excitement to get home grew, and less than half an hour later, he walked into the house. Willard wasn't at the door, but Karl didn't think much of it. He'd caught an earlier train than he'd anticipated, so it was only after eight in the evening. This morning, he'd phoned Willard and said to expect him home around midnight.

He went directly to the stairs and hurried up them, to Elsie's room, assuming that's where he'd find Bridget.

His knock was immediately responded to, but as the door opened, he froze.

"Hello, Mr. Wingard. Elsie's asleep, but—"

"Where's Bridget?" he asked, glancing around the woman to look into the room.

Chapter Nine

Bridget didn't wait for Willard to open her door as he pulled the vehicle up beside the house. The carriage house door was open, and Karl's car was inside. He'd called this morning, said he was coming home from Washington this evening, but Willard had said he probably wouldn't arrive until after midnight.

She'd missed him during his absence and had so much to tell him. He'd called several times over the past few days, but she had never spoken to him and sincerely hoped the inquiry hadn't been overly trying for him.

Determining she'd check on Elsie first, so that when she did see Karl, she wouldn't need to feel rushed, she hurried to the stairway.

"Good evening."

Spinning quickly on one heel, she grabbed ahold of the stair post to stay upright. The sound of his voice had her heart pounding. So did the sight of him. He stood in the doorway of his office. Looking as handsome as ever. He'd removed his coat and vest, and the top few buttons of his white shirt were undone.

"Hello," she greeted. "I saw your car. I was going to run up and check on Elsie before coming to say hello."

"She's sleeping. I've checked on her. And I would like to talk with you."

He sounded cold. "All right. I'll just go put my coat—"

"Now. I'd like to speak to you now."

Even as a heavy disappointment washed over her, she nodded. The inquiry must not have gone well. Holding a smile on her face, she crossed the front foyer and entered his office as he stepped aside.

She took a seat on the davenport and closed her eyes for a moment. The past few days, while he'd been gone, she'd been able to bury, somewhat, the memory of Sunday, of when they'd stood on the back porch and he'd kissed her.

Burying the memory had been her only option, because she'd been putting too much time, too much thought into it. However, seeing him, sent it all into the forefront again.

Huffing out a breath, she opened her eyes, smiled up at him as he lowered onto the armchair next to the fireplace.

"We didn't expect you until after midnight," she said.

"And I didn't expect to arrive home to a stranger taking care of my niece. Did I, or did I not, hire you to be her nanny?"

A shiver rippled over her. She truly hadn't expected him to be upset. "Yes, but—"

"But? But nothing. I expected you to be here when I returned home, but you weren't. You were out gallivanting around town."

Her spine stiffened. "Gallivanting? I wasn't gallivanting. I was at the church. They were having a bazaar to—"

"Yes, a social event, which you thought was more important than Elsie's care."

"I did not!" Fully exasperated, she had to withhold her urge to jump to her feet. Crossing her arms, she settled a straightforward gaze on him. "You heard about the bazaar last Sunday. It was announced at the end of the service. As was how they needed baked goods for the cakewalk and other activities. Mary, Elsie, Catherine and I spent all morning baking so the items would be fresh and then I rode with Willard to deliver them."

"Mary and your friend Catherine told me all about that," he said, "and how you decided to stay at the bazaar rather than return home with Willard. It's my understanding you've been there all afternoon and evening."

"They needed help setting everything up! And Willard returned home to pick everyone else up and bring them to the church to attend the bazaar. Elsie, Mary, Catherine and Sean."

"Sean?" He shook his head. "You invited Catherine's brother to stay here, too?"

"Yes. They are brother and sister, and had nowhere to go upon being released from the hospital." He still sounded so cross, so ornery, her ire continued to grow. "I didn't think you'd mind. Willard said you wouldn't. So did Mary."

"Yet, no one mentioned it to me."

"You weren't here!" she pointed out. "And everyone was at the bazaar until it ended." Elsie had truly enjoyed all the games she'd played, but Bridget wasn't going to point that out, because he was too ornery to care. It was as if he felt they shouldn't leave the house without him.

"I stayed to help with cleanup while Willard brought everyone else home, and then he returned for me. Mary and Catherine said they'd put Elsie to bed."

He looked at her for a long moment. "So the bazaar was more important than taking care of Elsie."

"No, it wasn't!" She wished he'd stand up, yell, rather than sit there so stoic. It would give her reason to stand up, because not doing so was killing her. She wanted to wave her finger before his face, and had to ball her hand into a fist to keep that from happening. "How dare you say that! The bazaar was to raise money for survivors! I thought you'd appreciate having your house represented at the event."

"How dare I? How dare you invite complete strangers into my home in my absence." He stood, walked around his chair. "You may want to own a boardinghouse, but I don't. And I won't. Furthermore, *servants* don't represent my house at any events. Church or otherwise."

Her anger was too strong for her to continue to sit still. Too strong to even look at him. She had to leave before she lost all control.

She stood and marched to the door, but unable to forgo having the last word at least, she turned, pointed at him. "May the curse of Mary Malone and her nine, blind, illegitimate children chase you so far over the Hills of Damnation that the Lord himself can't find you with a telescope!"

Willard was in the front foyer, eyes wide, when she slammed the office door behind her. Head up, she marched straight to the stairway and up the steps. She had never met someone who could irritate her so quickly, so completely, as Karl Wingard. The man was a complete horse's ass at times.

She could have asked Willard to ask Karl about Catherine and Sean moving in here, but when Catherine had called from the hospital, saying they were leaving and didn't know where they were going, Willard had been the one to suggest they come here. He'd also been the one who'd gone and picked them up.

Not that she was attempting to shuck the blame on him. She wasn't. They were her friends, and she was grateful to be able to help them. It's just that Willard had assured her that Karl wouldn't mind. That there was plenty of room. She'd thought the same thing. Hadn't thought it would be an issue.

Catherine and Sean had insisted they'd stay in the servant's quarters in the basement, which they claimed were nicer than anywhere they'd ever lived.

As far as the bazaar, she'd been sure he wouldn't mind about that, knowing the money was going to survivors. Especially after Mary had said that Annette had served on the bazaar committee and that helping with the event in her honor felt wonderful.

It had.

Until she'd arrived home to Mr. Horse Poop.

She had half a mind to march back downstairs and curse him a second time. Several were rolling about in her head.

At the top of the stairs she turned, knowing she couldn't go back down to his office, no matter how much she wanted to. He'd been right. She had been hired as Elsie's nanny.

It was just so hard. She'd never been a servant and didn't know anything about being one. She knew how to take care of Elsie and how to clean, cook, wash clothes—all the things that servants did. What she didn't know were the rules. She hadn't even thought about them until Catherine and Sean had arrived.

They knew far more about the rules of that than she did. They'd questioned going to the bazaar. Had said they'd stay home. She'd been the one to insist they attend. There had been nothing that needed to be done at home. They'd all eaten at the bazaar, and with Catherine and Sean's help, the house had already been cleaned from top to bottom this week. Besides, there had been people from all walks of life at the bazaar, both helping with it and attending it.

She opened the door to Elsie's room and couldn't help but smile at how Copper raised his head, checking out who was entering the room.

"It's just me," she told the puppy quietly.

Curled in a ball on the bed near Elsie's feet, Copper laid his head back down.

Bridget patted him, gave Elsie a soft kiss and left the room, wondering if Karl would be upset to know Copper was sleeping in Elsie's room. He seemed to be upset about everything else she'd allowed, so why not that, too?

She entered her room, but other than taking off her coat—irritated all over again that she hadn't even had time to take it off before Karl had started badgering her—and hanging it in the closet, she was too flustered to do more than pace the floor. The bitterness inside her wasn't all directed at Karl. There was plenty of it going out to her own good self. Or not so good self.

There just was no history for her to draw upon, to have learned from or to compare to what she was ex-

periencing right now. Not when it came to being a servant, or when it came to a man like Karl. Just when she
thought she might be figuring him out, he changed.

He was like an old tomcat. All nice and purring one
minute and biting the very hand that feeds it the next.

All in all, she just wasn't cut out to be a servant. Da
had known that. All his reasonings aside, he'd known
that her temper, the very thing he'd warned her about,
was too strong to be subservient to anyone.

She huffed out a breath. *Oh, Da, what am I going
to do?*

No answer suddenly appeared to her, and she truly
hadn't expected one, but it would be nice. Catherine
and Sean hadn't had anywhere to go, and neither did
she. Not until they could at least recoup the money they
would have had upon arrival. There had been boardinghouses and hotels that had opened their doors to people the night the *Carpathia* had arrived, but they were
full now, even overflowing. Society aid programs had
assisted those traveling elsewhere to obtain train tickets and traveling vouchers, and others, like the church
with the bazaar today, were raising more money to help,
but there were so many who, like Catherine and Sean,
had been injured, and now owed money for their hospital stays.

Maybe she should take the twenty-five dollars from
the White Star Line, request a travel voucher and go
to Chicago. Catherine and Sean could go with her, but
that would be letting Karl down. She had agreed to stay
until Mrs. Conrad returned.

She'd have to quit. Tell him that she'd stay and take
care of Elsie, but not be hired by him. Like she'd stated
in the beginning.

No, she couldn't. Then she wouldn't have any money to give Catherine and Sean.

If only the same Karl who had left on Monday had returned tonight, instead of the ornery one that had made her so mad.

She was still mad at him. The fact he'd thought that anything meant more to her than Elsie's care was maddening. Insulting, that's what it was.

Pausing midstep at the sound of a knock, she pivoted and marched to the door. Before answering it, she drew in a deep breath and painted a smile on her face. Most likely it was Willard, coming to check on her after having seen the way she left Karl's office.

She pulled the door open, and the fake smile disappeared as she stared at Karl. He had one hand planted on the doorframe, was leaning slightly to that side and had a cockeyed, sheepish grin on his face.

"We need to talk," he said.

"Why? Have you not insulted me enough already this evening?"

"Yes, I have." He stepped into the room. "That's why we need to talk."

She shook her head. Turned away from him as he walked into the room and closed the door.

"What was it your father said? Don't let the sun set on your anger."

She turned, gave him a head to toe scathing look sharp enough to make him bleed. "Da never met you."

He grinned again. "True."

So much for making him bleed with her eyes. She took ahold of the doorknob to open the door for him to leave. "And it's don't let the sun go down on your anger, not set."

"What's the difference?" he asked.

She had no idea, was just too mad to agree with anything he said right now. "The sun had already set when you made me mad." She opened the door.

He sat down on the bed. "I'm sorry. I'm sorry I made you mad." He stood and paced the floor at the foot of the bed like she'd been doing. "I'd expected to come home to…people. Instead no one was here."

She closed the door. "Elsie was."

"Yes, she was, sound asleep, and well taken care of." He stopped pacing, looked at her. "I shouldn't have taken my anger out on you."

She had no idea how he did it, but he could make her so mad she wanted to spit one minute and then make her heart melt the next. "Why did you?"

He looked away. "Blame it on my mother."

The anger that crossed his face was like what she'd seen downstairs, and Bridget was momentarily taken aback. "Did you see her?"

"No. No." He shook his head. "I shouldn't have said that. She has nothing to do with any of this."

He sounded disgusted, but also wounded, and she stepped closer to him. "The inquiry? Is that why you were so mad?"

"Yes," he said quickly. "I've never seen people try so hard to circumvent responsibility in my life."

"It was an accident."

"I know." He ran a hand through his hair. "I'm not saying they hit that iceberg on purpose, that they meant to sink the ship and kill all those people, but it happened, and the White Star Line is responsible for all those deaths. For all the children left without parents, for wives left without husbands, for people having lost so much."

He looked pained and tired, and that, too, made her heart melt. "What do you expect them to do?" she asked.

"I want them to listen to everyone, find out how they can prevent something like this from happening again."

"Isn't that what they are doing?"

"No! They're only listening to a select group. Mainly officers, shipmates. The passengers they have called to witness, they sequestered in private rooms."

"Why?"

"To make sure all the stories jibe. The only person they are casting blame on is the captain of the *Californian* for not responding."

"The other ship we saw that night?"

He frowned. "Are you sure you saw one? Reports show the *Californian* was twenty miles away. Even on a clear night, it would have been impossible to see that far."

"I'm sure I saw one. I'm sure I rowed toward it, but I don't know how far away it was. It just kept getting further and further." She sat down on the bed. "No one else saw it?"

"If they did, I haven't heard their testimony." He sat down beside her. "But the inquiry isn't over."

"Maybe I didn't see a ship." She was sure she had, but she was also sure there were things she didn't remember from that night. "Just because I said it happened, doesn't mean it was true. Like when you think you see something, but when you look again it's not there. Maybe it was like that."

He took ahold of her hand. "No, don't second-guess yourself. I believe that you saw a ship. That you rowed toward one." He touched her face with his other hand. "Just like I believe nothing is more important to you than Elsie's care. I hope you can forgive me for that. For the other things I said."

She leaned her cheek against his hand. "I have to forgive you. I won't be able to sleep tonight if I don't."

"I won't be able to sleep tonight if you don't, either."

He was looking at her so intently, her lips started to quiver, remembering the moment his had brushed over them. She twisted, looked away, knowing kissing him could not happen again. It was sure to make her heart skip rope. "I'm sorry about inviting Catherine and Sean to stay here. I'll—"

"We'll let them stay," he said, removing his hand from her face. His other hand was still holding hers and he squeezed it. "I was going to have to ask you where they were. This way, I know."

"Why?"

"Because I've been working with a lawyer, Charles Braddock. He's representing a large group of those traveling third class to see they receive compensation and has agreed to include Catherine and Sean, and you, on his list. A large class action suit will hold more weight than individual ones."

"What does that mean, a class action suit?"

"It means that one hearing will provide restitution to a large group of clients, instead of one at a time, which is ideal for those who may not be able to afford a lawyer who is capable of actually bringing a lawsuit before the courts."

"Sue them? This group is suing the White Star Line?"

He nodded. "It's the only way they are going to receive anything."

"How long will that take?"

"I don't know, but I will call Charles tomorrow, invite him over so the three of you can ask him any questions you might have."

"How much will that cost, for him to include us?"

"His law firm is offering this service for free."

"Why?"

He smiled and softly said, "Because it's the right thing to do, just like it was the right thing for you to help with the church bazaar."

She laid her hand atop the one holding hers. Couldn't help it. She was glad he was home. "Annette served on the ladies committee at the church. Mary, Willard and I helped today in honor of her."

"She would have liked that. I like that you did that, I was just too grumpy to see that earlier. I was anxious to see all of you, and when you weren't here..." He shrugged. "I don't know what it is about you, but you really bring the worst in me out at times."

"And the best," she said. "Elsie and Copper have become best of friends."

"I noticed that. I believe he growled at me the first time I walked in the room."

She giggled. "He does that to me, too. I think he just doesn't like to be disturbed."

"Or maybe he's afraid he shouldn't be sleeping on the bed."

Teasingly, she slapped his arm. "I knew you would mention that. I knew it." Giggling, she added, "You'll be glad to know that he does eat in the kitchen. There won't be any begging at the table. I promise."

"Do you ever eat in the kitchen?"

Her stomach did a little flip-flop. "Why?"

"Because I'm starving. I haven't eaten since noon, and I don't want to eat alone."

She stood, and pulled on his hand until he stood. "I'll confess something to you."

He raised his brows. "Oh? What?"

Walking beside him to the door, she said, "We've all eaten in the kitchen while you've been gone." She opened the door. "It's not where you eat, it's who you eat with that's important."

"I like the sound of that."

Smiling up at him, she determined that tonight she wasn't going to worry about what he did to her heart and just enjoy the fact he was home. "Do you like the sound of eggs and ham?"

"Very much."

Happy, she asked, "What about rum cake? It's my mother's recipe and very delicious. Elsie won it at the cakewalk today."

"She won the cake you baked?"

"I told her she could pick whatever one she wanted, and that was the one she picked."

"Because you baked it."

"She helped." No longer mad at him, she knew she could tell him a few other things. "Catherine and Sean are staying in the servant quarters in the basement, and they both have been doing chores around here, but I'll pay them out of my nanny salary."

He laid a hand on her back as they started down the staircase. "If they are working around here, I will pay them. As you stated, Mrs. Dahl is helping her daughter, so there are things around here that need to be done. Do you know if Sean is any sort of a carpenter?"

"I don't know, why?"

"Because I've been thinking about having a playhouse built in the backyard for Elsie, like Reggie's girls have. Perhaps Sean could do that."

The urge to kiss him was so strong her toes curled inside her shoes. "There it is again," she said. "The best of you."

Karl couldn't say there was anything good about him right now. He felt rotten for the way he'd treated her. That comment about his mother had come out because that is who he blamed. Bridget not being home had reminded him of being young, of wanting to have his mother there when he came home, like other children. When she wasn't there, he'd remembered a time when he'd been with his father downtown and seen his mother. He'd pointed her out, and his father had said that she was always out gallivanting around.

Bridget wasn't his mother, and she hadn't been gallivanting around. While he'd been wallowing in self-pity at her not being here, she'd been out raising money for those who needed it. Then she'd cooked him eggs and ham and sat beside him in the kitchen, where he ate two pieces of the best cake he'd ever tasted, and they talked. Talked until after one o'clock in the morning. They conversed about little, insignificant things and larger, important subjects like what was being done for the survivors and how more was still needed.

Their discussion was still with him when he entered his office the following morning. Sitting in the kitchen last night had reminded him of years ago, when he and Benjamin would sneak down there and talk. He hadn't had that in a long time. A friend to confide in. Not since Benjamin had gotten married. His brother had then had Annette. Benjamin had been so happy. Karl didn't trust that what he was feeling for Bridget was anything close to what Benjamin had felt for Annette, but he did have to believe that all women weren't like his mother. Some women did care. Some women were loyal.

"Good morning, Mr. Wingard," Julia Robertson said as he entered the front room of his office. She'd been with the company before him, helping his father keeping things moving smoothly. "There is a stack of messages on your desk and I have a few things to discuss with you."

He rested a hand on her desk. "Your things first," he said, knowing they needed immediate answers.

She slid on a pair of glasses and went through a small list of business concerns, and he quickly agreed with her suggestions for addressing them. He'd always appreciated her, but the last two weeks had proven how much he also needed her, and he made a mental note to increase her salary.

"There is one final thing, sir," she said. "The Metropolitan Opera Company is hosting a benefit concert for Sunday night. The performers are donating their time, and the opera has contacted us about purchasing a balcony suite. All proceeds will go to groups assisting *Titanic* survivors. Would you'd like me to purchase the suite and offer it to branch managers to attend?"

He nodded. For the past five years, Benjamin and Annette had attended public events on behalf of the company. Something else he'd have to take over. "Yes. Please do."

"Very well." She opened her little book full of telephone exchanges. "Just let me know if you need me to follow up with any of the messages on your desk."

"I will." The benefit concert continued to filter through his mind as he walked toward his office, but so did Bridget, and how last night she'd said that she'd never eaten at a restaurant until boarding the *Titanic*. Pausing before opening his door, he turned. "Are there two balcony suites available?"

"Yes."

"Then purchase two, please. Offer one to employees, and let them know they are also welcome to make a donation of their own, if they'd like to. I will fill the second one."

Nodding, she glanced down at her desk and then back up at him with a very large smile. "I will, sir. Thank you."

He nodded, feeling good with his decision. Then, realizing he had no idea, he asked, "How many seats are in a suite?"

"Twelve."

"Perfect." He entered his office, and though there was a stack of messages, he made five phone calls and within a short time had the suite full of prominent citizens, who also pledged to make significant donations to the event. His father had said that he had the gift of being able to convince people of what were good investments, and he was glad to use that in this situation.

He went through the messages then, which included a telegram from Mrs. Conrad. Her grief was evident in the message as was her promise to return home as soon as she was able to put weight on her foot. She had been his nanny and was very dedicated to his family, yet he felt that Bridget had handled the situation far better than Mrs. Conrad would have been able to. She may not have had the stamina to survive the ordeal.

Later, as he was leaving to be in attendance at the meeting between Charles, Bridget and her friends, he asked Julia, "Do you know where a person would obtain an evening gown for the opera?"

"Down the street, where you purchase your suits. They have a full woman's department." She opened her desk drawer, pulled out a slip of paper and held it out to him. "Here's the size you'll need."

"Thanks." He grinned. "The items you bought for her fit perfectly."

Smiling and nodding, she said, "You are very welcome."

Chapter Ten

Karl chose a dark blue dress, the same blue as Bridget's eyes, with cream-colored lace, and purchased everything else the salesperson suggested, including a hat and matching evening cape. With his back seat full of boxes and ribbon-tied packages, he drove toward home.

The sun was out, and the sky bright blue. The birds were tweeting in the budding trees, and people walked along the sidewalks and hurried across the cobblestoned streets. It was all normal, yet he seemed to be looking at it through a new set of eyes. At everything. He felt good inside. Good about the opera's fundraiser, knowing he was finally doing something that had the potential to actually help the people who had been affected.

A grin formed as he thought about taking Bridget to the opera. Or, perhaps, about convincing her to go with him to the opera.

She was sure to say no at first, and it was up to him to convince her otherwise. They would go to dinner afterward, downtown, make a full evening out of it.

He wasn't sure how she'd done it, but it almost felt as if she'd picked him up like an old rug last night, hauled him outside and shook out all the dirt, the debris, that had been weighing him down for years.

"Well, Lordy be, but look at that smile," she said as he entered the house via the front door a short time later.

He laughed because he couldn't grasp her waist and pull her close, kiss her, which is what he really wanted to do. "It's been a good morning."

"I'm happy for you," she said. "We didn't expect you home for lunch, so it will just be a moment while Catherine sets the table. Elsie just ran down the hall to wash her hands." Her smile grew even wider. "For the second time."

He lifted a brow. "Didn't pass inspection the first time?"

"No, she and Copper found a puddle in the corner of the backyard and made mud pies. He's on the back porch until his paws dry."

Her eyes were sparkling and he held out his hands. "Let me see your hands."

She held them out to him. "Why?"

He took ahold of both hands, flipped them over and back again before giving her a nod. "Because I'm sure you're the one who showed her how to make mud pies."

Slapping his chest with one hand, she laughed. "Guilty."

He curled his fingers around her hand that was still on his chest.

"Mud pies are a true sign of spring, just like daffodils." She glanced up the steps. "Look who is home for lunch, Poppet."

"Uncle Karl! I made mud pies!"

"I heard that." He released Bridget's hand and caught

Elsie as soon as she was within reach. "Are we eating them for lunch?"

"No, silly, they are full of mud!"

"Oh, so how did you make them?"

She told him with great detail as he carried her into the dining room. He'd loved her since the day she'd been born, bought her gifts, hugged her, teased her, but the bond he felt growing with her since her arrival back home was far stronger than before, and that, too, was because of Bridget.

After they'd eaten, he was dragged out into the back-yard to see the mud pies and the puddle, which was well on the way to being dried up by the sun. Copper was with them, and as Elsie took chase after the puppy, Karl pointed to an area in the yard where five split pieces of wood were laid out. "What's that?" he asked.

Bridget took ahold of his hand and pulled him toward the wood. "I told Sean you were interested in him building a playhouse and he staked out the dimensions."

Her eyes were sparkling, and he couldn't stop staring at her. He liked her eyes. He liked a lot of things about her. Admired how she didn't waste time when it came to anything. Her honesty. Her zest for life. More than that, he admired how she was an inspiration. She certainly inspired him. In a way no one ever had.

"I hope you don't mind. He's also drawn up a plan."

"I don't mind," he answered. "I look forward to seeing the plan."

"Good." She glanced left and right before whispering, "It will be two houses. One for Elsie and one for Copper."

Once again, his mind became fully preoccupied with kissing her. Tasting those soft warm lips again

"I haven't mentioned it to Elsie," she said, still whispering. "I'll let you do that."

He leaned closer, whispered, "Or maybe we'll just let her guess what he's building."

She bit on her bottom lip until her smile was too big to contain. "She'll be so surprised!"

He couldn't put his finger on just one thing that she'd done to change him, but she had, because this, all of this, was what he'd missed while being in Washington. Every day with her was fresh and new.

She twisted, and he caught the side of her waist before she could take a step. "Where are you going?"

"I need to put Elsie down for her nap. You said the lawyer will be here soon."

Regrettably, he nodded, but then tightened his hold on her side. "I'll help you."

She giggled again. "All right, you can catch Copper."

"Catch Copper?"

Eyes full of mirth, she nodded.

That would be simple enough. The dog, now boasting a bright blue collar, followed Elsie everywhere. "All right." He gave her side a gentle squeeze and then released her to kneel down. "Elsie. Come here."

Just as he predicted, the puppy raced beside Elsie as she ran toward him, but the moment he reached out to scoop up the pup, he turned and shot around Bridget.

She giggled.

He whispered to Elsie, "Help me catch Copper."

She shook her head. "Only Bridget can do that."

"Oh, no, we can, too," he assured her.

She shrugged and then took off after the dog. He did, too. For every turn he made, the pup made one in the opposite direction, and with ever near miss, Bridg-

who had indeed sketched out a plan of a playhouse and doghouse.

"Are you a carpenter by trade?" Karl asked, viewing the very detailed drawing.

"I haven't mastered any one trade," Sean said. "But I've been doing most of them my entire life. I was always big for my age, so everything from picking rocks to swinging a hammer, I've done it."

"These drawings are very good." Karl ran a finger over the drawing, along the scalloped eaves of the little house. "Very detailed."

"I didn't do them," Sean said. "I can build it, but I knew I couldn't draw it. Catherine did. She's got a knack for that."

"She does." Karl appreciated the man's honesty; he also appreciated the way Bridget was beaming. "Do you know how to drive?" he asked Sean.

Sean admitted he didn't, and Karl told him he'd have Willard drive him to the lumberyard after their meeting with Charles. He also asked how Sean was feeling,
wing from the hospital visit that both his and Cath-
feet had been frozen by the icy waters.

sir." Sean shifted his stance. "Willard loaned
f his boots. They feel a lot better than my

ught about that. How Sean and Cath-
everything and needed everything.
that." Karl made a mental note
hem to other stores besides the
clothes and other essentials

he project when Willard

et's laughter rang in the air. Enjoying the sound, and the game, he continued to chase the dog, making both Bridget and Elsie laugh.

After about the tenth miss, Karl decided in this endeavor, he'd claim defeat. He sat down near Bridget, huffed out an exaggerated breath and looked up at her. "I give up. What's the secret?"

Still laughing she knelt down beside him. "The trick is for him to think you don't want to catch him." She winked at him. "Like a leprechaun."

"A leprechaun?"

She nodded, stood and walked away. "Come along, Poppet, time for your nap."

Elsie ran over and took ahold of Bridget's hand. The image of the two of them, walking hand in hand was so precious, he stared at it for several moments.

Near the door, Bridget knelt down in front of Elsie and said something, too quietly for him to hear. Too quietly for Copper to hear, too, yet the dog slowly sneaked closer, as if wanting to know what was being said. The pup walked all the way next to her knee.

Karl found himself mentally telling her to snatch up the pup before he ran away, but she just kept talking to Elsie.

As he watched, she reached down and petted Copper's head until the puppy sat on his bottom. She then turned her attention away from Elsie and spoke to the pup, before reaching down and scooping him up with both hands.

The grin she flashed his way as she stood, pup in hand, made Karl laugh out loud. He leaped to his feet and clapped. "That's quite the trick."

She gave him a graceful curtsy.

He walked forward and scooped up Elsie. "I'll carry her upstairs. You carry the dog."

"You're the one who brought him home," she reminded him quietly as they stepped onto the porch.

"With your permission," he replied just as softly, while opening the door.

"I must concede to that." She kissed the dog's head.

Who would have thought he'd ever be envious of a dog? Not him. But he was.

"He will learn to come when called," she said as they entered the house. "He's just too young right now. All he wants to do is play tag."

"You mean catch me if you can."

He liked her expressions, how animated she was, and how lovely. She was also so natural. There was nothing fake or deceiving about her. He'd never known anyone quite like her.

In Elsie's bedroom he watched Bridget tuck his niece into bed along with her puppy and her doll, and then she sat down on the bed with a book in hand.

"Close your eyes, Poppet," she said quietly. "So you can see the pictures."

Arms crossed, he leaned against the wall, intrigued how that would work. Her lyrical voice was soothing and animated as she read the storybook. By the time she closed the book, Elsie, along with the pup, was sound asleep. He also felt an interesting sense of peace inside him.

She stood, kissed Elsie on the head and then, setting the book on the shelf, crossed the room.

Once in the hallway, with the door closed behind them, he said, "You are just full of little tricks, aren't

you? Having her close her eyes while you read, so she falls to sleep faster."

Smiling, she shook her head. "I had her close her eyes so she'd learn to use her imagination in creating the images I was reading about."

He was reminded of what she'd told Elsie in the car, about closing her eyes so she could see Benjamin and Annette, and how Elsie said she did that. "You are a very wise woman."

She giggled. "I know." Flashing him a sparkling-eyed grin, she added, "Because it does make her fall to sleep faster."

Laughing, he draped an arm around her shoulders and pulled her closer for a quick sideways hug. "I knew it."

Their shared laughter floated in the air as they started down the stairway. She was givin...

normal, and he liked it.

"I'll find S...
of the pla...

Giving...
"Join us."

"All rig...
"We'll see y...

He nodde...
shoulders. A...
foyer and ent...
this new norm...
experienced.

She returned...
Karl had only...
ably not twenty...

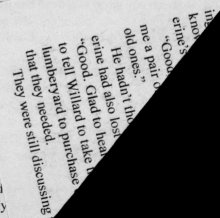

knocked on the door, announcing Charles had arrived for their meeting.

Catherine joined them in the office, and Karl listened as the lawyer explained the processes honestly and openly. He made no outlandish promises, but did offer hope.

After the meeting ended and Willard, Sean and Catherine—who had asked to go along to pick out the paint—had left, Bridget followed him back into his office.

"You seem awfully thoughtful," she said. "As if you didn't like what Charles had to say."

"I don't," he admitted.

"You don't think it was a good idea for us to sign his papers?"

"No, I think that was the right thing to do," he answered. "I just don't like the idea that you have to go about things this way."

"Because it will take so long?"

He nodded. Charles had said it could be nine months to a year before resolution. People who had saved, sold everything to come to America were now plunged deeper into poverty than before. Loss like that had never personally affected him in the past, but it was different now. It wouldn't have been if not for Bridget. If Mrs. Conrad hadn't broken her foot and had arrived home with Elsie, he knew, deep inside, that his life wouldn't have changed—he wouldn't have changed—not like he had the past two weeks.

She laid a hand on his arm. "I do wish there was a way for you to understand it was an accident and it's not up to you to try and make anything right about it."

"But it is. I've been very fortunate in my life. I have the financial ability to go anywhere, do anything, buy anything, but that doesn't make me any better than anyone else." He wasn't exactly sure where his thoughts were going. They were just... Going. "Look at you. You arrived in this country with nothing, yet you have given Elsie so much. It has nothing to do with money."

"There are many things that money can't buy," she said.

The frustration that had filled him while in Washington had returned. "Exactly. And it shouldn't dictate worth. Every life is worthy. Every person is worthy."

"You're right, Karl, but that's not the way of the world. I know you are thinking that every third-class passenger should be compensated to the same level as the first-class ones, I saw it on your face while Charles was talking." Looking up at him, she shook her head. "But those first-class passengers paid a lot more for their tickets. They paid to be served mutton and beef and salmon. Paid to be served at fancy tables and chairs. In all honesty, the food served to the third-class passengers was better and more plentiful than some people had ever had."

"I understand that," he said. "But a life is a life."

"It is, but there is also nothing wrong with having money." She placed a hand on her chest. "That's why Da wanted me to open a boardinghouse. So I could make money. Have money. Be independent. I'm not going to feel bad when that happens because I will have worked for it, earned it, just like you do, and your father did, and your grandfather."

"This isn't about money," he said.

"Isn't it? You want everyone to be compensated at

the same rate." She shrugged. "That's impossible because there is no set rate that will ever satisfy everyone. Some people feel rich when they have a hundred dollars, and for others, a million isn't enough."

He huffed out a breath. She was right. He walked to the window, stared out it. He didn't know what he wanted; all he knew was that something had changed inside him and he didn't know what, or what it meant.

Her hands came around his sides and she hugged him from behind, her body up against his. He laid his hands on her forearms folded across his chest. Her embrace was comforting, yet torturous. He wasn't sure why until she spoke.

"That emptiness you feel inside," she whispered, "is grief, Karl, from losing your brother. Someone you loved very much. Making the White Star Line compensate everyone, at the same level, won't make it go away. Part of it will never go away, but the pain can't be released until you admit it's there. Once you do that, day by day, it'll get better. I promise."

That couldn't be it. He was stronger than that. Only the weak showed their pain. He'd done that once, years ago, and was punished for that. He couldn't do it again. Wouldn't. Yet, as those thoughts raced across his mind, something inside him broke loose, spreading an intense pain. He tried to breathe through it, to not react, but her arms tightened as she pressed closer against him.

The comfort of her embrace was a stark contrast to the hurt inside him, and in some ways, it felt stronger. Her comfort was stronger than his pain? That was impossible. The pain inside him was rioting. He had to push her away. Tell her to leave, so he could be alone, bury the pain back inside him. That's how he had to deal with it. That's how he'd always dealt with it.

He twisted, grasped her shoulders.

Tears were on her cheeks as she looked up at him, and her arms, still around him, held on as tight as before. "Benjamin's gone, Karl, but I know in my heart that he's so glad you're here. Still watching out for him, like always."

His throat burned as he swallowed a vibrating growl. The pain inside him was like a storybook ogre. Trapped and clawing to get out. He didn't want to expose her to that. She was too beautiful, too kind and caring. He shook his head, fighting against the desire to pull her close while believing he needed to push her away.

"I want to help you, Karl. Please let me."

Her plea was barely a whisper, yet echoed in his head as if she'd shouted it, like she was holding out a hand for him to grasp as he was falling.

"I promise it will get better. I know. I've been there."

Her words struck him again, echoed in his head, but it was the touch of her lips against his cheek that he reacted to. He looped his arms around her, pulled he up against him and buried his face in her hair. She had been there and the pain inside him hurt for her, too. Then, it was as if a dam had let loose inside him, releasing a river of dark raging water. Benjamin was dead. Gone. Forever. He hadn't wanted to admit that, not even to himself, but it was true. So very true. And that hurt, knowing he was gone forever.

Annette was gone, too. So was Bridget's father. He held her tight as thoughts—pain—kept flowing and flowing, until there was nothing left to flow, leaving him feeling drained. As he breathed in the soft, enchanting fragrance that was uniquely Bridget, a sense of calm, tranquility filled him.

He lifted his head and couldn't think of a way to express his gratitude to her, other than to kiss her. In appreciation. He leaned forward and pressed his lips to her forehead and held them there, eyes closed, absorbing just how precious she was to him at this moment.

They shared another smile when he ended the kiss and looked down at her again.

"I'll see who is at the door."

Confused, he asked, "What?"

"Someone is at the door," she said. "Willard's not here, so I'll see who it is."

"I'll come with you."

Phil Weinstein was at the door, and removed his bowler hat. "Hello, Karl, I have some news for you."

His heart sank. He knew the news. "Benjamin and Annette?"

Short, with round glasses and a barrel chest, Weinstein nodded.

He waved a hand, inviting the man in, and his heart sank a bit deeper as he saw the moisture in Bridget's eyes.

She squeezed his hand briefly and flashed him a trembling smile before she turned and walked toward the staircase.

He led Weinstein into his office and closed the door. "Where are they?"

"Here," Weinstein said. "The ship just docked. They've been embalmed and are on ice, but an immediate funeral is advised. The bodies are being transported to the undertakers on Twenty-Ninth Street." He held out an envelope. "I've been directed to give you this, as well."

"What is it?"

"Compensation for your niece and her nanny, from the White Star Line."

Karl's jaw locked tight as he opened the envelope. Two checks, both made out to him. "Why do they both have my name on them?"

Looking confused, Weinstein said, "Your niece is a child and the nanny is employed by you."

"The only reason Bridget—Miss McGowen—is being compensated is because she's employed by me?"

"You paid for her ticket, didn't you? Or your brother?"

Karl laid the checks on his desk. In the beginning, he'd wanted to see Benjamin and Annette's bodies brought home, buried here. That was insignificant now. Bridget was right; that wouldn't bring them back.

Pushing the air out of his lungs, he turned. "Thank you, Phil, for bringing the news. For coming over."

"We do hope this settles things for you." Weinstein curled the brim of his hat into his palms. "Your presence at the inquiry has, uh…um, been stirring the pot, so to speak."

So that was the true reason for the checks. "Has it? I wasn't aware of that."

"Other investors lost family members, too, Karl. Large investors. Prominent people. It's important for the company to be assured that you're satisfied, as satisfied as you can be with the circumstances as they are."

Weinstein was merely the messenger. Karl had to tell himself that to keep his temper in check. "Circumstances that should never have occurred."

The other man nodded. "Very unfortunate circumstances. New regulations will be put in place. The inquiry will require that."

Yes, it will, because that's their goal. Nothing else. Karl walked to the door of his office, opened it. "Thank you again for coming over."

"Shall I convey your satisfaction?"

Karl crossed the foyer and opened the front door. "You may convey that you completed the task asked of you."

Weinstein stumbled slightly, but walked out the door.

Promptly shutting the door, Karl glanced up the staircase, at Bridget standing there. He couldn't take his eyes off her as she slowly walked down the steps and straight to him, into the arms he held wide.

Bridget wrapped her arms around his waist and held on tight. For him. For her. For Elsie. For Benjamin and Annette. She wished she could do more to help him, but knew only time could do that. When she felt able, she eased her hold, rubbed his back and softly kissed his cheek. "We need to call the church."

He gave her another tight hug, then leaned back and nodded. "Is Elsie still sleeping?"

"Yes, so I can help you with whatever you need."

"I don't know what I would have done without you these past two weeks," he said.

It was the other way around. She didn't know what she'd have done without him. Listening to Catherine and Sean speak of what they'd gone through, including their hospital stay, made her feel guilty that she'd been welcomed into Karl's home immediately. Given food, clothing, a place to stay, a job. She owed him so much.

She shook her head. "You would have been fine."

He grinned. "I wouldn't have been cursed, twice."

Pinching her lips to keep from smiling, she took a step backward. "How do you know? Maybe someone else would have done that."

His hands slid to her waist. "Probably, but theirs wouldn't have been as cute as yours."

The warmth of his palms penetrating her dress made it difficult to think. "Cute? They weren't meant to be cute."

He kissed her forehead, and she closed her eyes at how that made her heart thud.

"Yes. Cute." He slid one arm around her back, while twisting toward his office. "And they were cute."

"Don't you believe in curses?" she asked, walking across the foyer beside him.

"I'm not sure how to answer that."

"Why?"

He stepped aside at the doorway, so she could enter the room, but kept his hand on her back as he walked in behind her. "Because if I say yes, you'll tell me why I shouldn't, and if I say no, you'll tell me why I should."

Twisting, she looked up at him. "That's because some curses need to be believed in, and others don't." Leaning closer, she whispered, "The trick is knowing the difference."

He caught her waist with both hands again. "How would I know the difference?"

She gave him a secretive look. "You'd need the luck of the Irish to know that."

"I think I have found that."

Her breath stalled, so did her heart as he leaned closer, until their lips met.

Warm, soft, his lips moved slowly across hers, as if teasing hers to kiss him back. She shouldn't, but the desire was too great. It was fun, the way her lips caught his, then moved, and his followed, catching hers, like a game of tag.

His hands on her hips pulled her closer. She pressed her hand against his chest, then curled her fingers beneath his suspenders, holding on as his lips captured hers over and over.

Some captures were longer, some were quick, fast. All she could think about was more. She didn't want any of it to stop.

She didn't know when his hands cupped her face, but that's where they were when he gave her a long, firm kiss and then leaned back. She opened her eyes, and a smile tugged on her lips at seeing how brightly he was smiling.

"Yes, I do believe I've found the luck of the Irish," he said.

Tilting her head, she replied, "And I believe you have kissed the Blarney Stone."

His thumb brushed over her lips as he shook his head. "It doesn't feel like a stone to me."

It was impossible for her to think straight. Her heart was pounding. No, it was skipping rope. "You are trouble, Karl Wingard."

He laughed. "I've been called worse." Releasing her, he stepped back. "But it's never sounded as charming as you make it sound."

She let go of his suspenders. If he could make her heart jump rope, he could steal it, too. Without her ever knowing it. "I—I need to go check on Elsie." She left the room, and hurried to the stairway, sucking in air the entire way. Losing her heart was not something she could do. Not now. She had promises to keep.

A long time ago, she'd thought she'd lost her heart, to Jamie Flannery. She'd been sixteen and Da had warned her then that losing her heart would change her life, and that she shouldn't let that happen until she was ready for everything to change.

Jamie hadn't stolen her heart, but he hadn't made it skip rope, either.

Elsie was awake, playing on the floor with Copper, and as Bridget made the bed she thought about Jamie, how he'd grown tired of waiting for her to want things to change and married Hannah Cooper. They had two children now; one was Elsie's age.

That could have been her. Having babies with Jamie. She'd still be in Ireland, living with Jamie's family.

Da had been right. She hadn't been ready for everything to change back then. She wasn't ready now, either.

She did like Karl, and wondered how long he'd wait for someone to be ready for everything to change.

A bark cleared her mind, and knowing what that meant, she said, "Copper needs to go outside. Let's hurry."

They made it outside in time, and while they were in the backyard, a truck arrived and two men helped Sean carry lumber in through the gate and pile it up near where he'd put stakes in the ground.

Bridget brought Elsie and Copper back inside so they wouldn't get underfoot, and upon seeing Karl in the hallway, she felt a pull inside her, like a rope. And he was on the other end, tugging it.

She wouldn't lose her heart to him, couldn't, because even though her life had already changed in many ways, it hadn't been in the way it was supposed to change. She wasn't supposed to be here. In New York. She had to go to Chicago, make Da's dream come true. That was her destiny. Furthermore, when the time came—if it came—for her to lose her heart, it would never be to a man like Karl.

However, right now, he needed her help. Not only with Elsie, but in finding his way through all that had happened. In a situation like this, even strong tough men like Karl needed help. When Da died, if it hadn't been for Mrs. Flannagan helping her with all the details, giving her a shoulder to cry on, things would have been harder.

She patted Elsie's shoulder. "Take Copper into the kitchen for a drink of water."

As Elsie carried the puppy through the kitchen door, Bridget walked down the hallway to where Karl stood talking with Willard.

She was about to stop far enough away to not be eavesdropping, when he held out a hand to her, encouraging her to come closer.

"I'll see to it immediately," Willard was saying as she stopped next to Karl. "Is there anything else?"

"I'm sure there will be," Karl said, "but that's all for now."

Willard nodded and glanced at her with such sad eyes her heart constricted as he walked away.

Karl took ahold of her elbow. "The funeral will be tomorrow. At the church. I need to drive over to the undertakers now."

She laid her hand atop his. "Would you like me to come with you?"

His smile was soft, sad, as he shook his head. "No, that's not necessary."

"I'm not saying it's necessary. I'm asking if you'd like me to go with you."

He rubbed the underside of her chin with one knuckle. "I don't want to expose you to that. So no, stay here."

She considered insisting, but had to respect this was something he felt he had to do by himself. "All right. Is there anything else I can do?"

He placed a soft kiss on her temple. "Just be here when I get home."

"I promise."

As she watched him walk away, she wondered how different things would be if he wasn't who he was. A rich man. A very handsome man. But instead, a man she could give her heart to, because she was afraid that she was falling in love with him. In fact, it was becoming impossible not to.

Chapter Eleven

The funeral drew a church full of people, and a large number of them stopped by the house after the service, mingling from room to room, nibbling on the trays of food set out and softly conversing about Benjamin, Annette and the tragedy that had brought about their demise.

Bridget had attempted to distance herself from Karl, because she was an employee, but he'd kept her at his side, introducing her by name and not as Elsie's nanny. The way that had made some people lift a brow worried her.

He was holding Elsie, and upon seeing her yawn, Bridget touched his arm. "I'll take her up to her room," she said quietly. "It's well past her nap time."

They were in the foyer and he stepped closer to the staircase. "I'll carry her upstairs for you."

Just then, as if the puppy had known Elsie was going up to her room without him, Copper came rushing down the hallway.

Laughter abounded at how his long ears flapped and his little paws stumbled, going in all directions at times while he ran around and even through the legs of people in his rush to get to the steps.

Bridget bent down and scooped up the puppy as he slid to a stop at the bottom of the staircase.

"My word," an elderly woman standing nearby said. "That was the cutest thing I've ever seen. When did you get a puppy, Karl?"

"Last weekend," he replied. "Copper and Elsie have become best friends."

The woman patted Copper's head. "That's wonderful. It's just what she needs right now."

Catherine slid up behind Bridget. "I'm so sorry. He slipped out while I was carrying dishes into the kitchen," she whispered. "I'll take him."

The laughter seemed to stop abruptly, and the silence that followed made Bridget's spine quiver. All eyes had gone toward the open front door, and the woman standing there.

The woman was tall, slender and dressed in black, including a short veil attached to a small hat that covered the upper half of her face.

"Catherine," Karl said, "would you take Elsie up to her room for a nap?"

"Of course." Catherine held out her arms.

Karl handed over Elsie, and Bridget looked at him as he took the puppy from her and put him on the steps to follow Catherine. Duty said she should follow Catherine, but everything inside her wanted to stay right here. Karl's face had turned to stone. The woman had to be his mother.

The entire house remained quiet as she stepped into the foyer and Willard closed the door behind her.

"Hello, Karl," she said.

* * *

"Mother," Karl replied. Stylishly dressed in black, as if she had anything to mourn, she'd taken the opportunity to make an entrance. A bitter chuckle stuck in his throat. The long-lost Harriette Wingard, now Apperson, returns home for another death.

In so many ways she was a stranger to him; in others, he knew everything about her. "There are refreshments in the dining room," he told her, when he really wanted to tell her to leave.

Twisting, he nodded toward the man approaching him, knowing others would be taking their leave now. "Adam, thank you for coming," he said.

"It was a lovely service," Adam Croswell said. "I also want to thank you for the invitation for tomorrow night. Clara and I are looking forward to it."

"Yes, we are," Clara said.

Moments ago, Clara had been smiling, fawning over Copper. Now her lips were pursed as she darted a gaze toward his mother.

Karl wasn't sure when he'd grasped ahold of Bridget's elbow, but he had and glanced down at her before he told the Croswells, "We are looking forward to it, too. Thank you both for agreeing to attend, and for your donation."

Others soon formed a line to bid their farewells. Karl was thankful that so many had attended the service and joined them at the house afterward, but the arrival of his mother soiled his gratefulness. For twenty-eight years she'd been soiling his life.

She was sitting in the front room, in the armchair near the fireplace, sipping on a glass of bourbon when the last of the guests left. Karl considered completely ignoring her, but she wouldn't go away.

Still standing near the staircase and holding Bridget's elbow after the last guest had left, he pushed burning air out of his lungs. His mother's timing was impeccable. Not just because of the funeral. Since yesterday, when he'd kissed Bridget, fully kissed her, they hadn't had a moment alone. He couldn't seem to get his emotions under control. One minute he was mournful over losing Benjamin, the next, he was lost in thought about how deeply that kiss had affected him. How it had filled him with something that was so light, so airy, he couldn't define it.

Right now, the last thing he wanted was for her to be subjected to his mother. "If she's still awake, keep Elsie upstairs," he said to Bridget.

"I will."

"I'll be up as soon as my mother leaves." He released Bridget and waited until she'd walked up the steps before he walked into the living room. The simple clink of the glass as his mother set it on the table struck a nerve. Everything she did struck a nerve.

"Need I ask why you are here?" He sat and leaned back against the sofa. There was only one thing she'd ever wanted.

"I brought Benjamin into this world," she said.

That was all she'd ever done for him.

"I never thought I'd live to see him leave it." She dabbed at one eye. "Never wanted to. No parent does."

He couldn't stay quiet. "Please, don't waste your acting abilities on me. Not now. Not ever. There is no reason for you to be here. Benjamin's holdings will all be put into a trust for Elsie."

"I'm not here for money."

"Good, because you won't get any."

She shook her head. "Your father taught you well, didn't he? To hate me."

"No one needed to teach me that." He rested one foot on his opposite knee. "You managed to do that all on your own."

Reaching up, she pulled the pin out of her hat and removed it from her head. She set the hat on her lap. "Do you honestly think I left this home because I wanted to?"

This home. Not him and Benjamin.

"I was sent away," she said with contempt. "Forced to leave."

He'd heard it all before, more than once, and wasn't any more moved this time.

She picked up her drink, took a sip, set it back down. "Your father loved money."

Karl almost cracked a smile. Not because of her. Because of Bridget. What his mother just said was the kettle calling the pot black.

"I thought I could make him love me, too. I'd been born in a house with a dirt floor. A dirt floor. As a child, I swore I would have it better than my mother ever did."

He'd never heard that, but still wasn't moved.

"You come from a line of hateful men. Your uncles had all left by the time I met Gerald. Your father lived here, alone, with your grandfather, Karl, whom you were named after. Your grandmother had died years before, when your father had been a little boy. That was part of the reason Gerald didn't think he needed a woman, a wife. Why have one when you can hire help. Someone to do your cooking and cleaning. But he wanted a son, and I promised I could give him one, and I did. You."

She pressed her kerchief to her nose, sniffed and looked away. An act. He had no doubt.

"That was my first mistake. The moment you were born, Gerald wanted nothing to do with me. I'd served my purpose."

He agreed. Giving birth had been the only motherly act she'd ever performed.

"I tried. Tried everything I could think of, but he'd already hired Sarah Conrad as your nanny. I wasn't even allowed to tuck you in at night. Then your grandfather died. Gerald didn't bother coming home after that, and I was fine with that. I made Sarah let me see you. Life was pretty good. Gerald was out opening new banks, I had a child, a home, more than I'd ever had, and then you became ill. Pneumonia. Gerald came home as soon as he heard."

She was watching him, clearly expecting some kind of reaction. Karl didn't have one. He couldn't remember it, but he'd heard about how he'd been very sick as a child, almost died.

"Your father brought in doctors, nurses, a priest, and he never left your side. I was amazed by that. You survived and the next few months were wonderful. Gerald was home, we…" She smiled, a distant smile. "Your brother was conceived."

The hint of joy that had been on her face faded. Regretting how she'd left shortly after Benjamin had been born? He doubted it.

"Two weeks after Benji was born, your father gave me an envelope full of money and the key to a home in Boston. I knew then that he'd used me. He only wanted a second son. In case something happened to one of you, he'd still have one."

He sucked in a breath of air. "Is there a point to all this?"

"I left," she said, her voice calm, composed. "But it wasn't because I didn't love you and Benji. I left because I did love you."

His composure was slipping, disappearing. There had been a time in his life when he'd prayed to hear those words from her. Prayed that she'd loved him and his brother, even just a small amount. "Again, is there a point to all this? Because I'm not seeing one."

"Gerald hated when I'd called him Benji." She shook her head. "'That's no name for a man,' he'd say."

Karl stood. He'd heard those exact same words, and he didn't want his father's memory tarnished. Not by her.

"Yes, there is a point to all this, Karl. My children were stolen from me, and I'm here to ask, beg if I must, to be able to see my granddaughter. Not once a year, on her birthday, but as often as possible."

"No." He withheld from expanding on his reasons. There were too many.

"Sarah Conrad is getting old, and—"

"I said no, *Mother.*"

She opened her mouth, but closed it and stood. "You are going to learn to love one day, Karl. It happens to everyone, and I pray that when that happens, she will love you in return, because I know the hell of loving people who don't love you back."

"So do I, Mother." The words were out before he realized they'd formed.

"There have been times that I resented you, your father, Benjamin, for stealing my joy, the happiness that I so wanted. I even pretended that I didn't care, but I still did, and I still do." She laid an embossed calling card on the table beside her half-empty glass. "Here is my number for when you are ready to learn the entire truth of why I left, and why I followed your father's rules of only seeing you once a year."

He already knew the truth and stood stock-still as she crossed the room.

At the door, she turned and looked at him with a sad, yet tender expression. "I know your father molded you in his own image, but I remain hopeful that you are wise enough to break that mold and become your own man. One who will give his niece a home full of love." She smiled. "I know it's possible. You're determined. You always have been. You learned to walk in a day. Made up your mind one morning and by that evening, you were walking all over the place."

Still smiling, she turned and left the room.

He remained where he stood as he heard her bid Willard goodbye. Heard the front door close and closed his eyes against an image that formed. Of her leaving when he was eight, after one of her visits. He'd run after her, grabbed her around her knees, held on, begging her to stay. That was the day he started hating her. Hating what she'd done to him. It was also the day he swore to never care about her again, and he'd stuck to it.

Bridget paced the foyer, each time taking a step closer to Karl's office before turning around, torn between the need to see him, talk to him, and the understanding that if he wanted to talk—to anyone—

he wouldn't be keeping himself behind his closed office door.

He'd gone in there last night after his mother had left and was in there still this morning. As far as she knew, he hadn't even eaten anything since yesterday before the funeral.

Huffing out a breath, she stopped one step closer to the door. What she'd told him about curses, about knowing which ones to believe in, was so very true. She was cursed. Had been her entire life. The curse was caring too much. Da had told her that over and over. He'd laughed about it, too, because he'd been cursed with it as well. He'd said the way to deal with it was to help those you can, and to use some good old common sense when it came to those you can't.

The trouble was, this time her curse of caring too much had gone one step further.

No, not just a step. It had leaped right into love.

That scared her.

Karl deserved to be loved. Truly loved. She just wasn't the right person. The people who had filled the church yesterday, filled the house afterward, had reminded her of visiting the first-class decks of the *Titanic*. They had been kind, nice, but she'd had nothing in common with them. She'd forgotten how out of place she'd felt on the ship while visiting some of the restaurants and other first-class areas, and how she'd been relieved to take Elsie to their cabin for her nap.

She'd stayed at Karl's side yesterday, but she'd have much rather been in the kitchen, preparing food, or upstairs with Elsie, filling her duties as a nanny because she knew that was where she *fit* in this world.

The world was made up of different people, which is

how it's meant to be. It would be very dull if everyone was exactly the same. The world would also fail to exist. It took all types, all walks of life to maintain a balance of give and take. Like Da had said, if everyone owned a pub, there would be no one visiting theirs, and if everyone owned a grocery, there would be no one growing the crops for the grocer to sell. He'd said the trick was to find what a person had to offer, and offer it to those who needed it. Like a boardinghouse, because she wouldn't be able to own the pub once he was gone. That wouldn't be seemly for a woman on her own.

Da had been right on so many things. A boardinghouse would not only offer a place for people to stay—something they needed—it would also allow her to care for others.

But where did that leave her feelings toward Karl?

She was about to turn away, leave Karl to his thoughts, when the door to his office opened. Her heart took to racing, as it did whenever she laid eyes on him anymore. He was extremely handsome. Dapper.

"I was just coming to look for you," he said.

She let her gaze settle on his face, looked for signs of… She wasn't sure, but hadn't expected him to be smiling. "Why?"

He stepped back, holding the door open and waved a hand for her to enter. "There's something I want to talk to you about."

Curious, she walked forward, into his office, eyeing the smile on his face that never faltered. She'd been worried that his mother's visit had upset him, but he seemed excited.

"Over here," he said, closing the door and walking

toward his desk. "The idea came to me last night. I've been working on it since then."

Glancing from the shimmer in his eyes to the stack of papers on his desk, she asked, "What is it?"

"A trust fund for *Titanic* victims. I've crunched the numbers to include an initial payout and yearly dividends to survivors as well as those who may have lost the family breadwinner, and it's doable. I'll need to raise more capital in order for the investments to be diversified enough to grow long and short term enough to make the yearly obligations, but I have ideas for that, too."

Her heart sank at him still being focused on everyone being compensated.

"I know what you're thinking," he said. "But hear me out. What you said yesterday was true. About me wanting the White Star Line to compensate everyone. That's not going to happen. I know that. And I know none of this will change what happened, but this is a way that I can make sure Benjamin and Annette are not forgotten, and help people in the process."

She glanced at the top of one sheet of paper, where he'd written *The Benjamin Wingard Family Trust Fund*.

"It came to me after my mother left." He shook his head, sadly. "I can remember the exact moment that I decided I was never going to care about her again. I was eight."

Bridget's heart tumbled at the idea of a child determining that. "Why? What happened?"

He shook his head, then shrugged. "She left. Again. I haven't cared about anyone since then. Except for Benjamin. He was four, and with our father working all the time, it was just the two of us. We had Mrs. Conrad and

Willard and Mary, but in my eyes, it was just the two of us. It was that way for years."

She laid a hand on his forearm, feeling his sincerity. His loss. "He thought the world of you. So did Annette. So does Elsie. They spoke of you from the moment I gave them Betsy."

He smiled and glanced at the papers. "They're part of the reason I want to create this trust fund." Taking ahold of her hand, he looked at her. "You are the other part."

"Me?"

"You are the reason that last night, after my mother left, I realized that not caring is no way to live. It's not a life I want for Elsie. I want her to care about people. Like you do. You care about everyone."

He had no idea what a curse that was. Every moment that went by, her heart was just filling up with more and more love for him.

"This trust fund is one way I can teach her to care about others. Not just right now, but going forward. Benjamin's life insurance policy will be the seed money to start this trust fund, along with money that I will put into it, which could provide every survivor with a lump sum now. It won't be enough to make anyone rich, but it could be enough to help. Help them now with what they need. Cover what they lost. And with the capital I know that I can raise, they'll also receive yearly dividends for the rest of their lives."

She could feel his excitement by the way his hold on her hand tightened. "You've really put a lot of thought, a lot of work, into this."

"I couldn't sleep last night. Had to run the numbers. See how much I'd have to raise." He took her other hand. "I know I can do it, but I need your help."

"My help?" Her pulse was racing, mainly from the look on his face. The eagerness, and the optimism. She didn't want to disappoint him, but had to admit, "There's nothing I can do."

"Yes, there is. You helped with the church bazaar, and…" He shook his head. "I don't know. I'm still trying to think it all through, but there are a lot of people that will need to be contacted. Survivors. People like Sean and Catherine."

A wave of relief and excitement washed over her. "I could help with that. So could Catherine and Sean. They knew more people on the ship than I did." Including the two men who had been at church this morning who needed work. And who would be helping Sean build the playhouse. At her suggestion.

Karl grasped her other hand and squeezed both of them. "I'd hoped you'd say that. I also plan on putting on a fundraising event of our own. Maybe we'll get some ideas tonight."

Frowning, she asked, "Tonight?"

"Yes, we are attending the opera. It's a fundraiser for the victims."

Bridget wasn't sure if he'd lost his mind or if she had lost hers. "I can't attend the opera."

"Yes, you can. I've already paid for the tickets, and I bought you a dress. It's—"

"No." She pulled her hands out of his and stepped back. "I'm not the kind of person who goes to the opera."

"What do you mean 'the kind of person'?"

"I'm a nanny. I can't go to the opera with you." Her stomach churned and she stepped back farther. She couldn't put herself in a situation like that. "I can't."

"Why not? You're the one who said you believed no one is above or below anyone else."

"I don't." Flustered, she shook her head. "I mean I do. I mean—I just can't go to the opera with you." She took another step back, and her foot caught on the leg of a chair.

Karl caught her before she tumbled, kept her upright. "Why?"

"Because I'm your employee. I'm Elsie's nanny," she pointed out, growing even more flustered.

"Then you're fired."

His spine stiffened. "You can't fire me."

"Yes, I can. I hired you. I can fire you."

That was true and the idea of being cast aside so easily made her insides go cold. "Who will take care of Elsie?"

"Catherine."

The air locked in her lungs. Not even tiny gasps would catch. How dare he? After all... Her anger snapped. *"Is ceann de's na h-óinseacha diabhail thú!"* His grin made her even madder. She wrenched out of his hold and walked away while repeating the curse in English, "You are one of the Devil's fools!"

"Probably," he said. "But I want you at the opera with me tonight." He grasped her upper arms from behind, rubbed them gently. "I can't do this without you, Bridget."

She gulped for air at how every part of her could feel the heat of his closeness.

His breath tickled her neck as he said, "You are the reason I'm doing it."

She shook her head and sighed. He was one of the Devil's fools. How else could he make the anger seep out of her as quickly as he instilled it in her. No, she was the fool for falling in love with a man she shouldn't have. Not now. Not ever.

He stepped around to face her. "If you hadn't been on that ship, if I hadn't met you, I would have gone on with life as normal. A life of not caring."

She looked away, had to. His gaze was too penetrating. "No, you wouldn't have."

"Yes, I would have," he said. "You make an impression on everyone you meet. You did me." He touched the side of her face. "Maybe it was the luck of the Irish or one of your curses," he said softly. "Either way, please attend the opera with me so others can see what you made me see."

"I didn't make you see anything."

"Yes, you did. Young or old, rich or poor, the *Titanic* carried some of the most wonderful people in the world. The opera tonight is a fundraiser for survivors, and the people who will be joining us in our suite have pledged to support the cause. They can afford to give generously, and I'm certain that upon meeting you, they will support the trust fund I'm setting up, too. I'm not trying to exploit you or asking you to do anything immoral. You just need to be yourself. Let people see you are just like them."

"But I'm not like them, Karl," she insisted. "I'm not like you. I was a third-class passenger for a reason. It was all I could afford."

"And that doesn't make you any better or worse than anyone else. You made me realize that, and you can make them realize that, too. To know the people these fundraisers are helping are real people. Not just someone they've heard about. Real people who need help because they lost everything through no fault of their own."

It must be her who had lost her mind, because she understood and agreed with what he was saying, but the opera? She'd never been to an opera.

"I know this idea is a risk, but risks are what make life worth living."

He had no idea it was her heart she was risking in all this, but it was to help others. People she knew who needed help. Lifting her chin, she nodded. "I'll go to the opera with you on one condition."

"Name it."

Chapter Twelve

Bridget was even more convinced she'd lost her mind as she watched Catherine in the mirror while the other woman secured the beaded headdress in place. It had two rows of ivory pearls that looped around her head, across her forehead, and were secured to her crown with a thick comb that had two ivory-colored feathers on them. Dipping her chin, to see the feathers in the mirror, Bridget pinched her lips together.

"You look beautiful," Catherine said, looking in the mirror over Bridget's head.

Bridget ran her hands over the dark blue dress. A sheer, soft material, with darker blue embroidered flowers throughout the several layers of the skirt. The under layer of the dress was ivory, with scalloped lace edges on the square neckline, elbow-length sleeves and the hems. The layers of ivory and blue were stunning. Truly the most gorgeous dress she'd ever seen. The shoes were blue, too, with square heels and made of soft leather that fit perfectly.

"I don't think I've ever been so nervous," Bridget said.

"Why?"

"I've never worn anything so delicate, so lovely." Her breath shook as she let it out. "Never dressed up to go anywhere, other than church, my entire life."

"No one will know that, not with the way you look," Catherine said, fussing with the feathers.

"I will," Bridget said. Her stomach hiccupped. "What if I trip or—"

"Trip?" Catherine said. "What are you talking about? I thought the shoes fit perfectly."

"They do. It's me who doesn't fit." She turned away from the mirror and rose from the chair. "I don't fit in any of this. These clothes. This house. I should be in Chicago. Working for my Da's cousin until I can make enough money to open my own boardinghouse. That's where I belong. That's where I'd fit. The pub I lived in my entire life wasn't much bigger than this bedroom. There was no fancy paper on the walls or frilly curtains on the windows."

"And that's why your father wanted you to come to America," Catherine said. "Just like my family. So we wouldn't have to keep living like that. Wondering if there would be enough food to feed everyone through the winter. Or if the spring would be so wet the crops would rot in the fields like they had the spring before. I never knew your Da, but I'm sure he'd be proud to see you now. Mine would be. I wrote them a letter. Told them about the fancy house Sean and I are living in, and I told them it's all because of you."

The air seeped out of Bridget as she looked at Catherine, with her curly red hair and bright green eyes. The other woman had thanked her over and over again for letting them come here, work for Karl.

Catherine glanced around the room. "This is more

than Sean and I dreamed, more than our folks dreamed. The clothes and shoes that were bought for us…" She shook her head. "We figured we'd work in a factory or something, never a home this beautiful, for people this nice. And Elsie. Goodness, you'd told me about her on the ship, but she is a true darling. Just a little darling."

Bridget's heart softened. "Yes, she is."

Grasping ahold of her shoulders, Catherine said, "Tonight is no different than those fancy restaurants you visited on the ship. They were full of fancy people and you did just fine."

"Because I didn't have to pretend to be anyone," Bridget said. "They all knew I was just a nanny."

"You aren't pretending now, either." Catherine spun around and picked up the dark blue embroidered cape that matched the dress off the bed. "You are a beautiful woman, inside and out. Who is helping so many others. Just think about that, Bridget. How many people you are helping, by just going to the opera. People like me and Sean, who wouldn't have anything if not for you."

Bridget swallowed hard as the cape was draped over her shoulders. For a moment she was convinced she could do this. Go to the opera. With Karl.

The moment left. "I'm afraid of him, Catherine."

"Him? Karl?"

Bridget nodded. "He's so handsome. So nice and kind and generous." Rattled, she added, "He barely has an ornery bone in his body."

Catherine walked around her, faced her. Frowned. "So what are you afraid of?"

"I'm afraid he'll steal my heart," Bridget whispered, not wanting to admit it, but needing to be honest.

Catherine smiled and leaned closer as she whispered, "And that you'll steal his."

Karl had never attended an opera. Had never wanted to, but now he wanted to do all kinds of things he'd never done before. Things that included having a woman on his arm. At his side.

Her.

A stubborn, strong-minded, caring and beautiful woman.

She'd been turning his head since the first moment he'd seen her holding Elsie in his front room, but tonight she was turning more than his head. Men and women, many of whom he knew, some he didn't, nearly stopped in their tracks as he escorted her into the Metropolitan Opera House. He paused to say hello to a few and introduced Bridget as they made their way to the balcony suite. She'd barely spoken a word since they'd left the house. He'd agreed to her stipulation and had hired two more men from the *Titanic* who needed jobs and a place to live. John and James. Brothers, who were now staying in the servant's quarters in his basement. Young men who Sean had vouched for, assuring he knew them from Ireland and that they were trustworthy.

Karl believed him, because he knew anyone who stepped out of line would find themselves face-to-face with Sean, and Sean would triumph.

He grinned. Bridget was well on her way to running a boardinghouse. He didn't mind. It felt good to know there was someone younger and stronger than Willard in the house while he was gone.

The other couples he'd invited to join them in the suite had all been at the funeral and the house yesterday, so introductions were more polite reminders for Bridget. Clara Croswell instantly invited Bridget to sit next to her while Adam suggested the men retreat to the back of the balcony to enjoy a beverage whilst waiting for the opera to begin.

"Where did you find her?" Art Kennedy asked, leaning against the back wall.

Karl let his gaze land on Bridget. She was nodding, leaning closer to the rail as Clara pointed over it. "She found me."

Art laughed. "Lucky you."

"Luck of the Irish," Karl said, although he wasn't Irish.

"I was under the impression she was your niece's nanny," Adam Croswell said.

Karl took a sip of his drink. "Elsie's nanny became ill and remained in England. Annette and Bridget became friends on the ship and she'd offered to watch Elsie so Benjamin and Annette could attend the captain's party the night the ship sank." He took another sip off his drink, let the rich alcohol slowly glide down his throat before continuing, "She promised my niece to not let go of her until she put her in my arms. And she didn't. Even as she took an oar, rowing the lifeboat all night in a sea full of icebergs and dead bodies, she held on to Elsie."

"You don't say," Adam whispered reverently.

"Dear Lord," Art said, just as respectfully. "What an ordeal for a woman to go through."

"You just gave me goose bumps, Karl," Jack McPherson said. "That's heroic."

"Hear, hear," Elwin Scott said humbly.

Karl nodded, slowly. "It was heroic," he said. "And

that is why we are here tonight. Every person on that ship went through hell that night. Those who lived are going to remember it for the rest of their lives."

"I've read the papers, heard stories," Adam said, "but until this moment, I never imagined…" He shook his head. "Such a tragedy."

"It was." Karl set his empty glass on the small table. "I have what I'd like to refer to as an investment in humanity that I would like to discuss with you gentlemen."

"You have our captive attention," Nathan Owens said.

"I've attended the hearings. There will be no admission of guilt, of blame. The majority of those who survived will not see a dime from the White Star Line. I'm setting up a trust fund, in my brother's name, to not only provide initial payments immediately, but yearly dividends to those affected by this tragedy."

"That is an excellent idea, Karl. Heroic in its own right. How can I help with that?" Adam asked.

Karl had crunched the numbers, and if all played out, the trust fund could provide each survivor the same amount of money as the check the White Star Line had given him on Elsie's behalf. Which had been higher than the one for Bridget—another thing that had duly irritated him.

"I would appreciate any involvement you might like to have," Karl said. "Financially and otherwise, but I had not yet thought of the trust fund when I invited you to join me this evening and I do not want it to take away from what you pledged here, for tonight's event."

"Of course not," Jack said. "I'll write you a check tonight, and another one every year going forward."

The others agreed, pledging initial and yearly payments both privately and from their businesses as well as friends and family.

"We've been looking for something solid to do, to help with all of this," Nathan said. "You just gave us a genuine way. With you overseeing it, it's sure to be a success, Karl. Your father would be proud."

His insides quivered slightly. Other than to his mother, his father hadn't freely parted with money. He hadn't realized that, but did now. He let the thought go, because the person he was truly proud of was Bridget. Her courage and stamina deserved recognition, and he was happy to provide that.

"Father, hell," Adam said. "I'm proud. Proud to know you. This is a hell of a thing you are doing."

"Hear, hear," Elwin said, livelier this time.

The overhead lights began to go out one by one, and Karl said, "Thank you, all, but what I'm doing is nothing compared to what Bridget did."

"We agree," Art said. "You are a very lucky man."

That he couldn't fully agree with right now, because she'd be leaving soon, going to Chicago. "I believe it's time to take our seats."

The women rearranged seats so their husbands could sit next to them, and as Karl sat down next to Bridget, his heart thudded at the smile she offered him. At this moment, he was a lucky man. He was sitting next to the most beautiful woman in the state. In the world, and truth was, he wasn't looking forward to her leaving. No matter when that might be.

Leaning toward her, he asked, "Enjoying yourself?"

"Yes. Are you?"

The sparkle in her eyes confirmed what he already

knew. "Yes, very much." He was enjoying the evening, because of her, and saw no harm in that.

The opera was interesting, but it was Bridget that he appreciated, watching as she pressed a hand to her lips at high points in the performances, sighed at poignant ones and clapped enthusiastically as each ended.

"That was the most amazing thing I've ever seen," she told him as they climbed into his Packard afterward.

He started the engine. "I'm glad you enjoyed it."

She laughed so brightly he glanced at her, frowning. "What?" he asked.

"My Da would have said those performers had good lungs," she said.

He nodded, fully agreeing with that. His back teeth were still clenched at how some of the high notes had reverberated in his spine so hard he'd had to force himself not to shake off a shiver.

She leaned a bit closer, eyes shimmering in the streetlight shining into the car. "He would have also said you were twice cursed by Adam's slipup."

Confused, he asked, "Adam? What did he do?"

Laughing harder, she said, "Not Mr. Croswell. Adam, as in Adam and Eve. When he ate the apple?" Still laughing, she slapped his shoulder. "I thought you were going to leap right out of your chair you were shivering so hard." She was laughing so hard she could barely talk. "I felt so bad for you."

Her lighthearted giggles made him laugh. "You sound like you felt really bad."

She covered her mouth with one hand as if trying to stop laughing, but couldn't. "I did. I really did." Once again, she touched his shoulder. "If you'd have walked out, I would have gone with you."

He'd honestly thought he'd hidden his reactions to some parts of the performances, but could have sworn she was captivated. "You didn't care for it?"

She gasped for air as her giggles eased. "No. I mean yes, I enjoyed it, but you looked so miserable that I would have left with you, just to ease your pain."

He knew she was being completely honest, because that was who she was, a genuine person, through and through. "I enjoyed that you enjoyed it," he said, being just as honest. Shifting the car into gear, he added, "I hope you'll enjoy dinner just as much."

Smiling, she leaned back against the seat. "I hope you'll enjoy it much more."

He did enjoy the meal, but again, enjoyed her company more. When he looked at her, watched her eating, he couldn't help but think about all that had happened since meeting her. How his life had taken a route he'd never traversed before, as if she'd been a new beginning for him. He also wondered if his life would turn around again, go back to how it had been once she left. Went to Chicago.

The idea of that, of her leaving, of his life turning back around, became even more unsettling.

He picked up his coffee cup and took a sip. "Why do you want to own a boarding house?"

She twirled a finger around the rim of her cup. "When my mother passed away, I was a few years older than Elsie is, and my Da's cousin Martha was leaving for America. She wanted to take me with her because there were no other female relatives to help Da care for me. I didn't want to go, so he told her no, maybe in a couple of years. Martha returned three years later, and was concerned about me living at the pub, but I still didn't want to go. Da said that I had to go, and I insisted that he needed me to stay with him, help him. He finally agreed with me, but said that Martha had become an accomplished woman here in America, by owning a boardinghouse and made me promise that I would do that, too. I said I would, as soon as he no longer needed me. Every couple of years, when Martha returned home, Da had still needed me. Then he passed away, so I left, came to America. Like I'd promised."

"So it was your father's dream for you, owning a boardinghouse," he said.

She shrugged. "It was our dream together. It's what he wanted and I agreed."

"Did you ever consider not coming? Of doing something else?"

A half smile formed on her lips as she sat quietly for a moment. When she lifted her eyes, met his gaze, she asked, "Truthfully?"

"Yes, truthfully."

"If my uncle hadn't stolen my money, and if I hadn't had to get it back, I wouldn't have left when I did. I would have stayed, ran the pub for a while."

"Your uncle stole your money?" He needed clarification before becoming too angry.

"Yes, the money my Da had saved for me to come to America. It was over five hundred dollars. I heard Uncle Matt talking about buying a ticket on the *Titanic*, and knew he'd taken it." She shrugged. "Sure enough, it was gone. I felt bad confronting him in front of customers, but I had to get it back."

He was irritated that she'd been treated so, but had to grin. She had more grit than men he knew. "And you did get it back."

"Yes, I did. And I left the next day." She let out a sigh. "I haven't thought much about it, because so much has happened since I left, but at times, while on the ship, I regretted leaving. Uncle Matt doesn't know anything about running a pub. Da left half of the pub to Matt and the other half to me, so that I'd have something in case I wanted to return to Ireland. I'd promised Da I would go, so I did, and I bequeathed my half of the pub to Uncle Matt."

"Why did you bequeath your half to him?"

She pinched her lips together and glanced down at her cup before saying, "Because I probably wouldn't have left if I hadn't."

"You didn't want to come?"

"Yes, I did, but I knew everything would change, and I wasn't ready for that."

His thoughts went quiet. Strangely quiet. He'd known what she'd gone through on the ship, but she'd been through so much more than just that. "Everything has changed for you."

"Yes, it has." She was staring at her coffee cup again. "Going to Chicago, opening a boardinghouse is all I have left of my Da. Of all we had together."

Karl remembered that feeling. The first day he'd walked into his father's office after his death, he'd had that same thought. Dispelling others from coming forward, he said, "You must still be angry at your uncle."

"No. He's family. I forgave him."

Not wanting to think about forgiving family members, he pulled out his billfold and laid several bills on the table. "Time to go home."

Chapter Thirteen

Bridget sat on the swing, watching Elsie play with Copper in the backyard, keeping a close eye that neither of them got too close to where Sean and the other two men were building the playhouse.

She wondered if someday she'd be able to think about things other than Karl. That's where all of her thoughts were centered. Including the opera last night.

A grin tugged at her lips. He truly had been miserable, but had sat through it because of her. That scared her. She could learn to live with the fact that she'd fallen in love with him, but the idea that she may have stolen his heart was frightening.

Pushing out a sigh, she picked the envelope off the swing seat beside her. The letter from cousin Martha. It had arrived today and included a train ticket as well as traveling money for her to go to Chicago as soon as possible.

Martha's letter held condolences over Da's death, and the tragic accident, but also excitement about having family living with her, helping her with the boardinghouse, and said that she'd expect Bridget by the end of the week.

A tiny groan rumbled in her throat. She couldn't be in Chicago by the end of the week. Mrs. Conrad wasn't here, yet, and though Catherine helped with Elsie, she also helped with other things around the house, which didn't allow her to dedicate time to being Elsie's nanny.

That was still her job.

Karl had left for Washington, D.C., again this morning, too. She couldn't leave without saying goodbye. That would be rude after all he'd done. Furthermore, she'd agreed to help him with the trust fund he was setting up.

Yet, she had promised Da, and Martha, before she'd promised Karl.

Still, she'd learned long ago that what she thought, what she felt, wasn't as important as what others thought and felt and needed.

That's why she couldn't let Karl fall in love with her, because then he'd want her to stay here forever, and she couldn't do that.

"Excuse me, Bridget," Willard said, stepping out of the back door. "Mrs. Apperson is here and has requested to speak with you."

Her heart leaped into her throat. "Karl's mother? Why would she want to speak with me?"

"It's about Elsie."

Oh, dear. Karl harbored a lot of pain because of his mother. She'd seen that yesterday when he told her about the trust fund. She was curious as to why, and what could be done about it. "Could you please ask Catherine to come watch Elsie?"

"Yes, right away."

When Catherine arrived, Bridget instructed her to keep Elsie outside, and then entered the house. At the doorway to the front living room, she pressed a hand to the butterflies in her stomach and squared her shoulders before walking through.

Karl's mother was standing near the fireplace, fashionably dressed from head to toe in olive green, even the hat decorated with a single silk flower. There was no veil today, and Bridget could see where Karl and Elsie received their dark brown eyes.

"Miss McGowen, I believe it is," the woman said.

"Yes, Mrs. Apperson."

"Harriette, please." She waved a hand. "Can we sit?"

Bridget gave a slight nod of acknowledgment. "Willard said you wanted to speak with me."

"I do." Harriette gracefully lowered herself onto the upholstered armchair. "You are in charge of Elsie?"

There was no hostility in her voice, or on her face. Her dark eyes held more of a pained, saddened glaze. Bridget sat on the sofa. "Yes, I am, but I'm only her nanny."

"Lucky child," Harriette answered dryly, with a hint of a grin. "When will Sarah Conrad return?"

"You'd have to speak to Karl about that."

Harriette nodded. "I assume he told you that I asked to see Elsie, and that he said no."

Bridget held her breath for a moment. He hadn't, yet, so she made no comment or sign of agreement.

"I owe you an apology, Miss McGowen, for a friend of mine you met on the *Carpathia*. Wilma Fredrickson has been a friend for years, and she knows I've never seen my granddaughter. Except from a distance. She truly didn't mean any harm."

Once again, Bridget chose to remain silent.

"I had hoped that after Gerald passed away, both Karl and Benjamin would be interested in learning my side of the story. A part of me had even hoped that Gerald had taken a portion of the blame, especially once Elsie had been born. But he hadn't, and the boys still believed everything was my fault. Gerald did, too. Karl's grandfather had told Gerald that he'd married beneath himself. I'd run away from home when I was sixteen, determined to have a better life. I met Gerald a year later and fell in love. Just like that. He was so handsome, and yes, rich."

Bridget questioned if Karl's mother was searching for empathy, or truly wanted her story told. She sounded genuine. Not cold or bitter, but rather casual.

Harriette removed her olive-colored gloves one finger at a time as she spoke, "I'm sure Gerald loved me in the beginning, until his father threw acid on that love, convinced him that I wasn't worth the ground he walked on, all because I'd been a sharecropper's daughter. A peasant. I don't know why that old man was so bitter, so hateful, but he was. All of his other sons left home, moved far away, except for Gerald. The old man had ahold of him, just like Gerald did Karl and Benjamin. I did everything I could to become a *lady*. Learned to walk, talk, act, like I was above everyone else. It didn't help, and I can tell you that I felt no remorse when Gerald's father died. That, too, drove a wedge deeper between Gerald and I, and for that I will take the blame. Karl was just a baby." She pressed a hand to her temple. "I'd never known such love, such undying affection for someone until I held him in my arms."

Goose bumps prickled Bridget's arms and she

clasped her hands together to keep from rubbing her forearms. Oddly, though, she didn't want Harriette to stop talking. She wanted to know more.

"I remember leaving here once." Harriette paused to swallow, press a hand to her throat. "It still breaks my heart. It was Karl's eighth birthday—the only days I could see my sons were their birthdays. Karl ran after me as I was leaving, wrapped his little arms around my knees, begged me to stay. Gerald grabbed him, spanked him, told him to behave or he'd never see me again."

Bridget covered a gasp with one hand and had to blink at the tears forming in her eyes for Karl. His eighth birthday. That was the day, the reason he stopped caring about his mother.

"It's the truth," Harriette said. "The God's honest truth. Willard saw it, so did Sarah Conrad, but they knew where their loyalties had to lie. They could have been ordered out of this house as easily as I had been. Four years before that, shortly after Benjamin had been born, Gerald had handed me money and keys to a house in Boston, and told me to leave. I refused. I couldn't leave my children, but ultimately, I had no choice. Gerald threatened to have me committed, put in the asylum." She sniffed and wiped the corner of one eye. "I knew I'd never see my children again if that happened, so I left, but not before I insisted that giving birth to them had to be worth something. Gerald agreed it was, and that I could visit them once a year, on their birthdays."

Instinct, and her life of hearing one man after another exaggerate, sharing unbelievable tales, told Bridget that Harriette wasn't lying. Her heart ached for Karl, for all the pain he'd experienced, and for his mother. "Why…" Her throat burned, as if it was coated with shards of glass.

"Why am I telling you all this?" Harriette wiped at the tears on her cheeks with an embroidered handkerchief. "Because I'm desperate," she whispered as the tears continued to fall. "I've lost one son forever and I'm willing to do whatever it takes to have my other son and my granddaughter in my life, even if it only means once a year again."

Bridget could feel the other woman's pain yet shook her head. "There is nothing I can do. I can't go against Karl's wishes."

"I understand that, but I'm hoping you might be able to plant a suggestion that Elsie should be allowed to see her grandmother."

The pleading in Harriet's eyes nearly gutted Bridget. "Karl's not in town. He's gone to Washington, to the inquiry."

"I know." Harriette shook her head. "My sons never knew how closely I followed their activities throughout the years, and I've learned to be patient, to take whatever I can get when it comes to them, their lives. It doesn't have to be today, or tomorrow. I know it will take time for Karl to agree, if ever. His father filled him with as much hate toward me as Gerald's own father had instilled in him."

There was truth in that. Bridget had seen the scorn on Karl's face both when his mother had arrived after the funeral, and the day at the hospital, when he'd said his mother was alive. Despite how she might feel at this moment, she shook her head. "It's not my place to plant any types of suggestions."

"You are Elsie's nanny. Your job is to see she has everything she needs. Don't you believe that should include her grandmother? The only other family she has."

In every other circumstance, Bridget would agree, but she felt a strong loyalty to Karl. To his happiness. She didn't want to jeopardize that. She didn't want to jeopardize Elsie's, either.

"I married again, over ten years ago, to Sylas Apperson. A very loving and kind man," Harriette said. "One who taught me how to love, how to forgive, and how to not forget myself in the process. For years I'd been empty inside. Thought of nothing but the calendar, the dates I would see my sons. When those days rolled around, and they'd look at me with scorn and hatred, I'd forgive them, and their father, and would look forward to the following year, hoping it would be different. I'd completely forgotten who I was, what I'd wanted out of life. Sylas pulled me out of that trap. Out of that dark, hopeless cavern, and I hope that someday someone can do the same for Karl. It's an ugly place to live."

Bridget couldn't help but compare what Harriette had said to what Karl had said yesterday about not wanting Elsie to live in an uncaring world.

The other woman stood. "I will leave now." She opened her purse and withdrew an envelope. "Would you please give this to Karl? It's for the trust fund I hear he's setting up."

Bridget stood and took the envelope. "Yes, I will see he receives it."

"Thank you." A faint smile appeared as Harriette gave a slight nod. "I don't mean to put you in an awkward position, Miss McGowen, but I must be honest. I will return."

Bridget had to be honest, as well. "I would do the same, if I were in your shoes."

Harriette nodded again. "I don't wish my shoes on anyone, therefore, let me say, don't let anyone force you down a path you don't want to take. Your happiness is as important as theirs."

The clatter of train wheels, the vibration of the seat beneath him as the train pulled out of the station had never excited Karl before. It did today.

It was only Tuesday afternoon, but he'd left the inquiry when it broke for lunch. A day and a half had been too long to be away from home. To be away from Bridget. She'd been on his mind the entire time. Every hour. Every minute. Since he'd left yesterday morning.

The inquiry was no longer a driving force inside him. Bridget was. The dream of opening a boarding-house wasn't hers. It had been her father's, not hers. Karl had no idea what it might take to convince her of that, but seriously wanted to. His home, his life, would be empty when she left.

If he'd needed proof of that, he'd gotten it the last day and a half.

Furthermore, Mrs. Conrad was getting old, as his mother had pointed out. His mother. Willard had said she'd stopped by the house, but that Bridget had kept her from seeing Elsie. That was what Elsie needed, what he needed, someone young, sturdy, stubborn enough to stand up to even his mother. That was Bridget.

He had to convince her to stay. Stay until Elsie no longer needed her.

He needed her, too. Word of the trust fund was spreading fast. The paperwork should be filed by now, as well as the accounts he'd asked Julia to set up ready to receive and distribute funds. There were people who weren't happy about it. More than one senator had questioned him about the precedent he was setting.

He'd told them that he hoped the precedent he was setting spread far and wide.

He did hope that. Of all the investment deals he'd worked on, all the banks he'd opened and expanded, this was the one that excited him beyond all others. He wouldn't have believed that. That something could ever be more important than Wingard's.

Karl rested the back of his head against the hard seat, wondering exactly what that meant. What it meant for him to have changed so much, without meaning to, or even realizing that it was happening.

He didn't find any answers on the long ride, but his excitement about returning home grew with each mile that rolled beneath the clanging iron wheels. When the train pulled into the station in New York, he nearly ran to his car.

The evening sun cast a golden glow on the house as he pulled into the driveway. He stopped, stared at it, convinced it had never looked so welcoming. Laughter filtered on the air, as did a few barks. Leaving the Packard in the driveway, he got out and walked to the backyard, peeked over the fence.

Exactly as it had looked on paper—except that it was painted blue and white—a playhouse stood in the backyard, complete with scalloped eaves and a gabled roof, with a matching doghouse beside it. People were admiring both little houses. He grinned, realizing the group of people all lived here. Sean, John, James, Catherine, Mary, Willard, Elsie and Copper.

He frowned, looked from person to person again, searching for Bridget.

His heart shot into his throat and he opened the gate. Halfway across the yard, his feet stalled when the door of the playhouse opened and Bridget, ducking to keep from bumping her head, stepped out of the miniature house. Something that ran far deeper than relief filled him.

"It's ready, Poppet," she said, stooping lower to look Elsie in the eyes.

"Yippie!" Elsie shot around her and into the house, squealing louder.

Copper ran into the playhouse barking.

The others all laughed, and were so interested in whatever was inside, they still hadn't noticed him. He walked up behind the crowd, all peeking in the door and the windows.

Bridget was near the rear of the group now, wearing a pale purple dress, her long hair tied back with a matching ribbon.

Quietly, he walked up behind her and whispered over her shoulder, "What are we looking at?"

She jumped and twisted, looked at him. Her smile lit up her face. "You're home!"

He had grasped ahold of her elbow when she'd jumped, and he rubbed a thumb over her soft skin. "I didn't mean to scare you." It took him a moment to pull his gaze off her because the desire to kiss her was nearly impossible to get past. Finally, he managed to glance at the playhouse. "What are we looking at?" he repeated.

"The playhouse was just finished today," she said. "I

put the table and chairs from her bedroom inside and set up a tea party for her and her dolls, as a final surprise."

The others had finally noticed him, including Elsie.

"Uncle Karl! Come see! Come see!" she said, waving at him from inside the playhouse.

He stepped forward and stuck his head in through the door. "This is a very nice house you have here," he said.

"I know!"

There was wallpaper on the walls, curtains on the windows, and a rug on the floor beneath a table set with miniature cups and saucers, and chairs where Betsy and two other dolls sat.

"Here!" Elsie picked up a cup and held it out to him.

He took the cup and pretended to drink something out of it. "Delicious tea. Thank you." Handing her back the cup, he said, "I believe Betsy wants some."

"Oh, yes!" Elsie picked up the tiny pot and pretended to pour into the cups on the table.

Laughing, he backed out of the doorway. "Good job," he said to Sean and the others. Then, looking at Bridget, he asked, "Does Copper's house have wallpaper and curtains, too?"

Her laughter floated on the air. "No, but he does have a rug."

"We didn't expect you home tonight, Master Karl," Willard said. "Mary will have something ready for you to eat shortly."

Everyone departed quietly, leaving just him and Bridget outside the playhouse while Elsie and her dolls had a tea party inside.

"I believe she likes it," he said.

"She loves it. And figured out what it was before it

was done." A serious expression formed. "How was the inquiry? Has it ended?"

"No, it'll be going for days, yet. And I'm convinced the outcome is pretty well set."

"Set?"

"Yes, there will be recommendations for lifeboats, radio coverage, design changes, but other than that, it will just become an accident, history."

"Those things could prevent it from happening again, and that is what you wanted to happen," she said.

"They could."

"You don't sound happy about that."

He looked at her, at how she had her head tilted to one side as if to really listen, her brows drawn downward, thoughtfully. How beautiful she was. Truly beautiful. "I'm happy with the outcome of other things."

"Your trust fund," she said.

He nodded but stepped closer, took ahold of her hand, threaded his fingers through hers. "And other things. I'm happy with the playhouse. I'm happy with Copper. With how well Elsie has come through the ordeal, and it's all because of you. Accident or not, none of that would have happened if you hadn't been here."

"I didn't do any of those things. You did."

He could feel the pulse in her wrist. Quick, but solid, steady. Like her. "Yes, you did, and I want those things to continue." Feeling a bit unsteady, he planted his feet firmer in the ground. "I want you to continue to be Elsie's nanny. Even when Mrs. Conrad returns. It's time for her to receive a pension. She will continue to live here upon her return, help when needed, but be able to relax."

She pinched her lips together and looked away. Her hand began to tremble.

"Bridget?"

"I can't stay here, Karl," she whispered. "I can't."

Chapter Fourteen

The amount of the check surprised Karl and pushed his anger to another level. Was his mother now trying to buy herself into his life? The exact same way she'd sold her way out of it. That shouldn't surprise him. No more than Bridget saying she couldn't stay. She'd told him that from the beginning. How she was going to Chicago to open a boardinghouse.

He sat back in his chair, ran a hand through his hair. Soon. That's what she'd said. She'd be leaving soon. He had to let her go, but damn it, he didn't want to.

His jaw set as someone knocked on the door. It opened before he had a chance to unlock his back teeth to say he was busy.

"I need to talk to you," Bridget said, entering the room.

He remained in his chair, watched her walk to the davenport. Talking to her right now was not on his agenda. He'd told himself he couldn't be mad at her, and he really wasn't, but he was disappointed. More than he wanted to admit.

"Willard said he told you about your mother's visit," she said.

Karl turned his chair to face her. "Yes, he told me about it."

"Did he mention that she left a check for your trust fund?"

He reached over, picked up the check, waved it and dropped it back down. "I'll be sending it back to her."

"Why?"

"Because I don't want her to have anything to do with Elsie."

"She is Elsie's grandmother. You and your mother are the only two people she has now."

She could have you. He bit the tip of his tongue to keep that thought to himself. "I will have to be enough."

"People can change, Karl," she said softly. "You said you've changed."

"She'll never change."

"How do you know?"

"Because I know her."

She stood and walked closer, until she stood near the corner of his desk. "You know, Karl, there are two sides to every story, and both sides are the truth. The truth as they each saw it. Like the accident. How people saw things differently than others. Like the boat I thought I saw."

"You did see it," he said. "It came up at the inquiry. It was a fishing boat. A sealer from Norway, but they were seal fishing in illegal waters. The ship's owner says they were nowhere near, but men on the ship reported seeing the flares and lights of the *Titanic*."

She lifted an eyebrow. "Two sides to every story, even from men on the same ship."

He knew what she was implying and it took all he had to not stand up, to not slap the desk. "What did my mother say to you? Not that it matters. It was all lies."

She avoided his gaze. "Even *if* it was lies, would it hurt for Elsie to know her? Did it hurt you to know her?"

He couldn't stay seated. Storming toward the fireplace, he said, "Hell yes." He slapped the mantel. "And therefore, no, Elsie doesn't need to know her."

"I don't want to upset you. I already did that today."

It was his turn to keep his eyes averted. She had upset him. Disappointed him. Hurt him. In a way he'd never been upset, disappointed or hurt before. Not even by his mother. "Then end this conversation," he said.

"I can't. Elsie means too much to me. You mean too much to me."

"But not enough to stay." That was out before he could stop it.

"I would if I could, but I can't. My cousin Martha sent me a train ticket. She's expecting me to arrive as soon as possible."

That was like a punch to the gut. He'd said he'd pay for her ticket, and would. Just like he'd promised. Damn it!

"When your mother left yesterday, she said she'd be back," she said quietly.

He heard her words like a shout. "She always comes back."

"I told her if I was in her shoes, I'd be back, too. In fact, if what had happened to her, happened to me, if someone denied me the opportunity to watch my children grow, denied me the opportunity to be with the people I love…"

He turned, looked at her. She was shaking her head, with three fingers pressed to her mouth.

"Forgive me," she said. "But it wasn't right. What your father did wasn't right. Not to her and not to you. And it's not right for you to do it to Elsie." Her hair flipped as she spun around and walked out of the room.

He didn't attempt to follow, because once again he was disappointed. He wished she'd have gotten mad. Cursed him. Instead, she'd looked sad, heartbroken.

He knew the feeling.

Damn it.

He crossed the room, opened the drawer and pulled out the calling card his mother had left. Enough was enough. He was putting an end to this. Hurting him was one thing, but he wouldn't let her or anyone else hurt Bridget, or Elsie.

The slam of his office door reverberated up her spine. Bridget held on to the railing tighter as she continued walking up the stairs, until she heard the front door slam, as well. Her feet stalled and she squeezed her eyes shut. What had she been thinking? He'd already been upset when she'd said she couldn't stay. She couldn't stay, but she could hope that he would look at both sides as to what happened years ago.

She didn't know his father's side of the story, but she had believed his mother.

Upsetting him, hurting him, made her throat swell and her eyes burn. She loved him. That was for sure.

She walked up the final few steps of the stairway, and then down the hall to check on Elsie. Both girl and puppy were sound asleep, and after several long moments of watching them, Bridget went across the hall into her room.

The letter from Martha was on her desk. Bridget sat, pulled out a piece of paper and picked up a pen. She tried to imagine what it would be like to have the freedom to say she wasn't traveling to Chicago, that she was staying in New York.

She'd never thought of it that way. Not having the freedom, but that's what it felt like right now. Flustered, she dropped the pen and stood. Paced the floor. She didn't have the freedom to love Karl, either. Moments ago, in his office, she'd wanted to hug him, but couldn't. It was all so confusing. She'd cared about people her entire life, and yet now that she'd found the man who made her heart skip rope, a man she wanted to love forever, she couldn't because she had to fulfill her promises.

Huffing out a breath, she sat at the desk again and picked up the pen. A thank-you for the ticket and money needed to come first, so that was where she started.

Several times.

So many times there was a pile of scrunched up papers in the small basket near her feet when she heard an odd thudding sound.

She hurried out of the room, peeked in Elsie's room, even though the sound was on the staircase, and then quickly walked down the hallway.

An elderly woman with snow-white hair and a cane was slowly making her way up the steps, with Willard carrying two suitcases behind her.

"Bridget," he said, "This is Sarah Conrad. She just arrived at the pier and caught a taxi home."

Bridget's heart sank at the same time it filled with empathy. She hurried down the steps, stopping next to the woman whose foot was in a thick plaster cast. "Hello, Mrs. Conrad. May I help you?"

"No, no, I'm fine," the woman answered, breathing hard. "Just got to get upstairs. To Elsie. Poor thing must be missing me terribly."

A wave of guilt washed over Bridget because Elsie hadn't asked about Mrs. Conrad lately. "May I carry your purse for you?"

Mrs. Conrad stopped. "Oh, yes, yes." She huffed out a breath. "That would help."

Bridget took the purse, which weighed more than Copper, and walked beside the woman up the stairs, close enough to grasp Mrs. Conrad's arm if needed. Both Annette, on the ship, and Karl, today, had said Mrs. Conrad was getting older, but Bridget had still expected someone slightly younger.

They paused at the top of the stairs for Mrs. Conrad to catch her breath, then proceeded down the hall.

Copper woke up as they entered the bedroom and let out a growl.

"What on earth!" Mrs. Conrad hissed.

"That's Copper," Bridget whispered, checking to make sure that Elsie hadn't been awoken.

"Master Karl bought him for the little miss," Willard whispered.

Mrs. Conrad let out a "humph," but didn't say more as they got her settled in her room.

"I told her that Mary and I had a room in our apartment for her, but she insisted upon coming up here," Willard said a short time later, in the hallway.

"She was worried about Elsie," Bridget said. "Maybe once she sees all is fine, she'll be more willing to not climb those steps again." Her heart did go out to Mrs.

Conrad. She obviously cared a great deal about Elsie, about the entire Wingard family. Bridget did, too. "Has Karl returned?"

"No, I'm not sure where he went."

Bridget had an idea, but wasn't completely sure. "You were here when his mother left, weren't you?"

"Yes, yesterday, when she left."

"No, I mean when he was a child."

His shoulders squared and he bowed his head. "Yes, Miss, I was. Good night, now."

She grasped his arm and shook her head. "Don't turn into a butler on me now." She wouldn't be able to leave until things had been repaired. "Karl's father is gone, but his mother is still alive. For his sake and Elsie's, I think everyone should know the truth."

"That was a long time ago," Willard said.

"Old wounds can still heal, if given the opportunity." She wouldn't force him to do anything he didn't want to. "You don't have to tell me anything. But Karl deserves your loyalty now, not his father. And so does Elsie."

He stood still for some time and then nodded. "You are correct." Grinning, he added, "Bridget."

She squeezed his arm. "Sunshine always follows rain," she whispered, and then softly kissed his cheek. "Good night, Willard."

With so many thoughts turning and twisting in her mind, sleep took a long time coming that night. Worse, though, was the following morning, when upon seeing Mrs. Conrad, Elsie wanted to know why her mommy and daddy couldn't come home like her nanny had.

Things didn't get any better when Mrs. Conrad insisted upon Elsie eating in the kitchen. Bridget didn't feel as if she had the authority to say otherwise, and had to hold herself back from saying too much, but was able to get Elsie calmed down.

Which didn't help because her compromise had been to bake cookies. She was quickly informed that young ladies of Elsie's caliber did not bake cookies.

Then, Karl entered the kitchen and requested Bridget to join him in his office.

He appeared pleasant enough, but there was no shine in his eyes, which suggested things may not have gone well with his mother, if that was where he'd gone last night.

She told Elsie she'd be back, and walked out the door ahead of him, aware of his movements behind her. How he closed the door, how he followed her all the way down the hallway into his office, how he closed that door.

Forcing her feet to continue, she walked to the davenport. Stood beside it, leaned a hand on the back. She tried, but couldn't think of anything to say.

"I thought you'd like to know that I talked to my mother last night and have agreed to let her meet Elsie."

"You are a very good uncle."

He lifted a brow. "I said meet her. One time."

She saw through that, but would play along. "And then?"

"We'll see."

He still needed some control. She could understand that.

He crossed his arms, leaned a hip against his desk. "You said if you were in her shoes, you'd be back, too. Is that true?"

"Yes."

He nodded. Didn't say a word. Just nodded and stared at her.

Her fingers dug into the heavy material of the davenport as the desire to cross the room, hug him, kiss him, became stronger as the seconds ticked past. If only she could do those things, life would be wonderful, rather than torturous.

"I...um...have the trust fund set up," he said, running both hands over his head. "I had asked you about the church, and—"

"It's all set up," she said. "I talked to the church. All you have to do is drop off the forms and they'll spread the word, have people fill them out."

"Wonderful. Thank you."

She rubbed her hands together, realizing her palms were sweating. "I also should mention that now that the playhouse and doghouse are done, Sean, James and John will start working on the carriage house. They are going to paint it, replace some shingles on the roof and the hinges on the doors. Willard has created a list of other chores he hasn't had time to complete over the past few years that they will move on to next."

"All right." He put his hands in his pockets. "That sounds good."

"And the steps are a bit much for Mrs. Conrad right now, so she will move into an extra room in Mary and Willard's apartment for the time being." Worried about the changes she had made, that now appeared to have all been wrong, she added, "If you liked Elsie eating meals with you in the dining room, you'll need to mention that to Mrs. Conrad."

His expression softened. "I wondered about that this morning. You didn't mention it to Mrs. Conrad?"

She shook her head. "It's not my place."

He was looking at her again, in that way that made her heart thud like it wanted out of her chest. Smiling, he walked across the room. "What do you want your place to be here, Bridget?"

She shook her head, shrugged. "That's not my place to say, either." That was true. So very true. There wasn't a place for her here. Never really had been. She'd known that, but had let her heart speak louder than her mind. Louder than the truth that had been right before her eyes the entire time. This was a place she'd never belong. Whether she loved him or not.

"I think it is." He touched the side of her face. "I think it's time you decide what you want. Not what others want. You have to have a dream. Something you've always wanted."

She had a dream, but it was as far-fetched as one she'd had as a child.

Her heart pounded harder as he leaned closer, and when his lips touched hers, the caress nearly paralyzed her. She wanted to love him, and have him love her in return. It just wasn't possible.

He kissed her again, coaxing her lips into action, into kissing him back. It made her feel so alive, like everything was possible, that she wrapped her arms around him and gave in completely. Kissing him as fast, as feverishly, as he kissed her.

She could have gone on kissing him forever, but suddenly, knew she had to stop because if she didn't, she might start to believe she could stay. That was impossible. She couldn't be here and in Chicago at the same time.

Breathless, she pulled back and then leaned her head

against him because her eyes were stinging. Drawing up her last bits of willpower, she pushed off him. "I have things to do."

"I have to go to the office, but I want to talk with you later, now that Mrs. Conrad is here."

She willed the tears not to come forward and nodded. Forcing her feet to walk to the door, she knew what had to happen, what she had to do now, while she still understood she wasn't the kind of woman who could ever steal his heart in return. As she grabbed the doorknob, she sucked in air, and flinched. Her lungs felt as if someone had broken a beer glass inside them.

She turned, looked at him, and at that moment, felt her heart breaking apart, piece by piece by piece. "Bye, Karl," she said before the ability to speak completely left her.

"Goodbye, Bridget."

As she walked out of the room, she thought of how Mrs. Flannagan had told her at Da's funeral that God would heal all the pieces of her heart, if she gave him all the pieces.

That couldn't happen this time. She didn't have all the pieces.

Chapter Fifteen

The kiss he and Bridget had shared lived with Karl all morning. She had changed his life in so, so many ways. He hadn't realized exactly what had happened until talking with his mother last night. He'd fallen in love. Had stumbled and fallen into a world that was so unknown to him he hadn't recognized what had happened.

How could he have recognized it? He'd never known love. Never knew what it was capable of doing to a person. Bridget did, and somehow, with little more than that first smile she'd graced him with, she'd found his heart and turned it on with some sort of magical switch.

Hands behind his head, he let out a sigh and leaned back in his desk chair. He'd never imagined he'd give marriage a thought, but he was giving it more than a thought. Much more. He'd never have believed there was someone he'd want to share his life with. Days and nights. Weeks. Months. Years. Never thought he'd want children, because children had meant a wife.

A wife.

His wife.

That's what he wanted.

A wife and children.

It had been hard to not say something to Bridget this morning. He'd considered it when he'd asked her about being in his mother's shoes and coming back. He hadn't meant it as in his mother's shoes precisely. Bridget still believed that she had to go to Chicago, complete the promise she'd made to her father. Those were the shoes he was referring to.

She'd said yes. Now he needed to figure out a way for her to see she could have her own dreams, her own wants. Coax her into seeing there was a place for her in his house. A very integral part.

Now that he knew what it was, this thing between them, this love in his heart, he was anxious to invest in it, watch it grow and protect it.

There was risk, but that too excited him. It always had.

The telephone on his desk rang, and knowing Julia would answer it, he didn't move, just kept thinking about the places he would take Bridget, the things they would do together, the fun they would have, both while convincing her to stay, and for the rest of their lives.

Tonight, he'd take her out to dinner again. Hell, he'd even sit through another opera if that's what she wanted. A hundred operas.

He dropped his hands and sat up at the sound of the knock on his door. "Come in."

"Excuse me, sir, your house is on the line," Julia said.

His heart skipped a beat, but he silently told it to settle down. Bridget wouldn't be calling him. More likely it was Willard with a question of some sort or another. The old man was happy to have the extra help around the house and had asked for his approval of the list he'd created for the younger men to complete before he'd left for the office this morning. "Thank you," he said, and waited for Julia to shut the door before picking up the telephone.

"Hello," he said into the speaker.

"Sorry to disturb, you, sir," Willard said, "But I thought you would like to know that Bridget has asked me to deliver her to the train station."

Karl held his breath for a moment. The old Karl would have instantly become angry, but to the new one—the one who now understood things differently—Willard's words came as no surprise. Bridget was convinced she had to go to Chicago. He just hadn't thought it would happen today. So be it. "Pack a bag for me and deliver it to the rail station along with her."

"Yes, sir."

He grinned at the uptick in Willard's voice. "I'm not sure how long we will be gone," Karl said. He'd been trying to come up with a way to get her alone. A train ride would do that.

"Very well, sir. I'm assuming I shouldn't mention this to Miss McGowen," Willard said.

Karl had to grin again, at how Willard had slipped back into his formal butler mode. "No, don't mention it to her. Thank you, Willard."

"You're welcome, sir."

Karl hung up the telephone and leaned back, rubbing his hands together and grinning. Time for the convincing to start. Chuckling aloud, he stood and grabbed his jacket off the back of his chair. He hadn't been this excited about something in… Perhaps ever.

Crossing through the outer office, he said, "I'm going to be gone for a few days, at least."

"Washington?" Julia asked.

"No. Chicago."

If that surprised her, it didn't show. "Very well, sir. Have a good trip."

"I will. I'm sure of that."

He whistled as he walked to his automobile, and had to laugh at some of the stares he received. Shocked stares. He accepted them and waved. He wasn't known as a happy man. Correct that. He hadn't *been* known as a happy man. Just as he'd never been known as someone who was concerned about those beneath him. That had all been before Bridget. As she'd said, no one was above or beneath anyone.

As he arrived at his Packard, he glanced up at the tall building with the Wingard name carved in the bricks at the very top. His father would be as shocked as those staring at him to hear him say that he believed no one was above or beneath anyone else.

Well, he wasn't his father.

His hand froze as he gripped the door handle. It was as if he'd just been struck with something hard and heavy. It didn't hurt. Instead it felt as if something had shattered around him. Something invisible.

He knew then what it was. The weight he'd carried. The chip on his shoulder of being Gerald Wingard's oldest son. The man who needed to walk in his father's shoes. Think like his father. Act like his father.

Once again, his eyes looked up at the building. At the name scrolled across the top.

He wasn't his father.

He didn't need to wear those shoes. Didn't need to think, to act, to be like his father had been.

He was his own man. One who knew exactly what he wanted out of life.

Opening the door, he climbed in and started the engine, fully ready to get exactly what he wanted.

His office was closer to the train station than his home, and he watched Willard arrive, park and carry two suitcases inside the building. Karl considered approaching Bridget, who was clearly sad—tearful—but decided to wait. It was hard because he wanted to comfort her, let her know it was all going to be all right, but he had to wait until the iron wheels of the train were already turning. She was committed to fulfilling the promise she'd made to her father, and he respected that. If need be, he'd stay in Chicago, help her buy a place and run it. Just to prove that he was committed, too. To her.

He caught Willard's eye and waved as the butler walked to the Studebaker. Bridget didn't notice. She had her eyes closed, was wiping away the tears with a handkerchief.

Karl balled his hands into fists, forcing himself to wait a bit longer. It felt like hours before the time finally came for him to board the train, and when he did, through the back entrance, he took a seat two rows behind her. She was wearing the tan coat and white hat she'd worn to the hospital the day they'd gone to see Sean and Catherine. From where he sat, he could hear her sniffles, and that tugged at his heart, made him draw up even more willpower to wait until the train left the station.

As soon as that happened, he rose from his seat, walked forward and stopped next to the padded bench she sat upon. "Excuse me, miss, is this seat taken?"

She went stock-still, and her head slowly notched sideways, like cogs of a clock, until she was facing him. Mouth agape, eyes wide, she stared. Then blinked. "Karl?"

Even with red-rimmed eyes, she was so very beautiful. "Hello, Bridget." He sat next to her.

Scooting closer to the window, she eyed him cautiously. "What are you doing here?"

"Did you think you could leave without saying goodbye?" He took ahold of her hand. "I think not."

She pulled her hand away, clutched both of her hands to her chest. "You can't be here."

He grinned, leaned closer. "I am."

"Why?"

"Because I'm going to Chicago with you."

"No, you're not."

"Yes, I am."

"The devil you say!" she hissed.

"Better the devil you know than the one you don't," he replied, using an old Irish saying he'd heard before.

She huffed out a breath and turned toward the window.

Unbeknownst to her, he could see her reflection. It was a faint, translucent image, but he saw her grin. His heart picked up speed as fast as the train was gaining speed for the long journey ahead. "I told you I'd see you to Chicago."

Her lips were pinched together when she turned back to him. "You can't go with me. You can't."

"Yes," he said, nodding, "I can. You helped me and my family, tremendously. Now it's my turn to return the favor."

A frown tugged her brows downward. "Return the favor?"

"Yes, I'm going to Chicago with you, and will help you pick out a boardinghouse, make sure it's a good solid investment. One that is sure to fit your needs and give you a good return of revenue."

"You're going to help me get a boardinghouse?"

"Yes, that's your dream, isn't it?"

"Well, yes, but—"

"No, buts, it's the least I can do." He was fighting to play nonchalant as hard as he'd fought to remain in his seat earlier.

"No. The least you could do is stay in New York."

He chuckled. "I thought you'd appreciate my help. I sincerely appreciated yours."

Still frowning, she said, "I don't need any help. Don't want any help."

He reached up, ran his fingers through the long black hair hanging over her shoulder, down her arm. "We are not so different, you and I. My father had a dream of his oldest son taking over Wingard's. He molded me after himself, made me follow in his footsteps, so that when the day came, I knew what to do. And your father had a dream of you owning your own boardinghouse. He laid your path by saving the money to send you to America. Here we both are, following those dreams."

She pulled her gaze off him, stared straight ahead for a time, before saying, "We are not alike, Karl."

"We both eat, sleep, laugh…love."

Looking at him as if he'd lost his mind, she shook her head. "Why are you doing this?"

He hadn't lost his mind, he'd found it, and his heart, and was going to do everything he could to convince

her that she didn't need to follow someone else's dream.
That she could have her own. He also hoped, more than
he'd ever hoped before, that he was a part of her new
dreams. "Because I want to."

This time, when she turned to the window and he
saw her reflection, there was no smile, but a frown instead.

He laid an arm along the top of the seat behind her
and stretched his legs out beneath the seat in front of
them. "Might as well sit back and relax. It's a long train
ride. Over nineteen hours."

She muttered something under her breath. A curse,
or a prayer, he wasn't sure, but would guess a curse. On
him. He swallowed his laughter, kept it hidden.

"You are needed at home, Karl," she said.

"I've been in Washington for a large portion of the
past couple of weeks," he pointed out.

"Yes, well, I was there then. I'm not now, so you
should be."

"And you shouldn't be?"

"No, Mrs. Conrad is back."

"Then why should I be there?"

She huffed out a breath. "Her foot is still in a cast."

"That didn't stop you from leaving."

Closing her eyes, she shook her head. "It's not my
home. It's yours, and you should be there."

He wanted it to be her home too, but she wasn't ready
to hear that yet. Just like he hadn't been ready to understand that he'd fallen in love with her until last night.
"I'll return once I know all is settled with your boardinghouse."

"I'm not going to start a boardinghouse right away.
I'll help my cousin first, learn what I need to know."

"What don't you know?" he asked. "It only took you a week to start one at my house."

She glowered at him.

He grinned and winked at her.

Tucking a clump of hair behind one ear, she asked, "Why are you really here, Karl?"

She'd missed a few strands, and he smoothed them behind her ear. "Growing up, I never had the opportunity to dream about being anything except a banker. My father took me to work with him for as long as I can remember. I passed out mail and counted change. At first, I thought it was fun, until I realized it was work, and it would be the work I would do the rest of my life."

"Then it was no longer fun?"

He shrugged. "I learned to accept it for what it was. What I do now is different, but it's still the same company, the work I knew I was destined to do."

"That doesn't sound fair."

"It's the same thing you are doing. Opening a boardinghouse because it's a dream someone else had for you."

She turned, looked out the window again. "No, it's not."

Figuring he'd give time for that to sink in, he asked, "Have you had lunch?"

"I wasn't hungry." She glanced to the floor, where a basket sat beneath her seat. "Mary sent sandwiches if you're hungry."

"I'm hungry." He took ahold of her hand. "Let's go to the dining car and have something to eat. I'm sure they are serving some sort of late lunch."

She shook her head. "I'll wait here."

He stood and tugged on her hand. "I don't want to eat alone."

She sighed, but stood. "Let me remove my coat."

He released her hand and helped her remove the tan coat, revealing a pale pink and white dress that merely added to her beauty. Something he truly couldn't get enough of. He would never tire of having her next to him. With him.

She held on to his hand as he led her through the passenger car and into the dining car. White tablecloths covered the tables lining both walls. He escorted her to a table and waited for her to slide onto the bench seat, then, instead of sitting across from her, he sat down next to her.

Bridget's heart was in a terrible state. The bench seat was as wide as the one in the passenger car, so she wasn't crowded, but having him sit next to her here, when the bench across from them was empty, felt very intimate.

That wasn't the only reason her heart didn't know how to behave. She'd been preparing herself—her mind, her heart—for never seeing him again as the train had pulled away from the station, when she'd heard his voice.

She'd thought she'd gone mad, hearing his voice like that, but then she'd felt him. Felt him so strongly she'd been afraid to look, fearing she truly had gone mad. Seeing him had been such a shock, she'd forgotten how to breathe, had used her last gasp to say his name.

"What would you care to drink?" he asked.

"Water will be fine." She removed her gloves and stuffed them inside her purse.

"They have a selection of wines," he said.

"No, thank you." She needed to keep her wits about her. The few she had left. When he'd first sat down next to her, she'd thought for the briefest of moments that he'd come after her because he loved her, until she remembered that could never happen. She couldn't let it. He deserved a woman from his world. A place that she would never fit.

He ordered water and coffee from the waiter, and then, holding the menu so they both could read it, he asked, "What would you care to eat?"

"I'm really not hungry," she said.

"Please don't make me eat alone." He bumped his shoulder against hers. "I've come to enjoy having you and Elsie share the table with me."

Refraining from stating how much she'd enjoyed that, too, she said, "I do hope you'll speak to Mrs. Conrad about Elsie continuing to eat in the dining room."

"You should have told her that this morning. Hmm. They have a hunter's soup. How does that sound?"

"No, I shouldn't have told her that," she said. "The soup sounds fine."

"Yes, you should have. You've been managing the house for weeks. Everyone respects your decisions. Salmon with hollandaise sauce sounds good, don't you think?"

"No, I wasn't managing the house, and the salmon sounds fine."

"Yes, you were, and it never ran so smoothly. I truly had no worries knowing you were there, even after you turned it into a boardinghouse. How about English ribs? Would you rather have those than salmon?"

"I didn't turn it into a boardinghouse, and the ribs

sound fine, as well." Carrying on a conversation with two completely separate subjects seemed to be delighting him. His smile grew every time she answered. Why did he have to be so charming? So perfect?

"That's right, you hired new employees, which, my dear, is managing the household." Without a pause, he asked, "How about dessert? There's apple pie, plum pudding, ice cream, fruit."

"I didn't hire anyone. You did. And you like apple pie."

"I didn't hire them. I agreed to pay them so you didn't have to pay them out of your own wage. And I do like apple pie, but I like rum cake better. Yours. It was delicious. I wish you'd make that again."

Theoretically, everything he'd said was true, but so was everything she'd said. "Not John and James. You hired them. And I left the recipe with Mary."

"I tend to differ. I did not hire them. I spoke with them after they were already working with Sean, and questioned him about them, to make sure you weren't boarding unsavory men. Mary will never be able to make rum cake as well as you do."

"They weren't unsavory, and yes, she can. It's a simple recipe."

"I didn't say they were unsavory. I said I spoke with them and Sean, to make sure they weren't." He laid the menu down. "And there is nothing simple about you. Not even a rum cake recipe."

She held her silence as the waiter returned with water and coffee. "May I take your order?" he asked.

Karl looked at her, brow lifted.

Knowing he'd order half the menu for her if she

didn't speak up, Bridget said, "I'll have the hunter's soup."

"And for your main course?" the waiter asked.

"Just the soup, please," she replied.

"Very well, and you, sir?"

"I'll have the salmon, and apple pie for dessert," Karl replied.

"Excellent choices," the waiter said. "Thank you."

Karl took a drink of his coffee, and as he set the cup back on the saucer, said, "I haven't been to Chicago in over a year."

"Why were you in Chicago?" she asked, picking up her cup.

"We have a bank there." He leaned back and stretched an arm along the top of the seat behind her. "Before my father died, I did a substantial amount of traveling all around the nation. Overseeing the acquisition of banks, branches and investment companies."

"You have more than one bank?"

"Yes. I hear they have an amazing opera in Chicago."

She pinched her lips together at his grin. "I still feel bad about that."

"I don't."

"You hated it."

"I enjoyed being there with you." He rubbed her shoulder. "They also have a playhouse in Chicago. We should attend a play while we are there."

"Karl—"

"Your soup is here," he said, nodding at the waiter.

She thanked the waiter as he set the bowl in front of her.

"Have you ever been to a play?" he asked as she filled her spoon.

"No. Have you?"

"Many."

He told her about plays, and other such performances that he'd attended as they shared the bowl of soup, and asked about places and things she'd done in Ireland. The conversation continued as his plate of salmon arrived, which he slid over so they both could eat off it, too.

They also shared the apple pie. She'd never done anything like that before, and enjoyed it far more than was proper, of that she was certain. But their conversation reminded her of just how different they were. The different worlds they had grown up in, Not just countries, but livelihoods, stations in life.

It wasn't as if she hadn't already known that, or that she'd forgotten it, but she had looked past it while living at his home. Mrs. Conrad's return had made several things clear. The other woman hadn't said anything directly, but her frowns and the way she'd clicked her tongue upon hearing things Bridget had allowed and encouraged Elsie to experience—like making mud pies, getting her hands and knees dirty, being called Poppet instead of Miss Elsie—had shown grave disapproval.

That had angered her at first, until she'd realized she was the one in the wrong. The outsider who knew nothing about the things Elsie would need to know in order to grow into a young lady of means. Her past was too different. She was too different.

She believed everyone had been created equally, and that it took all walks of life to make the world work, but she now understood something else. People were born into stations—classes—and though they might dream, even acquire ways to move up in the world, they needed to look at how that would affect others. Especially those they loved.

That's what hurt the most. She loved Karl, and therefore had to do what was best for him, even though it hurt.

Chapter Sixteen

"Did you have a dream, when you were little, of what or who you wanted to be?" Karl asked later, when they were once again seated in the passenger car.

Most everyone who'd known her as a young girl knew about her far-fetched dream, and the memory made her smile, at how her parents had kept that dream alive.

"You're smiling," he said. "What is it?"

She'd learned long ago that it could never come true, but it had been fun. Lifting a shoulder, she said, "A leprechaun."

He tilted his head, looked at her with a broad smile, yet a doubtful shine in his eyes. "A leprechaun?"

"Yes." Memories made a giggle tickle her throat. "Da pointed out they were boys, but I said I would be the first girl one. My mother used to let me set old shoes out by my bed and I'd fight to stay awake at night to catch one. Once, when I was upset about falling asleep, Da tied a bell on a string and ran it from a shoe to my bedpost."

"Why?"

She studied him for a minute. "Do you know what a leprechaun is?"

"Yes. Little green men who play tricks on people and have pots of gold at the ends of rainbows."

Exaggerating a sigh, she said, "They are much more than that." Until this moment, she'd forgotten how much she'd enjoyed her leprechaun years. That's what Da had called them. "They sneak into homes at night and repair shoes, and if you catch one, they will grant you three wishes. That's why Da tied the bell on the string, so I'd wake up when it rang."

He nodded. "So you wanted to catch one, not be one."

"I wanted to catch one, so when they granted me a wish, I could wish to become one." A warmth filled her. "Then I would be able to repair all the shoes of the people I knew, and when they caught me, I could make their wishes come true. Da's wish was to be taller, so he could reach the top shelves behind the bar without the stool that was always getting in his way. Mother's wish was to have blue eyes like mine. Which always confused me because her eyes were the most beautiful shade of green. Bright green."

Another memory made her laugh.

"Tell me more," Karl said.

"One day, we were walking home from church and there was a rainbow that looked like it was ending right on top of the pub. I was sure there would be a leprechaun in my bedroom. I searched and searched, and was about to be very disappointed that a leprechaun hadn't been there when my Da shouted for me to hurry downstairs. There, in the kitchen, flour had been spilt across the counter, and there were tiny footprints in the flour. I was so excited and Da helped me make a little net with a handle, so when it came back, I could catch him."

"Did you catch one?" he asked, eyes gleaming.

"Not yet," she said.

He laughed. "Still looking to catch one, are you?"

She leaned back, looking at him. He was so handsome in his white shirt and green silk vest. Pulling her gaze off him, she shook her head. "No."

"When did you stop?" he asked quietly.

Something lodged between her ribs. The old forgotten knife of pain. It wasn't as sharp as it had once been, but like so many other things, it was there. Had become a part of her. "Not long after that rainbow day, my mother became sick. Died. My Da brought home Shadow."

"Your dog."

"Yes. Da said Shadow had been bred for the purpose of sniffing out leprechauns, and we looked for them, all three of us some days, but before long the dream of finding a leprechaun faded away." She sighed. "So did the years."

His arm was on the back of the bench, and he lowered it onto her shoulders, pulled her against him and kissed the top of her head.

"I'm sorry, Bridget," he whispered. "Sorry about your parents, and that you never found a leprechaun."

The touch of his lips, the feel of his arm around her, his shoulder beneath her cheek, caused a yearning so strong it became painful to breathe. She closed her eyes, swallowed.

His other hand tucked her hair behind her ear, rubbed her cheek.

It was impossible. Him. Her. As impossible as catching a leprechaun. She opened her eyes. It was hard to let go of dreams, to face the cold harshness of the truth. Someday, he would find a woman who could be exactly what he needed. "Going to Chicago isn't about dreams, Karl. It's not even about promises. It's about me. About who I was born to be. About who I will always be."

He cupped her cheek. "You can be who you are anywhere."

"Yes, I can," she admitted, knowing that was possible. What wasn't possible, was having him near. "But this isn't about just me. Life isn't about any one person." She moved, separated herself from him, needing the clarity. "We are from two very different worlds."

"They aren't so different," he said.

"Did you ever believe in leprechauns?"

"No, but—"

"Karl?" a man said, stopping in the aisle. "Are you traveling to Chicago? Is something wrong?"

Karl didn't look happy about the interruption, but introduced her, "Bridget, this is Theodore Klein, he heads our acquisition division in Chicago."

She said hello in return to the man's greeting and then, taking advantage of the opportunity, she excused herself. Once Karl stood, she left her seat and found the restroom near the front of the car.

Afterward, she wished for an excuse to not return to her seat. Being near Karl was making the inevitable so much more difficult. He was still talking with Theodore as a young woman with a baby on one hip and holding the hand of a child not much older walked toward her.

Bridget held open the door of the restroom for the trio.

The woman was thin, with fine brown hair and a blue gingham dress. "Thank you," she said softly.

"Would you like me to hold the baby for you?" Bridget asked. "There's not much room in there."

A look of relief filled the woman's face. "You wouldn't mind?"

"Not at all." Bridget held her arms out. "We'll be right here."

The woman handed over the baby and entered the facility with the other child in tow.

Bridget tickled the towheaded baby beneath the chin and was rewarded with a toothless grin. She talked to him softly and bumped his nose with the tip of her finger, hoping to keep his attention away from realizing she was a stranger and not his mommy.

"Thank you very much," the woman said, upon exiting. Glancing over her shoulder, she added, "You're right, there's not much room in there."

Bridget handed the baby back to his mother. "Are you traveling to Chicago?"

"No." Her eyes were sad as she glanced at her sons. "Oregon."

"The three of you?"

"Yes. My husband bought an apple orchard there."

"That's sounds lovely." Sensing a deep sadness, Bridget asked, "Is he there, waiting on your arrival?"

"No." The woman's hold on the baby tightened. "We were on the *Titanic* and..."

Bridget laid a hand on the woman's arm, understanding the woman's husband hadn't survived. "So was I. My name is Bridget."

"I'm Maria." She glanced at the baby. "This is Thaddeus." Nodding towards the child holding her hand, she said, "And this is Frank Jr."

Karl had only been half listening to all Theodore Klein had been saying. The manager had been filling him on how well the territories he oversaw were doing, as if assuring him there was no need for him to visit Chicago. Karl hadn't yet said he wasn't visiting Chicago for that reason. He'd been too busy watching Bridget, who had exited the ladies' room and was now sitting on a bench with a young woman and two children.

"What hotel are you staying at?" Theodore asked.

"I'll let you know," Karl said, catching Bridget glancing his way again. "Excuse me."

He walked to where Bridget sat and placed a hand on the back of the bench in front of her. "Is everything all right?"

She laid a hand on his wrist. "Karl, this is Maria Aks, and her sons Thaddeus and Frank Jr."

"Hello," he said, noting the frown on Bridget's face more than the woman and her children.

"Maria and her family were on the *Titanic*. They've been in New York since the accident, but are now traveling to Oregon, where her husband bought an apple orchard before he'd traveled back to Poland to get them." She looked at him and shook her head. "The Women's Aid Fund gave her traveling vouchers to get to Oregon and I was telling her about the trust fund you've set up."

They may have come from different backgrounds, and he may not have believed in leprechauns, but he did believe in Bridget and wanted her to believe in him. "Do you have the address of where you'll be living in

Oregon, Mrs. Aks? So your payments can be mailed to you?"

"I never filled out any papers. I never knew anything about it," the woman replied.

He smiled. "Bridget will take care of that. Just give her the information. Do you have enough money for you and the children to make it to Oregon, and for a time after you arrive there?"

Her response was delayed. "We'll manage."

He withdrew his wallet from his pocket and removed several bills, handing them to the woman.

"I couldn't," she said. "People have already been so kind."

Knowing Bridget could handle this better than him, he handed the money to her. "I'll be at our seats."

It was some time before she returned to their bench, and he'd spent every moment thinking about the things she'd said.

"Thank you," she said, upon sitting down.

He twisted in his seat, took ahold of both of her hands and glanced toward the family she'd just left. "That is who you are, Bridget McGowen. The girl who wanted to become a leprechaun, so she could grant wishes for people."

"I didn't grant anyone's wishes." She glanced toward the front of the train, where the woman and her child sat. "If anyone did, it was you."

"No. If you weren't here, hadn't offered to hold that woman's baby, she would never have known about the trust fund, about the money she and her children deserve." He squeezed her hands. "And if not for you, I would never have set up that trust fund."

She shook her head.

He nodded. "You said going to Chicago isn't about dreams or promises, that it's about you. That's why I'm going there, too. For myself."

Frowning, she asked, "For your company? To visit your bank?"

"No. This is completely personal. You see, I met this woman. The most beautiful woman I've ever seen. She opened my eyes to other things besides outer beauty, because she is just as beautiful, just as special, on the inside. I didn't know what was happening at first, how she was changing my life. She keeps on changing it, too. For the better. The idea of living without her, of never seeing her again, is one I refuse to consider."

"Karl, stop." Her bottom lip quivered, and she bit down on it.

"No. I won't stop. I can't. My father would never have let me believe in leprechauns. There would never have been flour poured on the counter and filled with miniature footprints just to make me happy. To encourage me to believe in the impossible. The only thing I was allowed to believe in was hard work, building up a fortune and then holding on to it with an iron fist." He felt no bitterness, just sorrow that it had taken him so long to see things in a different light. "His teachings have served me well, but I want more for my children. I want them to believe in the unbelievable. I want them to eat at the dining room table. And I want their mother, my wife, to be stubborn enough to curse me in a foreign language when I step out of line."

There was a single tear dripping out of one corner of her eye.

"I won't force you to become my wife. I won't beg, plead, or threaten. I will ask you, Bridget McGowen, to consider that possibility. I love you. Something I also hadn't believed in until I met you. I will give you anything you want. Just ask, and I'll give it to you. If you want ten boardinghouses, I'll buy them."

She was shaking her head again. "Karl—"

"I'm not done. I know you think we are from two different worlds, and I agree with that, but that is also why I love you. There is nothing pretentious about you. You are as genuine as the sun. As determined as a flower that grows in the cracks of the cobblestones, outside of the flower bed, and that makes your bloom all the more beautiful, all the more special."

He lifted one of her hands, kissed the back of it. "I know you think there's not a place for you in my home, but you are so wrong. So very wrong." He refused to believe there was anything they couldn't overcome together. "My home is exactly where you belong. Proving that no one is above or below anyone. I now believe every life on the *Titanic* was worth as much as the next. Every life on this earth is worth as much as the next."

"They are," she said. "But it's more than that, Karl." Her voice was shaky. "You may see it that way, but others never will. I can't put you in the position of being ostracized. Being ridiculed for marrying beneath you. I can't put Elsie in that position, either."

He thought of his father, who would have thought exactly as she was suggesting. The man he'd loved, and would continue to, but would not follow in his footsteps any longer. "If that were to happen, it would be by people whom I wouldn't want to be associated with, and most certainly wouldn't want Elsie exposed to."

"But she will be," she whispered.

"And we'll be there, together, to show her how wrong

that principle is. Allow her to form her own opinions. Her own beliefs."

She closed her eyes. "My temper can get away from me at times. I've been known to say or do things that I shouldn't."

That was just one of the things he loved about her, but he could tell she felt it was a real issue. "So what if you do? It won't bring about the end of the world. Furthermore, it will make people think twice about their own behaviors." It had for him.

"You make it sound so simple, but it's not," she said.

"I believe it is simple. As simple as loving you. As simple as you letting me be your leprechaun. If you grant me the wish of being my wife, I'll give you the means to grant all the wishes to anyone you want." He'd said he wouldn't beg or plead, and because he was about to start doing just that, he drew in a deep breath. "Don't say anything, Bridget. Just think about it." He kissed her forehead, stood. Walked away.

Once again, Bridget forgot how to breathe as Karl walked through the gangway into the other passenger car. When he disappeared, she gasped so hard it made her cough. Several times.

The coughing might have made her eyes water; there was no way of telling with the tears that were already flowing. With blurred vision, she found her purse on the floor and took out her handkerchief.

The handkerchief Karl had bought her.

The purse Karl had bought her.

Everything she had right now, Karl had bought her.

He was the one who was as beautiful on the inside

as he was on the outside. He also did make it sound so simple, but it was not.

Still wiping at the tears on her cheeks, she turned, looked out the window. Fields of spring-green grass, as green as the grass back home, rolled past the window. The fields went on and on, for as far as she could see.

Oh, Da, I don't know what to do. I truly don't. I love him. I love him so much I don't want to see him hurt. Not now, not ever.

Huffing out a sigh, because she knew her father couldn't answer, she leaned her head against the window. She'd known he'd stolen her heart, but hearing him say he loved her had made her chest burn, ache at the need of telling him that she loved him in return. Him. A man who she believed had never received the love he deserved. Not as a child. Not as she had. She'd been showered with love. A love that had taught her how to love in return. But she didn't want that love to cause problems for Karl.

May those that love us, love us. And those that don't, may God turn their hearts. And if He doesn't turn their hearts, may He turn their ankles so we'll know them by their limping.

A shiver tickled her spine. She sat up, looked around. She could have sworn she'd just heard Da's voice, saying the very curse she'd heard him repeat many times.

She must have thought it. Thought the curse… *May those that love us, love us.* Her gaze went to the door to the gangway that Karl had walked through.

He deserved to be loved. Loved completely. Day in and day out.

Her spine stiffened.

She did, too.

Squaring her shoulders, she stood and stepped into the aisle. Then forward. Through the gangway and into the other passenger car.

She saw his back; he was sitting near the window, staring out as she had been only moments ago. Refusing to allow her steps to falter, even with the rumbling, rolling wheels making the car sway, she walked forward. Sat down next to him.

He turned away from the window. She could feel his gaze on the side of her face, but continued looking straight ahead.

"I want you to know that I'm mad at you," she said.

"Oh?"

She nodded and forced herself to still not look at him. The moment she did that, it would be over. "Yes."

"Why?"

"Because we can't very well have an argument on a train full of people."

"You want to argue with me."

"I want to argue a point."

"And you can't here?"

She blinked several times, so her eyes wouldn't try to sneak a peek at him. "No."

"May I ask what the point is?"

The hint of humor in his tone almost broke her resolve. She knew his eyes were twinkling. She loved when they did that. Sucking in a breath, she said, "I don't want your money."

"What money are you talking about?"

Keeping her chin up, she said, "The money you'd use to buy ten boardinghouses."

"All right, I won't buy ten boardinghouses."

"Good." She had to fight harder to keep staring straight ahead.

"Is that your only point?"

"No, I don't want you to be a leprechaun, either."

He leaned closer, ran a hand through her hair hanging over one shoulder. "Good, because I'm a little tall for that."

She pinched her lips together. He was much too tall to be a leprechaun.

He ran a finger along the edge of her face, under her chin, then used it to gently force her to look at him. "Is there more?"

That's all it took. One look into those sparkling, amazing brown eyes. Her heart began to swell, to meld back together. "I don't want you to get hurt," she whispered.

"The only way I'll get hurt is if you don't agree to marry me," he said. "If I can't hold you, love you, for the rest of my life, I won't be able to live with that pain."

"I won't, either," she admitted.

He cupped her face with both hands, stared into her eyes, almost as if he couldn't believe what he was seeing.

She shrugged. "I love you, Karl. Love you so very, very much."

His lips landed on hers, a hard, fast kiss. "Are you saying what I'm hoping you're saying? That you'll marry me?"

She grabbed ahold of his forearms, curled her fingers into the material of his shirt as her heart soared. "Yes. Yes, I'll marry you."

He kissed her again, then pulled her up against him,

hugging her so tight, so wonderfully tight. "Now I'm mad at you," he whispered next to her ear.

She lifted her head, looked at the smile on his face. "You are? Why?"

"Because we're on a train full of people where I can't kiss you, love you, the way I want to."

She giggled, and ran a finger over his lips. Her heart was so full of happiness it threatened to burst. Being married to this man was going to be glorious. Truly glorious. She didn't even mind the idea of him being mad at her right now. Leaning closer, so their faces almost touched, she said, "My Da always told my mother the best part of arguing was the making up afterward."

His grin grew. "Your father was a very smart man."

"He was." Although it didn't seem possible, her happiness grew even more, remembering the curse she'd heard inside her head a few minutes ago. Da had planted that there, so she'd hear it at the exact moment she'd needed to. Recalling the entire curse, she leaned back. "There's one more thing you need to know."

He kissed her forehead. "What?"

"Don't trust anyone with a limp."

Laughing, he agreed, "I won't. Is that it?"

She nodded, then whispered, "Unless you want to kiss me again."

"I do."

He kissed her, and she kissed him back with all her heart and soul. All the love that had been growing inside her since the first time she saw him, rushing into the room to see Elsie. That's when he'd stolen the first piece of her heart.

Maybe he hadn't stolen it after all. Maybe she'd given it to him, piece by piece, because he was the man she wanted to have her heart. Her whole heart. Now and forever.

"I love you," he whispered as their lips parted.

"I love you," she replied.

Chapter Seventeen

Bridget wanted to go on kissing him and kissing him and kissing him. She glanced around at the people filling the seats and huffed out a breath. Looking at him, she shook her head. "You picked a fine time to ask me to marry you. We truly are stuck on this train."

"You're the one who said yes."

"Did you want me to say no?" she asked. He was grinning, and she knew the answer to that, but liked their back-and-forth banter.

"No, but you could have waited until we arrived in Chicago."

She pressed her forehead against his bicep. "We would both have been miserable by then."

"We still will be!"

Her happiness just kept stepping up, like it was climbing a ladder. She patted his cheek. "We are going to have so many arguments to make up from by the time we get off this train."

He groaned. "You're not helping." Pulling her to her feet at the same time as he stood, he said, "Let's go."

"Go where?"

"Back to our seat. Where our belongings are."

She'd forgotten about that. Holding on to his hand with both of hers, she followed him along the aisle, into the gangway, where he kissed her. A wonderful long kiss. Then he opened the second door and led her back to their seats.

Sitting down, she leaned her head back. "Now what?"

He took ahold of her hand, threaded his fingers through hers. "Are you hungry?"

"No." It hadn't been that long since they'd eaten. "Are you?"

"No. I just thought it would kill time."

She rested the side of her head on his shoulder. It was as simple as he'd said. They loved each other and would make it work, different worlds or not. "I need to see Martha when we get to Chicago. To let her know that I'm fine and getting married soon."

"Should we get married there?" he asked. "So she can be there? She is your family."

"But your family won't be there."

He touched the side of her face. "As long as you are there, nothing else matters to me."

She felt the exact same way.

"Or we could wait until we get back to New York," he said. "Have a big wedding at church."

"Is that what you want?"

"I just want to marry you. If this was a ship, I'd find the captain."

She laughed. "Let's get married in Chicago."

"Good. As soon as we arrive, we'll go see your cousin and then to the courthouse to get the license."

"Good." The satisfaction inside her was short-lived. "Now what do we do?"

He groaned. Shrugged. "Are you hungry?"

She laughed, so did he, and despite all the people surrounding them, he kissed her again.

Karl had never claimed to be a patient man, but holding Bridget as they tried to get some sleep sitting up and sneaking kisses every now and again, had him about ready to explode by the time the train rolled into Chicago.

If he'd been a bit more clearheaded he also might have realized the wait until being alone with her wasn't over. Even collecting their luggage and securing a taxi to take them to her cousin's house took twice as long as he'd have liked.

Martha McGowen was a middle-aged woman, with a full head of dark hair piled high, and a laugh that filled a room. She was delighted to see Bridget and grilled Karl soundly about his intentions of making and keeping Bridget happy.

Evidently, his simple and honest answer of loving her beyond all else, forever, was correct because within no time, Martha was planning a wedding for the following day, insisting she would take care of everything.

She allowed him to stay for lunch before sending him off to find a hotel, with stern instructions to not return until tomorrow at two o'clock.

What had he expected? That she'd let him stay the night with Bridget, at the boardinghouse? A boardinghouse for women only.

He had the taxi drop him off downtown, at the same hotel he used to stay in while visiting the bank here, and booked the nicest room. Then he called Willard and Julia, telling them both that he and Bridget were getting married, and explaining that he wasn't sure when they'd return. That would be up to Bridget. If she wanted a honeymoon trip around the world, then that's what he'd give her. He'd never been so happy, so overjoyed in his life.

Or so impatient.

He left the hotel and visited a jewelry store, bought a wedding ring as well as another ring for Bridget. A sapphire because it matched her eyes. He bought the necklace and earrings that matched the ring before he left that store in search of another.

At that next store, he asked to speak to the owner, gave the woman Martha's address and asked her to take every wedding dress in the store to that address and let the bride pick out the one she wanted. At another nearby store, he bought himself a new tuxedo. He almost went with the blue vest, but changed his mind and went with a leprechaun-green one instead.

After that, he was at a loss as to what to do next. It was barely midafternoon. He was only a few blocks away from the bank and started walking in that direction, but stopped. That was something his father would do. Work.

He wasn't his father. He was his own man. Would soon be married to the most amazing woman on earth. A woman who would be a wonderful, fun, loving mother to his children.

Spinning around, he walked back to the hotel, took the elevator up to his room. There, he stared at the phone for several minutes before he sat down, picked it up and waited for an operator to give the exchange to.

When the other end answered, he drew in a breath at the sound of her voice. "Hello, Mother."

"Karl? Is—is something wrong?"

"No, I just wanted to tell you that I'm getting married."

"You are?"

If there was a place to make sure Bridget was never injured, this is where he needed to start. "Yes. To Bridget."

"Miss McGowen? Oh, Karl! You just brought tears to my eyes. She is such a lovely woman, and so very dedicated to you. I could tell that right off. When? Where? May I attend?"

A wave of guilt struck him. She sounded so excited. So happy. "In Chicago. That's where we are. We're getting married tomorrow."

"You eloped! How romantic! I like her. Really like her, and I'm so happy for you. Tell me more, please?"

An image flashed in his mind, of the day he'd wrapped his arms around her knees, begged her not to leave. She'd had her arms around him when his father had pulled him off her, and there had been tears on her face when his father had spanked him, told him he'd better never do that again. That had been the reason he'd hated her, because his father had spanked him. That hadn't been her fault. He'd never looked at it that way before. He sat down in the chair. "I'm sorry, Mother, for never—"

"This isn't about me, Karl," she interrupted. "This is about you and Bridget. Why Chicago? Does she have family there?"

"Yes. Her cousin. Bridget had promised…" He told her far more than he'd intended when he made the call, and continued to talk until the operator broke in and said the line had been tied up too long. He then bade his mother goodbye and hung up the phone.

He felt lighter, freer, than he'd ever felt. Laughing, he leaned back. "Bridget McGowen strikes again." He laughed harder. Lord, but he loved her.

Not only because she was so lovable, but because she made him a better person. Someone he could like. Someone he wanted to be.

The following day, Karl arrived at Martha's boardinghouse fifteen minutes early. He'd fought hard to stay away for the twenty-six hours that he had.

Martha welcomed him with a hug and thanked him for sending over the dresses, winking when she said Bridget picked out the loveliest one. She was gone then, off to take care of last-minute details.

The living room of the three-story home had vases of flowers sitting on the tables and rows of chairs lined up in front of the big, bay window. He did a double take when he saw Theodore Klein walk out of the kitchen.

"Congratulations," Theodore said, holding out a hand. "You could have told me about this on the train." Slapping his back, Theodore, as he was known to do, continued, "When Martha called, asked if I'd be interested in being your best man, I said of course. I didn't realize you knew Martha. She's been a member of our bank for years and has taken advantage of some very good investments that I've told her about in the past."

Karl, no longer stunned, nodded. "Thank you for agreeing to stand up for me. I appreciate it."

"Number one employee of Wingards, right here," Theodore said.

Karl wouldn't go that far, but Theodore was a good guy, and he did appreciate him being here. He dug in his pocket and handed him the ring box. "Here. Don't lose it between now and the wedding. Or I'll have to fire you."

Theodore laughed.

"Karl, this is Father Bittner," Martha said, leading a robed man into the room. "You three can get in position, right there in front of the window. And don't you dare faint when you see your bride for the first time."

"I won't," he assured her.

Famous last words.

The room had filled up with men and women taking their seats in the chairs, but they'd become invisible to Karl. When the music had started, his eyes had gone to the back of the room, to the woman dressed in white and wearing a long veil. He could see her face, her eyes, her smile, through the thin material, and the blood rushed through his veins so hard and fast there was a swooshing sound in his ears.

She arrived before him, clasped onto his hands, and he knew he truly was the luckiest man on earth. He wanted to tell the priest to hurry up, make her his, to have and to hold, for richer, for poorer, until the end of time.

Bridget responded, repeated her vows of loving Karl forevermore with heartfelt sincerity, and rejoiced with a squeal when she was proclaimed as Mrs. Karl Wingard for the first time.

She rejoiced again when Karl lifted her veil and kissed her. His lips were soft, warm, and the pressure sweetly reverent.

As he started to pull back, to end the kiss, she whispered, "Oh, no you don't."

He chuckled and then gave her a kiss that made even the angels watching from above rejoice.

"Was that better?" he asked.

Breathless, she nodded and then laughed. Still gasping for air.

There was cake, punch and coffee afterward, and she made a point of introducing Karl to all of Martha's friends who'd helped with the wedding, and joined him in thanking each and every one of them.

As they prepared to leave, she promised Martha they would visit again before returning to New York. Then, holding on to Karl's hand, she hurried out the door with him, through a shower of rice, into the taxi waiting to take them to the hotel.

"We don't have to return to New York right away," Karl said once they were in the back seat. "We could take a honeymoon around the world if you'd like."

She kissed him. "I want to go home. To our home." She slid her hand inside his coat, ran her palm over the smooth silk of his vest. "But not today."

He laughed. "Your wish is my command."

The moment she'd seen him standing next to the priest, waiting to become her husband, tears of happiness had stung her eyes. The best dream she'd ever have had come true. She was Mrs. Karl Wingard!

She snuggled up against him. "I didn't know a person could be this happy."

"Me, neither." He hugged her tighter. "Me, neither."

It didn't take long to arrive at the hotel, thank goodness, because she hadn't known how overpowering her physical desires could be, either. She loved him so much and wanted to share that love with him in every way.

As he escorted her into the hotel, a bellhop collected

her suitcase and accompanied them in the elevator and up to their room.

As Karl tipped the young man, Bridget crossed the room, stopping near a table, where there was a bottle of champagne on ice and two glasses. "You ordered champagne," she said as Karl closed the door.

"The hotel must have."

She picked up the card that said Mr. and Mrs. Karl Wingard—the most wonderful name in the world. Turning it over, she read more. A simple congratulations and best wishes. "It's from your mother."

He walked closer and she handed him the card, watching his face and biting her bottom lip.

A smile formed as he set the card down. "I called her. Yesterday."

She was overjoyed at the steps he'd taken to repair his relationship with his mother. Looping her arms around his neck, she stretched on her toes and kissed him. "I love you."

"I love you." He gave her several small kisses. "Everything about you."

His hands lingered on her sides as he stepped back, looked at her with such affection her insides began to throb.

She rubbed his shoulders, loving the notion of being able to touch him whenever she wanted. However she wanted. Running her fingers up his neck, into his hair, she said, "Thank you for the dress." She'd planned on wearing one he'd already bought her because it seemed silly to only wear a dress once, but Martha had made her understand that Karl wanted to buy things for her—it was one of the ways he knew to show love. That made sense, and she'd never deny any form of his love.

"I'm glad there was one you liked," he said.

"I do like it." She kissed his chin. "But there is one issue with it."

He frowned. "What?"

She kissed the side of his neck. "I can't take it off by myself. It buttons up the back."

His hands slid around her, to the center of her back, to the buttons there. "That could be an issue." He kissed her ear. "If you weren't married to me."

A thrill zipped through her as she felt the first button being released, and then the next and the next.

That was just the beginning.

Their kisses weren't only kisses, they were a sharing of love. A love so great, so unbound by any restrictions that it grew with each caress. Each exposure of skin. Each exploration of touching, looking, kissing. He not only made her feel love, he made her feel cherished. The way his hands fit upon her skin, her curves, her sensitive spots that had her reeling, wanting more and more.

"I've never held anything so precious," he whispered, cupping her face as they lay on the bed.

His mouth was hot, his kiss as stimulating as it was tender. "I want you so badly," she whispered. "So very badly."

"I don't want to hurt you."

She'd heard the first time could hurt, but wasn't afraid. Not in the least. Her heart said it would be magical. "You won't."

"Tell me if it's uncomfortable, and I'll stop."

She wouldn't let him stop. Not ever.

Even though she was completely willing to give him everything immediately, all at once, he took his time. Like he had her love, he coaxed her body, piece by piece, until there was a scalding hot pressure building inside that had her gasping.

She was ready for him, burning and hot, when he slid inside her. There was a short snap of pain that didn't take anything away from the pleasure flowing over her like waves rolling onto a sandy shore, growing stronger with each thrust forward and each backward pull.

A sense of wonder, so grand, so powerful, overtook her, taking her higher and higher until she was at an invisible peak that had her teetering on the brink of reality. Karl was with her. His skin hot, his body hard, his breathing coming as fast as hers.

"Sugar and shoot!" she shouted as the pleasure exploded into something so intense it completely stole her breath, her ability to think.

The ecstasy slowly faded into an aftermath that was pure bliss. She sank deeper into the mattress, marveling at how she was slowly floating back to earth.

Karl kissed her several times before he rolled off her and laughed. "Sugar and shoot?"

Too exhausted to do more than flop an arm onto his chest, she nodded. "It was either that or curse you."

"Curse me?"

"Yes, but I don't know one for something that amazing."

Chuckling, he kissed her temple. "I couldn't agree more. There are no words."

Energy was returning to her body, making her feel even better, happier than ever. She flipped onto her side, snuggled up against him and kissed him. "I want to do that again."

He laughed. "So do I."

"We are pretty amazing," she said. "Don't you think?"

Rolling onto his side, so they were face-to-face, he kissed her. "Yes, I think we are amazing."

She sighed. "You are so amazing. All the things you do. I'm in awe."

He shook his head. "I'm nothing compared to you." Running a finger along the side of her face, he said, "Just think what we are going to be able to do together."

Flipping a leg over his, she whispered, "I am."

Epilogue

K arl slipped on his suit coat while watching Bridget twist to look at herself in the mirror. The hem of her emerald green dress flipped and flopped at each of her turns, but it was her hand, placed on her stomach, that held his attention. With his heart overflowing, he walked up behind her and wrapped his arms around her, rubbing the firm roundness of her stomach, their baby growing inside her. Seven months of marriage had made him want her more, not less. He was convinced that's how it would continue to be, even after decades.

"Does this dress make me look fat?"

She wasn't due for five more months and could not be called fat. Her stomach was barely noticeable. Hiding his grin, he asked, "If I say yes, are you going to get mad at me?"

"No, you are just being honest."

He kissed her neck and sighed before saying, "Then the answer is no."

She spun around in his arms and straightened his tie while frowning. "Why did you say it like that?"

Acting nonchalant, he kissed her forehead. "Because if I made you mad, we'd have to make up later."

The sparkles appeared in her eyes one at a time. "I do believe I'm angry at you."

He cupped her bottom, pulled her closer. "Why?"

Her giggle floated on the air. "I'll think of something by the time we get home." She kissed him. "So we can make up."

He caught her lips and gave her a solid, sensual kiss that told her he'd hold her to that promise.

She had taken New York by storm. Half the time people didn't even know what had hit them until she was gone, off on another task of granting wishes. All for the good. Anyone who may have ever said a bad word about her whispered it so quietly that no one else heard because she had too many friends, too many people in high places who would defend her to the hilt.

Including him. He was her greatest fan. And her greatest love. As she was his. They never let each other forget that.

"We need to leave," he said, releasing her and picking her coat off the bed. "It's snowing again."

"A white Christmas," she said as he held the coat for her to slide in her arms. "I'm so excited about that."

Like everything else she did, her all or nothing had overtaken the house. There were three Christmas trees that he knew of downstairs. Probably more in the rooms he didn't regularly enter. Red velvet bows and green garland decorated the staircase and doorways, and big wreaths hung on all the doors, smaller ones in the windows. The house had never looked so festive. It had never been so full of love, either.

They paused in the front room, long enough to say

goodbye to Elsie and Catherine. Mrs. Conrad was still in the house, but had asked for retirement, stating she was too old for the day-to-day duties. She was still regularly at hand though, which was nice for everyone.

Other than the two nannies, and Willard and Mary, Karl was never quite sure who worked for them and who was merely doing odd jobs until they found something more permanent. Bridget knew, and he wouldn't have it any other way. She was amazing at keeping the household running smoothly, even as she took on other community tasks.

"I am so excited they are awarding you for your work with the trust fund," she said as they drove along the snow-covered roads. "You deserve it. Every person has received their initial payment."

He nodded, but once again kept his smile hidden. "You found the last two?"

"Yes, they had returned to Poland, but I found them."

She had no idea that the award was not being given to him. The city had called him last month, wanting to proclaim him man of the year for the money he'd raised for *Titanic* victims. He'd refused. Said if anyone deserved the award, it was Bridget. The class action suit that Charles continued to work on was still in litigation and from the sounds of it, would be for years. Without Bridget's help, people wouldn't have received any financial compensation. And because of her work, the White Star Line had set up a pension for the families of boatmen and employees on the *Titanic* who had perished.

The mayor had suggested that Karl could accept the award on her behalf, because she was, well, a woman, and there was no such thing as woman of the year. Karl had disagreed, and after he'd made a few phone calls to others of like mind, the mayor had called him again. Said there would be a woman of the year award this year, and in future years.

Karl glanced her way. She would never fail to amaze him. And others. Sean, James and John now ran a business that she'd encouraged them to start, building playhouses, doghouses, sheds and offering repair work. There were others, too, people she'd found one place or another, and helped to take the first steps to success. She had the ability to give others a sense of pride and determination that made the difference for them. It was amazing, and the pride he felt for her was indescribable.

"Look." Bridget pointed out the window, at a couple entering the hotel. "Your mother and Sylas are here. She didn't mention that last night at dinner." She sighed. "Silly me. Of course, she'd be here. You're her son. She loves you."

"She loves you, too," he said, parking the Packard. His mother did love both of them. Their past was now where it needed to be, in the past. He did wonder at times if his father had been afraid that loving a woman would have made him less of a man. A notion Karl knew was completely false. Loving Bridget had made him more of a man. A far better man than he'd have been without her.

He held her arm tightly, making sure she didn't slip on the snow as they walked into the downtown hotel. The same one that had hosted the inquiry eight months ago.

"Oh, it looks so lovely," Bridget said, referring to the holiday decorations.

"Yes, it does," he replied, referring to her face. She

had a natural glow about her that lit up every room she entered.

She grinned and bumped his shoulder with hers. "I'm still mad at you."

"Good."

They found their seats at a table full of people he'd known for years, but now considered friends rather than acquaintances. His mother and stepfather were also at the table, and he kissed her cheek before he and Bridget sat.

"I'm so excited," Bridget said, giggling. "To be married to the man of the year."

Knowing glances made a round of the table, but she didn't notice. Several people knew the truth, but he wanted it to be a surprise to her, and others had allowed that to happen.

Conversation rolled freely around the tables as they enjoyed a meal before the mayor took a stand behind the podium at the front of the room. He was a long-winded man, and a lot of his speech was centered on how New Yorkers came together to help the victims of the *Titanic*. He handed out awards to the opera, several society groups, churches and business owners for their acts of support and fundraising efforts that had provided places to stay, clothes and food during those first few weeks after the accident.

"And now, ladies and gentlemen," the mayor said, "it's time for our final and most prestigious award."

Bridget giggled and clapped, looking at him with stars in her eyes.

He grinned and lifted a brow.

"There is a change this year. There will not be the man of the year award," the mayor said.

"What?" Bridget snapped.

Karl grabbed her arm before she stood.

"For outstanding," the mayor continued, "above and beyond, actions of generosity…"

"This is an outrage!" she hissed. *"Go dtachtar le d'anáil thú!"*

"Calm down," Karl whispered.

"Calm down? Now I am mad at you! If anyone deserves to choke on his own breath, it's him!" she said, explaining the curse she'd cast upon the mayor. "You deserve that award! He won't be voted in again, I'll—"

"Mrs. Karl Wingard, New York's woman of the year!" the mayor said, pointing at their table.

The crowd cheered.

Her cheeks turned red as she smiled at the crowd, offering a small wave as she looked at him in question. "You did this."

"No, you did this. You deserve this award."

"Bridget, can you come up here please?" the mayor asked as the clapping slowed.

She grabbed his arm. "I'm not going up there without you. We are in this together. Have been from the start, and will be until the end."

Karl agreed and kissed her cheek before standing, helping her rise. The crowd rose, gave a standing ovation as he escorted her to the podium, where she was presented with an inscribed plaque. The crowd continued to applaud louder and louder. He'd never been more proud and knew this was the first of many awards his adorable, loving wife would receive during her lifetime.

It was hours later when they arrived home and finally climbed into bed.

"I still can't believe you did that," she said, snuggling up to his side.

"I didn't. The mayor decided who should receive the award."

"With help from you."

He kissed her. "I know it's not becoming the first female leprechaun, but becoming the first woman of the year has to be close."

She sat up. "I knew you had something to do with it."

He cradled her face, pulled her close for a kiss. "That award is yours. Completely. For all the work you've done. For all the people you've helped from the moment you saved Betsy from falling in the water. I'm just your husband. Who loves you very, very much, and who you were mad at, but now want to make up with."

She flung a leg over his waist, straddling him. "You're right. I do want to make up."

He grabbed her hips, lowered her onto him and sucked in a breath at the ecstasy. "Sugar and shoot!"

* * * * *